ROTTEN

AARON DICK

Copyright © 2020 by Aaron Dick

First Edition

Book Cover Illustration by Simon Ripley
Book Cover Design by oliviaprodesign

ISBN 978-0-473-53916-0 (Paperback)
ISBN 978-0-473-53917-7 (eBook)
ISBN 978-0-473-53918-4 (Kindle)

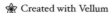 Created with Vellum

This novel is dedicated to my first daughter Annalise.
In return for all the sleepless, anxious nights you've given me.

No one saw them at first. Thick heavy bugs like cockroaches, covered in a film of oil, nauseatingly damp-looking, like a glutton's forehead after they have finished eating a large meal. They were hunch-backed bugs, rising sharply at the front into a small hillock of chitin and then sloping away in rounded segments to a narrow point; faecal brown and vomit orange. They didn't seem to have any obvious eyes and their legs and mouth were hidden beneath the sickly armour of their shell.

They skittered along tiled floors and inched their way up porcelain toilets. Occasionally one would scrape its heavy body out onto the asphalt of a street and crunch beneath the wheels of a taxi, the black-green muck of its innards smearing across the road and slicking the surface of rain puddles left in the dark early hours of the morning.

One blindly followed the warm smell of buttered popcorn. It bent and squashed between the cabinet sized popcorn maker and the wall of the cinema as it climbed upward. Each needle shaped leg poked and tore at the soft decorations wrapping the popcorn maker, ripping out tiny holes as it rose. Eventually it managed to squeeze out of the gap behind the machine, nosing towards the pile of soft white popcorn that sat in drifts beneath a glowing heat lamp. The cinema lobby was empty and quiet.

On the other side of the lobby, far from the popcorn machine, too far away to see the creature that was sliding into the piles of food and leaving a trail of glistening liquid behind it, an employee of the cinema was brushing spilled popcorn into a long-handled shovel with his broom. He was muttering to himself, like most seventeen year olds employed by people they think of as dumb adults, and who work with members of the public; also categorised as fools by such teenagers.

"Fuck this," he said, and he propped the broom and shovel against a wall and began to walk towards the serving counter.

He looked quickly left and right and, seeing that no-one was watching, spun around so he could sit on the polished wood of the counter. Then he lifted his knees to his chest and spun around again, swinging his legs to the far side of the counter before bringing them down again.

"I don't know why I keep coming back to this fucking job," he said, and he pulled a cardboard box off the pile sitting next to the popcorn machine. He pulled out the stainless steel popcorn scoop and opened the glass door to the prepared corn.

Under the fluffy corn, the creature twitched. Though warm, the popcorn had turned out to be lacking in certain qualities that the creature needed in order to feed and sustain itself. But now there had been movement and sound, registering in the almost non-existent neurons of the creature's nervous system by way of organs and senses that did not rely upon ears or eyes. It could feel the approaching metal scoop, but it ignored that completely. What set it shaking was the flesh that followed behind. That soft, warm, moist and, above all, fresh flesh that held the metal scoop. Beneath the lip of the creature's shell, tiny mandibles unfolded in a multitude of razors and claws.

CHAPTER ONE

Jayden turned into the pathway to the house and pushed his phone back into his pocket. A thin dark house sat squeezed between its neighbours, the small window in the front door illuminated by a faint glow from within. He groaned and rubbed his face. *It's been a long day and now this,* he thought. *May as well get what awaits inside over with.*

James swung open the door and smiled broadly. The streetlights outside caught the brilliant gleam of his teeth and they shone from between his lips as if he had swallowed a halo. His eyes twinkled in recognition too.

"I see you got spruced up for our little get together Jay!" He reached out and plucked at the collar of Jayden's work shirt, then stepped forward, spreading his arms open to enfold Jayden in a hug. Jayden accepted the hug without returning it, standing like a fencepost wrapped in vines. "I'm so pleased to see you're taking a bit more of an interest in getting out and seeing people. You know we were quite worried about you for a while there." James stepped back with his hands on Jayden's shoulders. The broad smile continued to reveal his shining teeth. Jayden wondered if they were artificial. It was like looking at a life size Ken doll's smile. *What do his real teeth look like? Are they still under there, some blackened nubs beneath the tiling?*

"I'm sure you were absolutely on your knees with anxiety," replied Jayden.

James blinked. "Yes. Well, yes, we are worried. But you've only just arrived, come on in."

I know I've only just arrived, you twit. I'm the one doing the arriving. But Jayden said nothing as he followed the other man into the flat.

James led Jayden through the hallway and into a lounge. Sophie was sitting on the chocolate coloured sofa with a glass of wine between her fingers, chatting happily with a woman Jayden had never met before. Jayden sighed as he noticed both women were wearing floaty tops that shimmered under the light, and clean jeans. He was still in the white collared shirt and black pants that he wore for work.

"Oh my god, Jay, you look so nice tonight," gushed Sophie as she stood up to greet him, leading the way with her wine glass like some elven comet.

"They're just my work clothes Sophie," Jayden answered. She shushed him with her hand and gave him a quick hug and kissed his cheek.

"Nonsense Jay, it's been far too long since I've seen you in anything except those horribly morbid band tee shirts you insisted on wearing all the time."

"She has a point you know," smiled James as he slid an arm around her waist. Jayden grimaced. He felt much more comfortable in those loose, worn-in clothes.

"They're just clothes too," he said, shaking his head. "I seem to recall you and James used to wear ripped fishnets and way too much pale makeup, I don't see why my tee shirts are any different." Sophie's cheeks flushed. *Yeah, don't forget that I know the real you,* he thought. Before she could reply Jayden turned to face the woman sitting on the other side of the coffee table, opposite the sofa that Sophie had been sitting on. "So, what's your name?"

The woman smiled and glanced away before she answered him. "My name's Katie, I work with Sophie." Sophie drew a deep breath and pulled James aside, talking softly.

"Oh yes, another one of these file shuffling number jockeys eh?" Jayden smirked. She smiled in return and he felt a twitch in his eyebrow. "My name's Jayden, though I go by Jay often enough. I imagine you already knew that if my friends have had any influence in your being here tonight."

"Yes, they told me a lot about you." Katie paused and her eyebrows creased. "Wait, what do you mean if they had any influence? Did they not tell you I was coming?"

Jayden shrugged. "They just have this habit recently, where they try to pair me off with chicks they know."

"Oh I see." Katie pursed her lips and tugged at the shoulders of her top with her spare hand.

"There is a good side to it," added Jayden. "It means that they've probably only told you the good things about me and none of the bad. So I won't need to show you how awesome I am because you'll already know." He grinned widely as Sophie came back over to the pair.

"Well, I'm glad the introductions are out of the way." Sophie sat down on the sofa again and motioned Jayden to sit beside her. "Why don't you get Jay a drink, honey? I'll try and stop him from embarrassing himself."

James set off towards the kitchen. "Just a beer for you I assume, man?" Jayden nodded. *He's such an arse,* Jayden thought. *"Oh look at me, I'm fetching you a drink, because I'm such a perfect host."* What does Sophie see in *him?* Jayden had known James for years, since before he left Wellington. But the James he had found when he returned, this cleaned-up toothy-grinned guy who had shacked up with Sophie? Who was he? Where had he come from? This wasn't the James he had known.

Sophie picked up the bottle of white wine from the coffee table and topped up her glass. "Dinner's on the way. James has a spectacular recipe for fish, you'll really love it. It just melts right in your mouth." Katie nodded and sipped at her glass. She had less of a smile on her face now.

Jayden looked around the lounge as the women talked about various fish meals they'd had in the past. The lounge hadn't changed much in the few months since Sophie had last forced him to come over and watch a rugby game with some of James' friends. What a thrilling night that had been. A bunch of tall guys with wide shoulders yelling and jumping around the small room while Jayden slumped on a chair in the corner.

The walls were painted a soft creamy faun and the carpet was impossibly clean. He rubbed the thick pile with his feet. Jayden often wondered how he had stayed friends with Sophie and James. They had changed so much more than the people he usually hung out with. Momentum seemed to explain it.

He had met them before he had left Wellington, long before he had been forced to come back. They'd seemed just like him then, and he could feel comfortable around them just being himself. But then they had changed. Maybe that was it. He'd made friends with the real Sophie who had eventually got together with the real James, and now they'd decided to become something else, something beige.

Oh god, he thought. *What if it's worse than that? What if this is the real them, and I made friends with them while they were pretending to be interesting people?* The idea made his skin crawl. He stared at the abstract art on their wall and let the women's chatter wash over him.

James walked back into the room with a glass of beer for Jayden who took it and gulped a mouthful down as quick as he could. James put the nearly empty bottle in front of Jayden on a coaster.

"I see you like that piece."

"What?" Jayden blinked and turned to face James who gestured at the art that Jayden had been staring at. Shades of blue filled the canvas, and broken glass had been attached as well. The colours and textures washed around each other in a spiral. Jayden rubbed his eyes and took another gulp of beer. "I guess so."

"What do you see," asked James, standing along-side Jayden and crossing his arms.

"Blue." Jayden didn't see the point in embellishing things.

James glanced at him then shook his head.

"So, Jay, I was hearing that you might be losing your job? What's going on?"

"Well done James, you'll definitely be able to set me up with your wife's friend by implying that I'm an unemployed deadbeat." Jayden took another drink from his glass and smacked his lips. Without looking up he lifted the glass a little. "But you're not wrong. Here's to telling The Man to go fuck himself."

Sophie grimaced. Jayden chuckled.

"Well, I've always thought that work isn't what defines a person really. What really matters is how they get on with people, you know? That's why I know I'm such a success." He swallowed a large mouthful of beer, forcing it to wash away the sour taste in his throat, and then poured the rest of the bottle into his glass. Jayden looked over at Katie. Her eyes were wide and bright and brown and the lights in the ceiling made her skin glow.

"Sophie, I must say that you've really let yourself go." Jayden kept his eyes on Katie and watched her forehead wrinkle in confusion. "Seriously, I don't know why James hasn't kicked you out yet."

James shook his head and sighed. "Jay, you know that we have put up with a lot from you recently. But you really can't keep on like this. It's not fair on us, and we'll tell you not to come back, just like all the others have."

"I don't know what you're talking about," Jayden interrupted, but Sophie shushed him and James kept talking.

"We asked Katie along for dinner tonight so you could meet her. But don't flatter yourself. She's way too good for you." Katie blushed. "We certainly aren't hoping you two will get together. We just wanted you to make some new friends!"

Jayden stood up. "I need to take a leak."

"Stop trying to push us away Jay," sighed Sophie. "You need some people around you. We know that you aren't seeing any of the old crowd anymore. Especially if you've lost your job, you need to keep your life busy!"

"Too much shit beer James, get better supplies." As he walked down the hall he could hear the others begin talking softly. *So long as I don't have to hear their pointless blathering.*

But even so, he caught the beginning of something Sophie said. "This isn't how he is really. It's just that he's been in such a bad place since... "Jayden stepped through a door and into the bathroom, banging the door shut rapidly behind him to cut off their conversation.

Jayden flushed and turned to the sink. He spun the tap and rinsed his hands then splashed some water on his face. He stared into the huge clean mirror above the sink and let the water drip off the end of his nose and chin.

Were they right about him? Was he pushing people away? He didn't feel like he was pushing them away, he felt like he was rightfully telling off people for all the little deceptions they told each other to try and get through the day without offending people. Was it his fault that they couldn't cope, that the old crowd was getting prissy, pretentious and giving up on a real existence?

Sophie with her small talk about dinner. Who cared? Fish was fish. Dinner might be good or bad, but either way how is it worth wasting time from your life discussing? Surely, people should just eat it? James with his bloody beer glass. He hadn't even brought out any expensive fancy foreign beer, something that sounded ostentatious. It was just something that came in a 24 pack off the shelf of the local supermarket, and yet he had to pour it into another glass instead of just handing Jayden the bottle. Wasting time on pointless rituals.

He didn't really know this Katie chick, but she didn't seem like she would be any different than the others. Trapped behind that smiley, make-up mask that she must think she needs in order to get through the day. As if she really gave a damn about finding out what he liked. Nobody actually gave a damn about what he liked.

Jayden grabbed the hand towel and wiped his face dry. *The fish better be good, that's all,* he thought to himself as he stalked back to the lounge.

Katie smiled at him as he sat down and he was sure he could see the cracks in her foundation. He smiled back then rolled his eyes.

"Come on, Sophie's just served up dinner. Let's head into the dining room," said James. Jayden followed the other two to the small table, set with two long thin candles. Sophie had just lit them both and blown out the match as she waved them in.

Dinner passed without anything catching Jayden's attention. He barely noticed when anyone talked to him and barely responded. The fish tasted like ash in his mouth, and he told Sophie so when she asked what he thought. Sophie shook her head and looked away. James frowned. Jayden smiled at them and forked another mouthful of the flaky white meat into his mouth, staring at them as he chewed.

James offered dessert and Katie gladly accepted. The others had managed to get her to talk about her job but Jayden had snorted a lot and so she had stopped, focusing more on her chocolate mud cake.

"Look Jay, you've been rude to our guest and insulted us. Do you even want to come along to the movies tonight?" asked James.

"I don't have anything else to do; I may as well come and be bored at the movies."

James pursed his lips. "Well if you do I have one warning for you: this will be your only chance to redeem yourself. If you keep acting like this, we won't ask you back. But if you can at least pretend to be human for the rest of the night, we might."

Jayden shrugged and stabbed his fork into a piece of mud cake. His mouth was dry and he had to chew for a while before he could swallow it.

CHAPTER TWO

There was a queue at the cinema but Jayden managed to keep his mouth shut by shoving his hands deep into his pockets and fidgeting with the loose change he found there. He nodded as Katie continued to try to talk to him. He watched her lips, slightly curved into a smile, as they slipped together and apart. She was wearing a very bright red lipstick, and the way she spoke so quickly was beginning to wear it away. He could see the natural colour of her lips coming through.

"... which is why they stopped asking him to help renovate! I feel sorry for him sometimes, he always means well."

Jayden blinked and cleared his throat. "I'm sorry?"

Katie's lip twitched for a moment, stretching her smile tight against her teeth. Sophie leaned over and punched Jayden just above his elbow.

"'Ow! Dammit, what did you do that for?"

"Because you're being horrible to our friend, jackass." Sophie was frowning over the fuzzy collar of her coat. She brushed some hair away from her forehead before tucking her hand deep into her pockets. "Katie's trying to tell you about her brother."

Jayden felt his mouth open, but James interrupted

him before he could speak. "Don't even think about asking why she's telling you that, man. You asked her what she's been doing today and the answer was 'Catching up with her brother'. Seriously, can't you just be a little bit nicer? Katie is one of our friends and we told her that you were kinda fun. I don't want to look like a blatant liar in front of my friends. It used to be true."

Jayden closed his mouth again. "Alright, fair enough." He shrugged at Katie who wasn't smiling anymore. "I'm sorry if I've been brushing you off. I haven't had the best time in the last few months and so I've been easily distracted."

James looked up and down the street outside the cinema foyer. "Distracted by what man? There's nothing out there but streetlights and rain."

James was right; the streets of Wellington were cold and wet. The wind was pushing a few empty pie packets and leaves of paper along the gutter. Water was gurgling down the storm water drains. Down at the corner of the street, Jayden could just see the silhouette of a person lighting up a cigarette. The tiny point of orange light glowed under the dripping awnings, standing out like a flare in the dismal twilight.

The person stepped away around the corner. A small round piece of trash blew up from the gutter after them.

"That's alright; I know how easy it is to let your mind wander when you're a bit stressed." Katie's smile had returned. *Jesus. Does the woman ever relax,* thought Jayden. "But that's why I'm so glad we're here," Katie's gaze swept around the foyer as they moved further inside, taking in the screens showing clips from upcoming movies and the counter where a small line of people trudged forward one at a time. A teenage couple had just made it to the register and were giggling over how much popcorn to order. The boy's hand was just edging under the waist of the girl's jeans.

"I suppose it's one way to kill an evening," agreed Jayden.

"It's certainly better than you sitting around in that dingy little apartment of yours," laughed Sophie. "You should see his place Katie! It's the size of our bathroom, seriously."

"It's not that small." Jayden shook his head.

"It is! It is!" Sophie undid the fastening of her coat now that they were inside and the cold air wasn't as noticeable. Jayden watched her shoulders shift as she slipped it off and folded it in her arms, then blinked and looked away. "We had some drinks with him before a concert once, do you remember?" She turned to Jayden for a moment. Her eyes were so green. "We were there before we went to see Lubricant, that English group?" She turned back to Katie. "Anyway, while we were there I decided to measure the rooms in steps." She stepped away from them, striding in a slow careful rhythm that reminded Jayden of cheesy 70's sci-fi and people pretending to be robots.

"Oh! I remember this!" James started to follow her, mimicking her exaggerated stride. "I think we managed to get about seven steps away from the front door, wasn't it?"

"That's right, seven or eight steps!" Sophie was nodding furiously. "And if we took another step we'd have to go through the wall!"

"Go through the wall and plummet to your doom," growled Jayden.

James laughed. "Oh cheer up. You only live on the second floor; no-one's going to do any sort of plummeting from your apartment."

Katie laughed too. Jayden sighed but couldn't help

smiling a little as well. They stepped closer to the ticket counter.

"God, you'd think people would know better than coming to work in that condition?" Katie pointed behind the counter. Jayden saw a short skinny girl in a deep blue work shirt and pale blue cap leaning against the wall by the popcorn machine. Her shoulders shook as she hacked and coughed into her fist, pressed against her mouth. They watched as she bent over and made a sickening clicking choking sound.

"Jesus, yeah." Jayden shook his head. "Some people are a total waste."

"Guys, a little compassion maybe?" James leaned over in between Jayden and Katie. "She should probably go home, but it's not like she's drowning puppies or something. I expected better from you Katie."

"Oh, but you don't expect better from me?" Jayden raised his eyebrows. James just stared back at him, until Jayden looked down. His stomach twisted. *I'm just being honest,* he thought to himself. *James is being a shit.*

The four of them walked towards the doors to cinema three. Jayden was holding a box of popcorn for James, who had his hands full with drinks, bags of chocolate-covered, chemically-coloured sugar lumps and more popcorn. Katie had a few ice creams and Sophie was carrying all the coats, handbags and tickets.

"I don't know, do you think this is enough? I might get hungry later, I think I want something else," said Jayden. Katie nudged him with her elbow.

"Oh shush you, we've got just enough for an old-fashioned night at the movies."

"I'm not sure I remember a good old time at the movies involving bloated stomachs."

Katie didn't reply, she just winked at him and fol-

lowed Sophie past the gangly teenager who was ripping tickets, into the cinema.

Their seats were in the back row. As mildly annoying music warbled out of tiny speakers hidden
around the room, Jayden watched the rows begin to
fill up. The touchy-feely teenagers were only a couple
of rows ahead of him. A very large hairy man was over
by the wall on the right, coughing periodically with a
horrible phlegmatic rattle. A variety of couples in
their inoffensive middle aged blandness filled most of
the seats. It was the uni students, already drunk at
7.30 in the evening and throwing handfuls of popcorn
at each other from opposite ends of the front row
that made Jayden squeeze the fingernails of his fists
into his palms.

"Man, I hate little punks like that," he muttered.

"Oh come on," said Katie. "James has told me all
about the silly things you and Sophie used to get up
to when you were younger. I'm sure you would have
been just the same."

"She's right you know," said Sophie from the other
end of the row. "Remember that time we were up in
Auckland and we were egging each other down
Queen Street? We nearly got cornered by those cops
but they got tired of chasing us." Her smile flashed
under the dim lights, echoing the spark of mischief in
her eyes.

"Okay, yes, we got up to our share of mischief,"
said Jayden. "But those guys are dicks about it."

Katie snorted.

"No really!" Jayden turned and chopped at the air
with his right hand. "You can see that they're self-im-
portant assholes with no thoughts for the experience
of the other people in this movie theatre!"

"Doesn't sound awfully different from the guy
who's been slagging off everyone around him all
night, does it?" This time Katie grinned, exposing

more of her teeth than before. Jayden was sure they looked pointed.

He slumped back into his seat and crossed his arms. "That's just unfair, turning my actions back on me like that."

"Lighten up. Here," she handed him a small plastic bag of sweets. "Have a pineapple lump."

He chewed as the first ads began to show on the screen. At the door to the cinema, the gangly teenager was scratching the back of his head.

The ads flickered past Jayden in a welter of flashing neon and pumping bass. The glazed expressions on the faces of the others in the cinema made him think that the advertising was doing its work and penetrating into the shallow depths of their brains. Katie crunched through the chocolate shell of her ice cream and leaned closer to him, whispering in his ear through a mouthful of vanilla ice cream.

"I think a lot of these ads are pretty funny, don't you?"

"These things? Funny?" Jayden looked carefully at the ad being projected in front of them. It involved a still photo of a small Asian restaurant with a smiling caricature painted above the door. Specials and location details were written in flashing letters on either side of the photo and some squealing guitar wound through the room. "I don't see anything amusing there at all."

"You don't?" Katie lowered her ice cream and tipped her head to one side. She looked over at Jayden's face and then shook her head slightly. "How could you not find these ads funny? Look at this car yard!" She pointed at the screen, where a new ad had begun. The screen displayed a stocky man who was trying to smile wide enough to split his face in half even while he spoke at length about the respectful way he and his employees would sell cars. The car yard behind looked small and appeared to be full of cars that were much older than the phrase 'New Vehicles' could possibly support.

"What about it? Some jackass with a bad wig wants to sell me a car when it's cheaper for me to catch a bus. Why should I be laughing at him trying to scam me?"

"Because you know he's trying to scam you!" The right side of Katie's mouth curled upwards. "Look at the sweat seeping out from under that shit wig. Look at the desperation in those squinty eyes. Can't you just tell his mortgage payments are due and he's not sure that he's going to make enough to cover it?" She took another bite of her ice cream. "You can imagine his dumpy shrew of a wife from those eyes, berating him whenever he comes home without making enough for her to be happy." Katie leaned over to her left, including James in the conversation. "Don't you think the desperation of these people is funny James?"

"Well, kind of. In that sad, pathetic way that tragedy happening to other people can be funny." He ran his fingers through his hair. "But I think that's a bit of a cruel way to look at the world, don't you?"

"It certainly is." Jayden smiled at Katie and they both started giggling.

The ads finished and trailers began to play. Jayden and Katie made short sharp observations about the trailers, enjoying pointing out the deficiencies of actors and directors to each other, revelling in the sub-par attempts of each film's marketing department to convince them that this movie would be worth watching. Jayden even took a handful of popcorn from Katie's cardboard bucketful.

The teenage usher stood at the door, flickering light from the trailers inside making his eyes look like fire-filled orbs. It was clear that he was anticipating the next brawny blow-em-up quite intently. His hair was scraggly but short, hanging in slightly wavy clumps just past his ears. His skin reminded Jayden of uncooked fish, including the strange slightly red areas. Jayden presumed that the blotches were acne trying to break through the mighty chemical warfare being employed against them. The youth scratched his arse lazily then turned and moved outside the cinema again. A few more people were turning up, struggling under their own popcorn containers.

A cartoon had begun to play, which surprised Jayden. It was unusual these days to get any actual pre-movie entertainment. A humanoid rabbit was climbing the walls in a small room that had been conveniently filled with an array of second-hand goods that provided slapstick humour in just the right violent amounts. Even Sophie was laughing from her seat on the far side of James. Her face lit up in the glow of the rabbit's antics, and her eyes were like stars.

Loud rock music played as a plump, bearded cartoon man entered the room and began to chase the rabbit in an ill-fated attempt to keep any more antiques from being destroyed. Jars shattered, stuffed displays of extinct animals were knocked into fires and burned to ash within a second; precious books and documents were torn or used to mop up spilled bottles of valuable wine. Jayden wiped away a tear from the corner of his eye and took a deep breath. He noticed a flicker of movement in the corner of his eye and turned his head to see what it was.

The ticket-taker was speaking quietly to an old woman. He had bent over to bring his mouth closer to her fragile ears. She refused to give up her ticket so that he could tear it in half and he appeared to be at a loss as to how to change her mind. The knot of her floral headscarf shook wildly as she argued back.

Jayden grunted and was about to turn back to the cartoon when he noticed the wet man.

He was wearing a well-cut coat over his suit, though it was soaked through. His hair was plastered flat across his skull and water was still dripping from the tip of his nose and the ends of his sleeves. At first Jayden thought he was dribbling water from his mouth as well, but then he realised that the liquid at the man's lips was a dark colour, not clear. The wet man had clearly just come in out of the rain outside. He even still had a cigarette in his mouth, though it too was sodden and totally useless.

The teenager straightened up as the wet man approached, preparing to deal with two customers at once. As soon as the wet man reached the old lady he reached forward with one hand, fingers spread wide open, and closed it in a fist around her neck. Jayden could hear the sound of splintering bone from his seat, far away from the doorway.

Blood spurted out between the wet man's fingers. His damp lips slithered apart into a smile that didn't touch his eyes, dark liquid spilled out from behind his teeth, staining the white enamel and then dripping onto his shirt collar. He let go of the woman's neck and her head flopped backward like a rag doll. Blood coughed out of her mouth as she dropped to the floor. The teenage boy stared at her body as it fell, not moving; he barely seemed to be breathing. Although the music playing along with the cartoon told him it only took a moment, Jayden felt like the boy took hours to raise his head and look into the eyes of the wet man.

For the tiniest fragment of a second the two figures faced each other, framed in Jayden's vision by the doorway. The lights in the cinema foyer seemed to swell, swamping the pair in a dirty yellow glow, obscuring the details of their faces. The wet man's face disappeared in the shadow cast over his flesh. The nametag on the boy's uniform flashed at Jayden's eyes.

Someone screamed from the front of the cinema and Jayden spun around to find out what was happening.

A girl in the front row was standing up and pointing to the slumped body of the old woman. The woman's pale cream clothing was stained dark red by the blood that flowed from the ruin of her neck. The screams paused as the girl at the front drew breath and then continued, a piercing wail that twisted in Jayden's ears like fingers being rubbed across wet glass.

People jumped to their feet, questions fired across the room like bullets. More screams joined the first, yells of anger and disbelief. Jayden felt someone climb over from the row in front of him, standing on his legs in an attempt to get closer and see what was happening. Jayden fought against the figure, and tried to climb against the press of people so he could head towards the front of the cinema. As he moved he heard a wet noise that reminded him of a damp brown paper bag being ripped apart slowly. He knew that the young man in the doorway had just died.

"What the fuck is going on?" Sophie was clutching James' shoulder and trying to look towards the door. There were too many people crushing around the doorway. A popping noise was accompanied by a ripple in the crowd and more screams. Sophie flinched and turned wide eyes to Jayden. "Why are you going that way? Jay, tell us what's happening?"

"There's a fucking maniac at the door." Jayden was already three rows ahead, clambering over the chairs in a straight line. He only paused long enough to look back over his shoulder and meet Sophie's gaze. He saw James watching him with a confused expression. He couldn't see Katie anywhere. "I know he's killed two people already. We've got to fucking get out of here."

"What do you mean 'he's killed two people already'?" Sophie's voice was hard to hear over the crowd. Thankfully there were only a few others heading towards the fire escape at the front of the cinema, and Jayden wasn't pushing against the crowd any more. He didn't stop to answer her.

He reached the open space in front of the seats at the same time as a middle aged man in a shirt and tie. Alarms began sounding as others moved through the fire doors. The man glanced at Jayden then pulled open the door nearest to them, bathed in neon green from the light above it. They both spared a second to look at the scene behind them.

The crowd had moved away from the doorway now. In the flickering light of the projector it was hard for Jayden to make out any faces. He thought the figure clambering down the seats not far from him might be Sophie. *But that's not right,* he thought. *Where's James? Surely he hasn't just left her, that bastard? I knew he was all front, that fucking coward.*

"I've seen enough mate. Good luck." The man in the tie ducked past Jayden and down the dim corridor beyond. Jayden watched the main entrance to the cinema, waiting for the figure that he hoped was Sophie.

Now the crowd was heaving down the cinema and past the rows of seats. The shouting hadn't quietened, though no-one was wasting energy screaming anymore. People were calling one another, giving instructions and trying to herd each other to safety.

Something thin spun through the air from the doorway at the back of the cinema, landing somewhere between the seats. Jayden tried to tell himself that it wasn't a foot he had seen on one end of the thing. Something small and round sailed across the back row and cracked against the wall. There was no mistaking the hair that trailed behind the head as it careened ingloriously through the air.

Jayden felt sick. His stomach was pulsing and he could feel his throat clenching. Sweat drenched his torso.

"Jayden!" Sophie reached him, only moments ahead of the panicked mob heading down the seats. A dark figure moved down the aisle, silhouetted by light from the doorway at the back of the cinema.

"Where's James?" Jayden grabbed Sophie's arm and began to lead her into the corridor.

"He went to try and help and said we should get out of here!" Sophie shouted above the din and shook off Jayden's hand. She glanced around the corridor. "Where's Katie?"

"If she's not with you, she's on her own. Come on!" Jayden pulled at Sophie again.

"No!" Sophie stepped away from him and lifted a hand to her mouth. "Did – Did you leave her back there?"

Jayden grimaced as the first member of the mob elbowed him aside. "This isn't the fucking time! Either we run or they trample us." He looked up in time to see the wet man had caught up with a straggler. The two figures tripped behind a seat. One figure rose. "Or he catches us. Neither looks pleasant. Now fucking move!"

The rush of bodies forced Sophie to follow him. They held each other's hands as they ran through the square concrete hallway, bouncing off other scrambling fugitives. Weak yellow lights shone as hard as they could, but Jayden felt the shadow pressing in on all sides through the entire passage. Some of the more athletic, or terrified, of the mob outran Jayden and Sophie and they were soon pulled further and further apart by the press of panicked figures.

"Jay!" Sophie's fingernails hooked into the flesh at the end of his fingers. He turned in time to see her stumbling and her arm stretched as far as she could towards him. A gaggle of middle-aged women was threatening to overwhelm her. He slowed his pace for a stride.

Then he turned his face towards the other end of the tunnel and pumped his legs as hard as he could. He tried not to listen to her voice behind him. "You bastard!"

Jayden managed to wonder, despite the noise and darkness and confusion, if he had done the right thing. But then Sophie was by his side, reaching up to slap at his face as she ran.

"You fucking coward! How could you just leave me!?"

"Look, I'm sorry," Jayden panted as he tried to avoid tripping over the feet around him. Someone to his left stumbled and fell. "How did you-"

"I picked her up." It was Katie. She was running with Sophie now. "I can't believe you would leave her behind." The woman's face was stiff and dark.

"I still maintain that this is not the fucking time!" Jayden felt cold night air on his face and felt his heart flutter in anticipation.

"Well, as soon as we get out I'm going to-" Something solid and rust-coloured burst through Katie's chest as she yelled at him. Sophie screamed and pushed him forward. The vision hung in his eyes though, a rough cone-shaped lump with the textured surface of a rotting apple. It hung on the end of a thick twisted length of white organic tissue, coated in bright red fluid. He could see the broken ends of her ribs that had been shoved out through her flesh. As Jayden backed away, something else struck the back of Katie's head, jarring it forward, and he felt his bile rise.

The streetlights glowered down on a confused collection of people outside the emergency exit. Some stood staring at distant traffic, but most were running in any direction they could. Jayden could hear their shoes clattering into the distance. Sophie pushed Jayden towards the car park. His legs felt as though they had been filled with wet sand, they were so heavy and sore. Blood pounded under his skull, pushing out most of his thought, and he panted, trying to suck air into his lungs.

"Did you fucking see that?"

"I don't know what I saw; get to the fucking car Jay!"

"Someone should call the police." He stopped and reached into his pocket, feeling for his cell phone.

"Jesus, Jay!" Sophie slapped him again, hard. The sensation of the sting remained on his cheek as though she had covered her hand in acid. He blinked and rubbed the skin. "Not only do you not check where Katie is, you run off without any of us, you leave me to be crushed, and now you're going into shock before we're safe. Would you come on!"

This time he followed her. A siren was whining between the city's buildings, getting louder.

CHAPTER THREE

The car park felt even more cramped than usual. Thick concrete hung low over their heads, covered in a mesh of rusty pipes, leaking steam. Flickering fluorescent lights illuminated the edges of the walls, reflecting off the faded yellow paint that marked out arrows pointing towards the exits. Sophie reached their car first. It was pointing out towards the suddenly silent city. Jayden looked out past the metal railing. *Where did those sirens go?*

Two stories below his feet was the city street. It was empty, even though the night was still relatively young. The sirens had stopped, but now Jayden could see red and blue lights cycling across a billboard at the intersection two blocks away. The police must be there. The moon was a thin crescent, high above the bay. The sea was a black abyss, darker than the shadows that hugged the buildings.

Sophie swore. "Where's my fucking key?" She had her arm buried in her handbag up to the elbow. A tube of lipstick was pushed to the surface and tumbled to the floor. It clattered on the smooth concrete, the sound echoing on and on down the empty building.

"I don't know. Are you sure it's in there?" Jayden

began to walk around to the driver's side of the car. "Maybe you dropped it back at the cinema?"

Sophie dropped the purse to her side and stared at him. Her eyes were huge and round and surrounded by dark skin. He knew those eyes so well.

"What?" Jayden asked. He had thought her makeup was running, perhaps from the sweat of their panicked escape or maybe even a few tears, but now he reconsidered. It looked more like stress was getting to her, giving her fake black eyes.

"What did you say?" Her voice was high and thin.

"Well, it's possible that you dropped the key earlier, isn't it?"

"How fucking dare you!" Sophie jumped at him with her hands outstretched like talons. Her fingernails slashed through the air by his face before she overbalanced and fell to her hands and knees on the ground.

"Jesus Christ!" Jayden scampered back behind the corner of the car. Sophie hung her head between her shoulders as she crouched on the ground. Silence rang off the square concrete columns around them. After a few seconds Jayden leaned forward.

"Sophie?" She didn't respond. "Soph, are you okay? We're okay up here, the cops have turned up. Even if you did drop the key back there, we'll be able to go get it soon enough."

"Who cares?" Sophie's shoulders were shaking gently. "Who cares if we can go back? James won't be there anymore."

Jayden stood watching Sophie. Distant voices echoed off the buildings, short muted yelps. *What am I supposed to do about it,* he thought. *I didn't tell the slick bastard to go running off into death and darkness, as if he could really save somebody.* Useless, frustrated anger burned the back of his skull and he felt as though the skin on his face had shrunk. The feeling passed and he blew out a single long breath. *It's not my bloody fault he bailed, don't take it out on me.*

He walked around to where Sophie had dropped her purse, where the contents lay strewn across the concrete. Eftpos card, coins, a cardboard box of tampons, Sophie's cell phone; and over by the tyre, a key on a short chain with a tiny fuzzy kiwi. Jayden picked up the key, then stood and unlocked the driver's door. The lock clicked quietly as he turned the key. Then he walked back over to where Sophie knelt on the ground. He leaned over and reached out to touch her shoulder, then paused, his hand only a whisker away. He swallowed and then moved forward to gingerly place a hand on her, but she didn't even seem to notice. He squeezed softly and felt a shiver move down his throat and chest.

"Sophie. Your key was in your purse. I unlocked the door. We should leave." Sophie didn't move. Jayden tucked a hand under her arm and pulled her to her feet. He was surprised to find that she rose to her feet with him willingly. She didn't struggle against his touch, or attempt to turn away and go running back towards the cinema; so he led her around to the passenger's door, unlocked it and manoeuvred her onto the seat.

Jayden walked back around the car and scooped Sophie's things up into her purse. He got into the driver's seat and reached up to put on his seatbelt.

"How could you do that?"

Jayden blinked. He was caught, twisted in his seat, facing out the side window. The fabric of the seatbelt scratched his fingertips. "What?" he asked as he pulled the seatbelt down and turned back to face her.

Sophie wasn't looking at him. Her slack face stared blankly out the windscreen and her voice drifted from her drooping mouth like a breeze from a mildewed cave. "How could you leave us all in the cinema?"

"I told you that there was some terrifying guy there." Jayden frowned.

"But you didn't help us leave. You just shouted and ran."

"You guys aren't paralysed or anything," Jayden said. He shook his head slightly and nibbled at his lower lip. "You can work your legs, so I figured you'd be able to sort yourselves out."

"James made sure we knew where to go before he left."

Jayden shrugged and put the key into the ignition. "Well, sounds like he left you guys to do your own running anyway. I don't see what's so special about that."

Sophie nodded, ever so slightly. "Yes, he left us to get out on our own. But he was running to try and help. He didn't want us to get into danger, even if he was."

"He was deluding himself to think that he could help. He didn't know what was at that doorway. I saw it, I knew we were fucked if we stayed. I tried to tell him." The car coughed and sputtered before rumbling into life.

"When?" Sophie cried and her anguished question caught in Jayden's ears. She began shouting, her head falling forward, her face twisted in grief. Tears burst from the corners of her eyes, dripping to her lap. "When did you try and warn any of us? You screamed something about needing to run and then bolted! You never tried to check on us at all, you didn't even care when Katie–" She couldn't keep speaking and clutched her stomach as she doubled up in her seat. Her breath came in slow heavy sobs.

Jayden wasn't sure how to answer. He put the car into reverse and slowly released the parking brake. "I wasn't happy when she... when Katie died." He swallowed. It felt like sand in his throat. He wiped his eyes to clear away a vision of Katie's face, being pushed open from behind by a blunt arrowhead of red gristle and bone. He remembered the way her nose had swung sideways, as her eyeballs bulged in their sockets. He shuddered at the memory of her skin, pulling and tearing away from her cheeks like an over-filled plastic bag. "That was not a happy time for me either. But so many people were dying and we just had to get away-"

"But you two weren't strangers! You hadn't been having a drink with anyone else who died! You hadn't spent the evening making fun of people with anyone else who died! You knew her!" Sophie turned to face him, her face blotchy and red, her cheeks wet with tears. She was like some glorious angel of righteous anger. "She was a girl who thought you were cute, and you were interested in her too, don't try to deny it!"

"You wanted me to keep running!" Jayden tightened his fingers on the steering wheel, frowning. "I was going to call the police, and you said we had to keep running!"

"You didn't care about what happened to her, you were in shock at everything. You didn't really want to call the police, you just didn't want to think about what was happening around you. You still don't." Sophie's voice was heavy with anger and disappointment. "I knew you had been a shit recently, but I believed in the man I used to know. The man who used to be my friend, who used to be..." she sucked air in through her nose, her chest rising as she drew in air. "That man would have shown some kind of emotion when Katie..." Sophie stopped talking abruptly, still staring directly out through the windshield. Her breath escaped slowly, in small shuddering bursts.

"I barely knew her." Jayden felt his cheeks burning. "I'm not happy that she died like that. But I'm not happy anyone died the way they did tonight. That doesn't mean I'm going to risk dying instead of them."

"James did."

And maybe James had his neck squeezed until it burst, like a piece of ripe fruit. Jayden was smart enough to keep his thoughts to himself as he put the car into reverse

On the far side of the street below them, a beam of light swung up the building. It shot skywards then dropped back before zigzagging its way to ground level.

"What the hell was that?" Jayden pulled the handbrake back on and switched off the engine.

"Oh nice, suddenly *now* you have a conscience. Just get us to safety, it's what you're good at isn't it?"

"No, seriously. We need to check what's happening before we try to drive out past it." Jayden got out of the car and moved over to the railing.

In the street below a group of police were jogging closer. They were shining their torches over the buildings that lined the street. As far as Jayden could tell, they were searching for something, but the way their lights zipped along meant he couldn't imagine what. *Oh Jesus, I hope that doesn't mean the wet man is somewhere in this fucking parking lot,* he thought. He could feel his heart begin to pound, and he clutched the railing as he turned to look behind him. Beyond Sophie's car he could see only darkness. Inside the car he could see her still glaring at him. With effort, he turned back to the movement in the street.

A pale figure appeared at the shadowed mouth of an alleyway behind the police. The officer in the rear, clearly nervous and moving their torch far too quickly, nearly missed the figure. But it moved slowly out into the middle of the street and the sound of it calling out was just audible to Jayden. Instantly every torch spun around and lit the figure as though it was centre stage.

From the railing Jayden was able to recognise James' clothes. They looked ragged and dirtied, but at least he was standing. He was carrying something, pale cloth bunched in his arms, as though he had found a bundle of laundry. The light from the torches cast thick bands of shadow beyond him.

"It's James," Jayden called back to Sophie.

She shoved open the car door and jumped to the railing, leaning far enough over that Jayden began to reach over so that he could grab the back of her clothes in case she toppled over it. For a second she held out an arm towards the distant figure, stretching beyond the safety of the barrier, but then she shifted her feet on the ground and settled into a more balanced position.

James took a step towards the police. They called out, voices full of alarm. The sound reached Jayden and Sophie like the concerned chatterings of mice. Slowly, as though he were a vine coiling on itself in cool weather, he bent to the road and put the bundle in his arms on the rough asphalt. It unrolled on the black surface revealing a head covered by a swathe of blonde hair. Limp arms and legs unfolded out along the road next to torn strips of clothing that had been wrapping the small figure. A vine stripped of its heavy fruit; James rose and lifted his hands to either side of his head, palms forward and clearly empty. One of the police officers began to move forward, motioning to James.

Jayden and Sophie were too far away to hear the police clearly now that they had stopped shouting or using megaphones. They were clearly being wary of something they considered dangerous and so Jayden assumed they had discovered the evidence of the wet man's carnage; he just wondered if they had seen the wet man or where he had gone.

"They aren't sure if James is the one who did it," Sophie whispered. Jayden glanced across at her and then back to the scene playing out below them. Her eyes had been wide and fearful.

"Maybe not. But he's rescued someone and he'll co-operate with them. That'll mean there's no danger to him."

"What makes you think he's rescued someone?" Sophie sounded more like her old self now that she could see James. Her voice was stronger and didn't sound like it was close to breaking. She was ready to argue with him. Jayden's mouth twitched into a half-grin.

"Maybe he recovered a body. Maybe she's the only corpse that wasn't..." Talking about people being torn apart like play-dough dolls made her choke. "Anyway, maybe it's not quite what you think."

"That does worry me about one thing though," added Jayden. James and the police officer were only a few meters apart now, talking quickly and gesturing to the girl slumped on the median strip beside James. "If they are worried that he might have been the killer then that means they haven't even seen the actual killer."

"Oh god." Sophie's voice crept closer to panic again and she pointed to the buildings next to the alleyway James had emerged from. Another figure was walking out of a doorway near the alley mouth.

It was the sick cashier that had been retching in the corner when they bought their tickets. She was still in her cinema uniform with its grey stripes and she still wore a cap over her hair. Jayden imagined that if she turned around he would see her ponytail sticking out from the fastening on the back of the cap. She was carrying something in her arms too.

"I don't think they've seen her. Should we try and call out to them?" Jayden looked at Sophie. She was breathing shallowly and the colour in her face was draining as he watched. "Sophie? It's okay; it's not the guy in the wet clothes." She didn't flinch. "It was definitely a guy I saw killing those people. This girl was just working at the cinema. I mean, she was really sick, but that doesn't make her a killer."

"Then how come she's still alive when everyone else is dead? It doesn't make sense." Sophie was beginning to shake again. Jayden moved closer and put his hand on her shoulder. He didn't know how to keep her from breaking into another panic attack. To be fair, he didn't know how he had avoided falling into a catatonic heap himself. He supposed it must be adrenaline or something keeping him upright, replacing the blood and energy with a fake rush that would punish him later. But for now, he just knew he had to keep functioning.

"James isn't dead. Maybe she survived the same way he did, however he did. And look, she has something in her hands too. Maybe she saved someone too."

A third figure staggered from the darkness in the alley, lurching from one foot to the other and halting abruptly next to the cinema girl. Its head lolled to the side and its arms hung limp. Its legs were awkwardly jutting from the bottom of its torso and there seemed to be a thin rope leading from its shoulders to the upper stories of the building behind them all, almost invisible in the darkness. The police still hadn't appeared to have noticed either of the two newcomers, although James and the officer he was talking to had moved closer so that they could shake hands. Behind them slumped the figure James had put on the road.

The two figures began walking out of the alleyway. The girl in the uniform stepped quickly in small precise movements, like an insect, shifting each foot only a tiny distance before setting it down and moving the other foot forward. She didn't even seem to be bending her knees, her legs ticking forward like clockwork. The other figure moved like it was being pulled and pushed from different sides. Its feet dragged on the concrete and its arms dangled by its sides. Jayden felt his stomach begin to knot up. Sophie was right.

"James!" he yelled into the night air. "James, behind you!"

Sophie joined him, desperately crying out in the hopes that the men in the middle of the road would hear them. She pushed her body out over the edge of the railing, leaning precariously and jutting her face centimetres closer to help her voice carry. But James and the police just seemed to keep talking.

James turned and gestured at the figure lying on the ground by him then froze. He jabbed a pointing finger towards the alleyway and all the police swung their torches onto the approaching figures. Everybody paused. The streetlights spread their orange light over the scene.

Now that the police torches were outlining the two figures from the front, Jayden could see them more clearly. The girl became fully recognisable, any doubts over who she was vanished in the torchlight. The other figure was a young man dressed in an awkward uniform, his collared tee shirt dark blue with a small white name badge glinting on his chest. Both the girl and the young man stared into the torchlight as if it didn't nearly blind them. Their faces dripped with dark liquid and their arms were stained.

There seemed to be two long dark ropes hanging from the young man's shoulders, lifting up into the darkness unlit by the police torches. Jayden thought they extended all the way back to a second story window in the building behind the figures, but it was impossible to be sure.

Jayden thought he saw some rubbish blowing across the street, catching in the gutter beneath the parking lot and then being gusted over the concrete lip and out of sight below.

James was the first to break the spell that had fallen, darting forward to try and pick up the figure he had placed on the ground. The girl in the cap screamed and lunged towards him. Her arms raised like birds' wings and her face wobbled on the end of her neck like a stuffed toy. She slid forward along the road, hardly seeming to move her feet at all. Jayden had just enough time to reach out and cover Sophie's eyes before the girl reached James and crashed a fist into his head. Even from the distant car park, so far away that their shouts hadn't carried across, Jayden could hear the sickening crunch of her fist making contact. It sounded like an eggshell slowly being broken in someone's hand.

"James!" Sophie began to climb up the shiny metal of the railing, stretching an arm over towards the distant struggle. Tiny shouts from the police echoed faintly down the street. Jayden refused to look, horrified by the sounds that accompanied the increasingly panicked police shouts.

"Sophie, what the hell are you doing? We have to get out of here!" Jayden grabbed her shoulder and pulled her roughly off the railing. She landed in a heap on the asphalt. She brushed the hair out of her face and glared at him, her face twisting with anger.

"I have to help him!" She tried to get up again, but Jayden grabbed her arms and knelt in front of her.

"Don't be insane, we're too far away! That's a sudden drop onto concrete over the railing!" He glanced behind him. There was silence from the street now, though from where they were crouched he couldn't see anything. "The best chance we have of helping would be to get in the car anyway." He risked a glance around the parking lot. It remained empty and silent, lit only by erratic orange fluorescents. They buzzed like insects, flickering on and off and on and off and on. "Come on."

He got to his feet and scurried around to the driver's side of the car. He pulled the door open, slid into the seat and fumbled the keys back out of his pocket. As he began to insert them into the ignition he looked at the empty seat next to him. *Oh for fuck's sake,* he groaned to himself, lying back on against the seat.

"Sophie?" He wound down his window and leaned his head out of the car. Sophie remained where he had left her, slumped on the ground near the front of the car. She looked at him and then slowly crawled over to the railings.

Jayden thought he heard a scratching noise and turned to look across the empty parking space over his shoulder. Between the darkness and the narrow window of the car, it was hard to see, but the space still seemed empty. *I'm jumping at nothing,* he thought. Even the shadows of the tyres looked threatening at the moment. He looked back at Sophie.

She was looking out between the railings, like a prisoner in an old western jail, mournfully watching their accusers drinking with the local sheriff. Jayden watched her eyes as they flicked from side to side and then rolled slowly down as she closed them. She slumped forward, all the energy draining out of her figure. It was as though she was melting into a doughy heap of person, with no bones left whatsoever.

"Sophie?"

She didn't open her eyes as she stood up and stumbled around the front of the car. Jayden tried to start the car as quietly as possible and grimaced as the engine grumbled then roared into life. Sophie opened her door and almost fell into the seat.

"The street was empty."

"What do you mean?" Jayden grabbed the back of her seat and twisted around to look out the rear window as he backed out of the parking space with a soft crunch.

"I mean just what I said. There was no-one there. No-one at all."

Jayden drove in silence for a few moments, navigating between the concrete pillars towards the exit ramp. He opened the glove box and pulled out the parking ticket for the automatic arm. "Well, if you didn't see James'... If there was no... Maybe James got away?" His fingers were shaking and his stomach felt nauseous as he tried to slip the small piece of card into the machine. He missed completely twice and then finally it slid home the third time. A pleasant female voice told him to drive safely and have a nice day.

The road was empty but felt emptier than Jayden would have dreamed. He was sure there should have been a few people walking around town at this time of night, on their way to a small bar or heading home after a meal perhaps. Nothing moved on the flat grey pavement. Cold fluorescent lights burned behind sheets of glass, as sterile as an empty surgery. Sophie's voice came as a shock to him as they drifted along the streets.

"That's true."

Jayden looked at her face. Her eyes seemed to shine, even as they passed through the shadows between street lamps. "What's true?"

"James must be okay." Sophie smiled so wide that Jayden's cheeks ached in sympathy. *A smile that wide had to hurt!* "He'll be waiting for us when we get home! How silly of me to worry, of course he'll be okay."

And, thus relieved, she settled back into her seat and closed her eyes, as if she was going to go to sleep. She even curled her legs up beneath her, resting her feet on the seat itself. Jayden shook his head slowly and squinted at the road signs while he chewed on his lip. *Which one gets us to the bloody motorway?*

There was a movement in the rear-view mirror. Jayden felt the hairs on the back of his neck slowly lift up until the cold air could stroke his skin. A silhouetted figure was stepping slowly and erratically down the footpath in the distance behind them. Jayden pressed his foot onto the accelerator and drove faster towards the main roads of Wellington.

CHAPTER FOUR

Jayden woke up and swallowed. His throat felt as rough as sandpaper and his eyelids were stuck together. The dregs of his sleeping drool made a gummy covering for his chin and he groaned as he tried to wipe his face with his hands.

The couch cushions felt like softened marshmallow, drooping under his shoulders and elbow. His head was propped up further than was natural by the solid-cornered wooden arm of the couch and his neck cracked noisily as he stretched.

The room was empty and silent. It was Sophie's lounge, Sophie and James' lounge. Jayden blinked and sighed as he tried to recover his memories. Why hadn't he just gone home? He'd had to get Sophie back to her place. Why hadn't he told her to fuck off, and just come to his place? He sniffed and gagged as his body fought to stay in its dreams. Right, because she insisted that James would be here. He must have got her to bed, and then fallen on the couch himself.

Jayden reached out to the coffee table and picked up the remote control, turning the TV on to one of the breakfast news travesties. The smiling faces and shiny logos washed over him and he leaned back against the couch. For a few minutes he waited, expecting to hear about the horrors of the night before, but there was nothing. He stared at the ceiling, where two flies were crawling around the light fitting.

It wasn't surprising really. People were good at presenting themselves exactly how they wanted to be perceived. Sophie and James wanted to seem like regular grown-ups, and they thought that meant cream furniture and dinner parties, so that's what they did. James had wanted people to think he was a hero, so he went running off into disaster, like an idiot. So it was the same with the news, they wanted to present a chipper face with no blemishes, especially first thing in the morning when people were still trying to clear their heads of the cobwebs and nightmares from the night before.

Jayden had lost patience with it, the effort of trying to predict what people would want and then the struggle to ensure that that was what they saw. In the end, what was the point? At least if he was honest, it was much easier to keep track of.

Slowly, Jayden stood up and moved into the kitchen. He picked up the empty kettle and shuffled over to the sink, where he filled it. He kept listening for any news of the nightmare he had survived, but still nothing. With the kettle now topped up, he put it back and switched it on before leaning at the sink counter, relishing the cool metal against the palms of his hands. The morning sun was shining through the window in front of him, peeking between the neighbours' houses. The kettle clicked off, steam leaking from the lid.

Jayden got two mugs out of the cupboard and made cups of tea. Gingerly holding one around the lip so that he didn't burn his hand but could pass the handle to someone else, he passed through the lounge, glancing at the movie reviewer on the TV, and into the hallway that led to Sophie's room. The door was hanging half open and Jayden paused, staring at the dark crack between the door and the frame. In the back of his head, the darkness held shouts and screams.

Somewhere in the room beyond Sophie was sleeping alone, without the man she had partnered with. The man who had become a part of her. Jayden wondered if she had discovered who the real James was. He wondered if the real James actually had been the idiot from last night, diving into chaos. *Maybe she was right, maybe I should have done the same thing.* Sophie had said that when they were together, she thought Jayden was someone who would have been upset by all that carnage. But maybe this numb and angry Jayden was the real Jayden, the one that she had never really wanted to see. The one that she had sent packing. Laughter echoed from the TV in the lounge and Jayden frowned.

What if James was actually in there? Maybe Sophie was right? What if Jayden had just had too much to drink last night, and had had terrible dreams. James was always telling him that he was an embarrassment when they went drinking. Had he finally gone too far? It wouldn't be totally outrageous for him to have dreamt something awful while lying in such a painful position on the couch, after skulling back too many beers and goading Sophie and James so much.

He nudged the door open and stepped into the room.

"Sophie? Sophie, I've got a cup of tea for you. I couldn't remember if you had milk or sugar, so it's just a plain black one. I'll get some if you want." The room was very dark. Sophie and James' curtains were thick and heavy, blocking out the morning light. "Sophie? Thanks for letting me crash on the couch last night, I must have been pretty out of it." He walked over to the edge of the bed. He placed the mug on the bedside table and paused, staring at the small lamp that he could just make out in front of him. He slowly moved his hand towards it. "Ja... James? Are you..." He turned on the lamp.

The bed was empty.

The covers were pushed down to the end of the bed. The room appeared empty; but, lit by the small bedside lamp, shadows thronged the corners, deep pools of black beside the drawers. Jayden stood up and swallowed tightly. He felt very conscious of the open door behind him and the unseen space beneath the bed. With stiff shoulders, he turned and stepped back to the door then through into the hall. The doorknob to the front door was rattling.

"Hey Jay!" Sophie burst through the door with a canvas bag full of groceries. She looked clean and fresh in a nice summery dress. It was blue and white, and there were tiny flowers embroidered around the edge. It made Jayden even more aware of the grimy feeling coating his skin and hair and teeth; the wreckage of having slept in his clothes. Just seeing her burst in, sunlight shining off her hair, made him feel like he should go and brush his teeth.

"Hey Sophie." Jayden watched her bustle into the lounge, swinging her groceries around the couch and almost skipping into the kitchen.

"Oh, is this tea for me? That's so kind of you Jay, thank you."

Jayden walked to the lounge and stopped beside the TV. Voices murmured from its shining surface. He felt uneasy about getting too close to Sophie. She leaned around the kitchen door and her eyes seemed too wide, too bright.

"Actually, that was my tea. I did make a cup for you though; I took it through to your room. I was... I thought you'd still be asleep after..." He shook his head slightly. "I mean, I just wanted to try and make up for being weird last..." Sounds of rustling came through the doorway. "Sophie?"

"Yes?"

"Where did you go just now?"

"I was out shopping'" Sophie came back into the doorway, this time carrying a frying pan. Jayden had to focus on staying still in order to keep his feet from stepping instinctually away from her. He watched the heavy metal object slip through the air as she casually swung it about. "I thought it would be nice of me to make some breakfast for my lovely boys."

"That's very nice of you." Jayden ducked his head slightly as the pan rose in a particularly high loop. "What do you mean, your boys?"

"You and James of course!" Sophie grinned and spun back into the kitchen. Jayden heard the click and whoosh of the gas stovetop being lit. He stepped up to the doorway and looked into the kitchen. Sophie was opening a carton of eggs and cutting off a thin slice of butter for the pan.

"But... Sophie, James isn't here. You know that, right?"

Sophie stopped, not looking at him. She drew a deep breath and cracked an egg into the frying pan, where it sizzled merrily. She turned to face Jayden. The morning sun through the window left half her face in shadow.

"What do you mean? Where is he?"

Jayden didn't know how to respond. He frowned and wiped his mouth with his hand, hints of stubble scratching at his fingers as they moved down his chin. "Sophie, we saw him... Last night there was... Sophie, James is dead."

Sophie laughed and turned back to the frying pan. "Don't be horrible Jay, that's ridiculous. I know you guys were having a bit of an argument last night, but that doesn't mean you need to say such awful things. Is he having a shower right now?"

"The shower isn't on Sophie." Jayden took a deep breath and searched through his memories. *Did we have a fight? I don't remember that. I know that Sophie was pretty pissed off with me, but not James. Did I dream this whole thing so my drunk brain could get rid of him?* The thought made his face burn. Sophie had been his friend for so long, she had welcomed him into her circle of friends when he moved back to Wellington after Mia. There was no reason that she should have done that. She would have been totally justified if she had ignored his texts and left him to figure out a new social circle. But she had hugged him, and brought him to parties with the old crew, she had met him for coffee. What did it say about him, that she was the one he was getting into fights with?

But the memories of last night were strong and horrifying. He wished that he was wrong, that none of it had happened, but couldn't think of any way that was true. He took a step into the kitchen.

"Don't you remember? We saw him on the street below the car park. And those... things... must have killed him."

"Shut up Jay."

"I don't mean to hurt you Sophie." Jayden wasn't far from her now. He wondered whether he should reach out to hug her, to comfort her in some way, as he used to. "But you need to remember that he died."

"I said, Shut Up Jay!" Sophie flung the scorching hot frying pan behind her without looking and Jayden had to dodge sideways to avoid being hit by it. Hot molten butter and half cooked eggs splattered across the wall and the pan smashed a hole in the panelling. "James is not dead! You're just an asshole!" She ran past him and threw open the door to the bathroom. "James! James, where are you?"

Jayden tried to follow her, glancing back to see if the kitchen was going to burn down. "Sophie, please, calm down!"

"Fuck you, you bastard! James?! Please, tell me where you are!"

Sophie paused, staring at the TV screen. Jayden took the chance to duck back into the kitchen to turn off the oven and make sure the pan wouldn't start a fire. By the time he ran back out into the lounge, Sophie was sitting on the couch with a puzzled frown on her face. "James didn't come back with us last night."

"No, he didn't," Jayden began, but Sophie interrupted before he could continue.

"Get out of the way." She was watching the TV closely. Jayden turned around so that he could see what was happening.

A view of the central city was being shown; while the corner of the screen held a rotating graphic that said "Breaking News!" A voice was in the middle of explaining something. Jayden noticed red flashing lights down one street between the skyscrapers as the camera moved across the city.

"... going on. We have spoken to emergency services and they have told us that resources are stretched due to circumstances beyond their control, but no-one is letting us know what's happening. Some bystanders are worried about terrorism or possibly an industrial accident of some kind. No-one is being allowed beyond a police cordon that surrounds five blocks at this stage."

"James didn't come home with us, which means he could still be in town."

Jayden swung his head around to stare at her. He felt a chill run down the back of his neck.

"Sophie, no, James isn't in town."

"He might be." Sophie looked deep into Jayden's

eyes and he was sure he saw insanity flooding the bottom of those pools. "I have to go and look for him."

She stood up and walked to the front door. Jayden shook his head and sighed.

"I'm not coming with you," he said. "I saw what was happening down there, and there's no way I would go back into that."

She didn't stop walking.

Jayden waited as the footsteps echoed down the hallway and the front door creaked open. It shut with a soft click as the latch slid into place. He stretched his shoulders backwards and rubbed the back of his neck. An angry ball was burning at the base of his throat, and another deep in his gut.

"Fuck her."

He walked into the kitchen to clean up the frying pan. Part of the floor tiling felt warm, but there didn't seem to be any danger. He was careful not to burn himself on the black metal of the pan as he picked it up and returned it to the stovetop. "If she's lost touch with reality, then she's only going to get more disconnected. Or worse." He turned on the tap in the sink and reached to grab a cloth, but there wasn't one. He opened the cupboard beneath the sink and crouched down to see if he could find a cloth in there.

He wished there was someone he could pretend to be talking to about all this. Even a cat or dog would have done. A pair of eyes to look into while he explained exactly why it would be monumentally stupid for him to go chasing after Sophie, to head back down into that chaos in the city. He needed a set of eyes that might look back into his own without judgement or disappointment. Instead, he had to imagine what such eyes might be like as they watched him clean up the house of his only remaining friend. He had to imagine them as he stayed safe in a small house that wasn't his own, and let her go back into danger for the sake of her loved one. He flinched and raised a hand to try and hide from the eyes that weren't there.

"I've got to get the fuck out of here."

He walked through the apartment to make sure he hadn't left anything behind. His jacket lay on the floor at the end of the couch and his shoes were by the front door. He found some loose coins on countertops and between the couch cushions, which he put in his pockets, just in case. Finally, he drew a glass of cool water from the kitchen tap and stood looking out the window as he drank. The liquid chilled his throat and he could feel it sluice down to his stomach. His shoulders felt more relaxed.

The car. There was no way he was going to be able to walk anywhere safe after what he saw last night. One of those things could stroll around the corner and then he'd be fucked. He needed to get far, far away from the city. *Why did I leave the bloody car up north with Mia? I should have told her it was mine really, should have made her let me take it.* He shook his head and rejected the idea. *I guess I could try and get a train or a bus.* He snorted. *Yeah, because public transport is a great idea when there's weird monstrous people walking around. I'm going to need Sophie and James' car.*

He looked for the keys where he had left them the night before, on the stand in the front hallway. There was an old white envelope with a clear plastic window displaying James' name, a scrawled message in ballpoint pen saying "Pay by 16th" but no keys. He moved through the lounge, lifting the cushions on the couch again and peering underneath, then sighing and lifting the couch itself to look underneath until his fingers ached he had to let go. The kitchen was bare, but took quite some time to search. There was an old jam jar that had been cleaned out and now contained twelve paperclips of assorted sizes and materials, eight blue pens, six black pens, one green pen, one glittery purple pen, a lighter, screwed up receipts from the dairy, including Sophie's from this morning when she got a pack of eggs, and several slightly grimy old keys.

The master bedroom was much easier to search. There were only a few level surfaces that someone might drop a set of keys as they entered and those were all kept clean and sterile; only a small bedside table on either side of the bed, each with only one drawer that was mostly empty. Jayden flinched when he saw a box of condoms but nudged them to one side as he pawed through the contents of the drawer. He even tried the bathroom, checking the medicine cabinet between packs of old flu tablets and bottles of chemical green mouthwash.

He frowned as he walked back into the lounge and slumped into the couch. "Where the hell did I put them...?" He stared at the face on the TV.

The morning presenter was smiling with a mouth that seemed too white and stretchy for this early in the morning. In Jayden's experience, mouths weren't generally very flexible things before noon. He ignored the man and looked at the live camera-feed that was being projected as a backdrop behind the presenter. It showed a street in the downtown area of the city, two police cars awkwardly parked across the road and three police officers holding their hands up to keep people back. No-one was really pushing forward anyway, but the look on those cops' faces said they were going to do this job because it was the only thing they had left to hold on to right now.

"She wouldn't have." Jayden licked his lips and tried to replay his conversation with Sophie in his head. Had she mentioned driving to the dairy? He remembered the eggs. "Oh shit, she fucking did."

As he opened the front door, Jayden could feel his

stomach quiver and turn cold. He didn't know which idea was scaring him more; the idea that maybe Sophie didn't still have the car keys in her pocket from her morning trip to the dairy and that he was heading straight into the nightmare he knew was waiting for him in the city for nothing, or the fact that he had waited so long before heading after her.

CHAPTER FIVE

School-children scurried past Jayden on their way to school, like little brightly coloured beetles wearing garish cartoon backpacks that were bigger than their bodies. The roads were full of cars nose-to-tailing it all the way to work, the drivers behind the steering wheels bored and mouths hanging slightly open. Jayden saw one man reading as he drove, with his newspaper propped against the steering wheel.

At first he was sure he knew which way Sophie would have gone. The hills around Wellington all sloped down to the city and the city was where she had decided to go, so he just kept taking whichever street sloped down the most. Occasionally he would walk down tiny flights of stairs wedged between wooden fences with peeling mud-brown paint and houses that looked in no better state of repair. He always moved as quickly as he could down these stairs, glancing over his shoulder. One time a school-boy had walked past the top of the stairs just as Jayden glanced back and the movement had shocked him so much he nearly fell over. Luckily his hand reached out and grabbed a fencepost to steady himself, or he may have rolled head over heels down another twenty-five feet of rough and broken concrete steps.

Before he could think through what he was doing properly and come up with a plan, Jayden was standing at a traffic light, looking across the road at the first building higher than two stories he had seen all day. Skyscrapers glistened behind it in the morning sun. Streaks of yellow-white light flared across his vision as he looked both ways down the street. There was no more slope.

The streets weren't as full as he remembered them usually being on a work morning. *But then,* he considered, *most of them would be either staying at work or heading over to see what the deal with the police is. Like most New Zealanders, Wellingtonians are virtually professional rubber-neckers.*

There was a broad middle-aged man with a thick grey moustache standing below the traffic lights across the road from Jayden. He was selling newspapers from a large yellow metal cage beside him. The headline that was slotted into the advertising part of the cage said something about some politician who had recently denied owning a property somewhere he shouldn't, but Jayden glanced away before the boring words could kill off too many of his brain cells. He waited for a break in the constantly crawling parade of dull white and taupe cars before jogging across to a small traffic island dividing the two directions of traffic. Behind him someone called out angrily but the cars weren't slowing down so Jayden didn't worry. The pedestrian light changed to an animated green man, strolling amiably to nowhere in his little black circle.

On the other side of the road, Jayden spoke to the newspaper man.

"Hey man, where's all the cops?"

"Would you like to buy a paper first?" The man raised his eyebrows hopefully.

"Why in the hell would I want to do that?" Jayden began but the man held up a hand to cut him off.

"I don't mean to be rude sir, it's just that everyone has been trying to find out what's going on downtown this morning and no-one's bought any papers off me. It's kind of embarrassing, I mean, it's not usually a difficult job I have but today..." He shrugged and made a face that seemed to say "Life always gives you what you don't expect."

Jayden slid one hand into his pocket. He could feel the loose change in there, the smoothness of the coins and the way their edges clicked past each other as he held them.

"Here." He drew out a handful of coins and dropped them onto the newspaper pile in the yellow cage. "I don't want a paper but you can pretend to sell one for whatever's there. Now which way is everyone heading?"

The man frowned and Jayden could see his eyes narrow, but he scooped up the money and tucked it into a pouch he wore at his waist. "Seems that everyone's heading down that way, then turning right, towards the waterfront." He pointed behind Jayden, down the street.

Jayden didn't say anything; he just turned around and began to walk briskly past the quiet shop fronts towards the corner the man had indicated. A café sat right on the edge of the corner, with tables cluttering the footpath and big umbrellas wobbling in the breeze, ready to collapse on the unwary. A cute young girl in a deep green apron stood by one of the tables and watched him hopefully as he approached. When it became clear that he wasn't going to be stopping in to get a coffee, even one to go, and that he was even less likely to be offering her any semblance of a tip; her shoulders slumped and she leaned against the doorway. In the brightly lit interior of the café, Jayden could see a young man behind the register, polishing the glistening steel tubes of his coffee maker with all the care of a botanist tenderly feeding and pruning a rare orchid.

The road beyond the corner was nearly as empty as the other streets. Cars crept past each other on their way to work, though the traffic was beginning to thin. *Must be nearly 9 o'clock,* Jayden told himself. He glanced around for a clock tower or a building with a digital display but couldn't see anything. *Ah well, doesn't really matter anyway.*

A siren whined in the distance, but without urgency. It didn't seem to be moving anywhere, just sending out a warning complaint to the world about something nearby. Jayden tried to judge if it was definitely coming from directly in front of him, down the new road, but the tall sides of the buildings reflected echoes from all directions, including the murmur of wind from the sea, the sharp cries of seagulls and the muted grumble of cars. He paused as a courier van pulled out of an alley in front of him.

What will you do if she didn't come down here? What if she has run off to some other place that she and James hang out all the time? Maybe you should have listened when they prattled on about their boring little weekends, instead of rolling your eyes. Jayden felt his throat clench up. *What are you even doing back down here? Of all the god-forsaken places in the world that you never wanted to go, why the hell would you come back here after last night?*

Jayden walked as he thought. What was driving him back? Maybe he wanted to be proven wrong. To know that what he had seen last night was simply the imaginings of a worn out mind. Had he been particularly stressed at work lately? He didn't think so. Maybe there had been something wrong with the food last night and he had gotten sick? It wasn't impossible for him to have hallucinated something like that, to have imagined the sight of people standing in the cinema before...

Jayden stopped and clenched his fists for a moment. Even if it had been a dream, it certainly terrified him. He could still see, in his mind's eye, the shadow of a man being torn in half somewhere in a corridor behind a movie screen.

Do you want to protect her? Surely that's a worthy heroic thing. No-one would argue with you if you said you were following Sophie back into this potentially nightmarish place because you wanted to make sure she was safe? You've known her for years, and she's still your friend despite everything, not the fights between you and her, nor the situation with Mia. She's always been so kind to you. Even if James is alive, you'll want to make sure she isn't going insane.

Jayden tried to convince himself that taking care of Sophie was his main motivation, that he had not followed her immediately because he was still shaken up by what he thought he had seen the night before. But he felt a small voice in the back of his head wondering why he hadn't even thought about it until he got to the city.

"I'll get those damn keys off her and we'll go to Kanuka Creek," he muttered. "At least it's far enough away there that we shouldn't be troubled until someone knows what's going on."

An old lady in a dark green headscarf blinked at the rough sound of his voice and tottered slightly further away from him.

Near the end of the street was a police car. It sat at an angle across a side-alley from the main road that Jayden was walking on. One or two people stood nearby, looking down the side road, but they wore expressions of only mild interest. They looked nearly bored enough to walk away. Nothing could have happened here.

And yet, the police car's front doors both hung open. The passenger side was thrown as wide as possible, while the driver's door was swinging gently back and forth in the wind. No-one sat in the car. The long flat red and blue lights on the roof spun incessantly, flashing colours on the walls of the alley mouth. The sun was high above the horizon by now, shining down into the city, reflecting off windows to illuminate almost all the shadows. But the car was empty.

Jayden stopped and nodded at the others looking down the narrow road. It contained rusty rubbish skips and thick black plastic bags, clearly the back entrances to a variety of shops. At the very far end, where the alley opened onto another street, Jayden could just make out the alternating concrete layers of what seemed to be a car park. His feet felt like they were full of lead, weighty and held to the earth; and as cold and unfeeling. His socks felt rough as sandpaper on his skin.

He walked slowly down the alley. The plastic bags around him rustled as the wind caught them, but he moved carefully, making sure nothing had room to hide behind them before passing them. The rubbish skips gave him more trouble, as they could easily have hidden a full grown man, or something the same size and shape as a fully grown man, By moving to the opposite side of the alley and peeking around the edge of the skip, Jayden managed to get past them without his heart pounding much harder than a diesel engine idling.

Something smelt disgusting. The pungent rich scent of rotting food spread into his nose. Brown lettuce leaves poked through small tears in some of the bags and flies hovered in the air. Occasionally the miniscule insects would buzz right up to his face, tickling his lips or nose before he could wave a hand to brush them away.

Water dribbled down from the distant overflowing gutters above him, spreading a dark shining film over exposed brick and grey pitted concrete. A few posters flapped their dog-eared corners at him, while others soaked up the water and peeled from the wall.

Something scratched over the asphalt and Jayden spun around, lifting his hands into a sad mimicry of martial arts in crappy movies. He could feel his face flush with heat as he realised how pathetic it was that he had lunged into such a useless position. *God, I hope no one saw that.* He didn't dare turn around to look at the slack jawed observers standing at the entrance to the alley. He let out a breath as he realised the sound had only been a large beetle or cockroach that had scuttled across the footpath and under a plastic bag.

He felt the skin on his neck shiver as he lowered his hands and continued to the end of the alley. It was a disgusting place, and he would be glad to leave.

Beyond the end of the alley, the road was desolate. No-one stood on its footpaths. No cars moved. Damp patches remained from the brief morning rain showers. Jayden studied the multi-level car park that rose up across the street from the alley he had just left. He was fairly sure it was the one he had returned to last night, the one he and Sophie had stood in as James and the police had...

He cleared his throat and looked to the left. If he was correct, then James would have been somewhere over this way when it happened.

The street seemed as empty now as it could ever have been. No trace of anything unusual remained. No scorch marks, or damage to the road as far as he could tell. *Perhaps I really was imagining things last night,* thought Jayden. He looked at a smear of oil in the centre of the road and then raised his eyes to the buildings around him.

"Sophie? Are you here?" His voice echoed softly off the glass buildings and he grimaced. He felt pathetic for offering such a weak timid voice to call for

Sophie. But he also felt scared, wondering what else might have heard him. Where were the police from that car? Where were the reporters who had been hanging around to broadcast for the morning news shows?

Something moved to his left, a flicker of shadow that was gone when he turned his head.

Jayden could hear every breath he took wheezing its way in through his nose and down his tight throat to his lungs. His nostrils flared with every intake of air, and he couldn't stop them. Sweat was forming at the small of his back, a hot pool of nerves and trepidation. He started walking towards where he had seen the movement.

A doorway hung open with venetian blinds hanging over glass panes that split the door into two sections, lifting and falling back in the faint breeze. They looked dusty and yellowed from lack of use. Jayden peered into the room beyond. There were lots of shadows in there. Jayden felt his eyes growing warm as he tried to pierce the darkness. His lungs burned as he tried to hold his breath, fearing to exhale.

"Jay?"

"Jesus fucking Christ!" yelled Jayden as he leaped away from the door, very nearly collapsing over the curb and onto the black surface of the road. He swore again as he twisted his ankle on the edge of the footpath and crouched down to hold his leg. He glared back down the street. Sophie was walking towards him along the footpath, rubbing her hands over each other in a never-ending cycle. "You scared the hell out of me!" he snarled.

"I'm sorry," said Sophie. She did look a little bit sorry, glancing down to Jayden's leg and pursing her lips. "I was a little surprised to see you, down here at least. Why are you here?"

"I came after you, didn't I? I couldn't exactly just let you go alone." Jayden tried not scowl as Sophie's gaze flickered past him to the street, never stopping its twitching, shifting focus.

"Really? But you didn't think James was down here. Why would you offer to help me find him if he's not even here?"

"Sophie, James is... Look, I'm not here to help you look for him. I was worried about the trouble you might get into." He grunted as he rose to his feet, wincing a little at the sharp pain that darted up from his shin as he did.

"What trouble? There's nothing going on out here after all. It's downtown Wellington on a weekday morning, not three a.m. in some mist shrouded New York alley."

"Weren't you watching the news before you bolted out of the house this morning?" asked Jayden. "There's police stopping people from coming in here. Reporters were running around like Chicken Little, terrified of the sky caving in. It's not safe down here!"

"Chicken Little was wrong if you recall," answered Sophie with narrowed eyes. She turned and looked over the empty street, still twisting her hands together, knotting her fingers and unwinding them over and over. Jayden noticed an empty mince-and-cheese pie packet quivering in the gutter and then coming loose and bouncing and skidding down the road. "Besides, where are all those reporters? Surely if there was something dangerous down here then they'd be filming it?"

"Maybe the morning shows are over. Even journalists have to sleep sometimes."

"That's silly Jay. You know they'd still be filming if there was a story." She looked back at him over her shoulder, but only for a second before her attention was drawn back to the street. The buildings around them mirrored each other, with their skewed panes of pale blue and grey. Vertical lines towered on either side while the horizontal divisions angled to converge at some distant point. "And another thing." Jayden could see Sophie's shoulders shifting as she rubbed her hands through one another. "How come those police didn't stop you joining me?"

Jayden wanted to answer but he couldn't think of what to say. He thought of the police car he had passed, sitting empty outside the alley. The fact that there were no police at that car to stop him scared him a lot more than any angry boys in blue could have. He stepped forward to stand closer to her as they looked down the street.

"I feel like we were here last night," she said. "Does that seem right to you?"

"Yeah," he said. "I think we were parked over there." He pointed at the car park. "And I was fairly sure the last place I saw James was over here." He started walking towards the middle of the road, towards the oil stain he had seen earlier. As he approached he slowed down.

"What the... Is that oil stain moving?"

Insects buzzed up from the patch of dampness as Jayden and Sophie shuffled nearer, but he held out an arm to keep her from continuing. She pressed against his arm for a second, as though she was going to force her way past, and then she stopped.

"What is that Jay?" she asked in a dull voice.

Jayden was trying to tell if he was overreacting in his assumption that it was actually a patch of blood, or whether it could be some other liquid that would attract clouds of tiny buzzing insects, when a loud bang shot out from behind them.

CHAPTER SIX

The door with the venetian blinds had closed. Had been closed, it would seem, by the man in the blue uniform who was standing in front of the door.

"Oh thank goodness," said Sophie. "A policeman. He'll help me find James."

"Wait!" Jayden grabbed the back of her tee shirt as she began to move. "Something's wrong with him."

The police officer stood with slumped shoulders and his head lolled backwards. He slid one foot forward along the pavement towards them and then drew the other up to join it. The sound of his black polished shoes scraping over the footpath sounded harsh in Jayden's ears.

"I think we should go the other way," he said to Sophie.

"But why?" she began to ask, though she didn't try to stop him as he pulled her down the street towards the car park. He resisted the urge to look back at the policeman. He knew there was nothing he wanted to see behind him.

"Look, we need to get out of here. Do you have the car keys?"

"What do you need the car keys for? It's my car."

"I know, I know, I just want to drive the fuck AWAY from here and I need your car to do it."

"Where's your car?"

"My car's in Kanuka Creek. Remember? I left it with Mia? Like, years ago?"

"Oh right. You know, you probably could have said that you needed-"

"I decided to bus in from Khandallah and crash at yours," Jayden interrupted, unwilling to get drawn into a discussion of history that should stay buried, especially right now. "In case we had a few drinks, remember?"

"Oh. So you want me to drive you back to your place? Well, you'll have to wait until we find James."

Jayden had to press his tongue against the roof of his mouth to stop himself yelling at her. They had reached the alley he had come down but as he began to head towards the flashing lights at the far end, Sophie shook her head.

"I can't go yet," she said. "Come on, I need to find James." She pulled her arm loose of his grip and moved across the road to the car park. Jayden groaned, but jogged after her. Without her keys he was stuck here anyway.

They walked briskly around the lowered red and white arm of the barrier and Jayden followed Sophie towards a flight of stairs in the far corner of the car park.

"Where are we going?"

"We're going to start looking from where we parked the car. I bet if we retrace our steps, we'll find him."

"Yeah right," murmured Jayden, scurrying to keep up.

There was a soft thump behind them as the man in blue stumbled up the curb and followed them into the car park. Sophie stopped and turned around, her eyes wide and bright in the morning light.

"Jay, why don't we stop and talk to this policeman? I'm sure he'll be able to help us."

"Really? After all the things that happened last night, you still think that the fucking cops will... Alright, let's try a small experiment." He stepped in beside a dark grey hatchback and turned around. He tried to pull Sophie's shoulders down near his own as he crouched closer to the roof of the small car but she shook him off and stood straight, lifting her chin and staring at the policeman crossing the car park.

"Um... Excuse me? Sir? Mr Police Officer Sir?" Jayden swore under his breath. Why did he always have to sound like such an idiot? "We understand if you're upset that we are in an area we aren't supposed to be. Could you tell us if you've seen our friend James? He got lost down here last night."

The policeman didn't answer. His shoes continued to scratch along the concrete floor. One clump as a foot was thrust forward, followed by a long scrape as the other was dragged up to it.

"He would have been wearing a nice striped dress shirt. He has short brown hair and he's usually very friendly. I'm very worried about him." Sophie's voice echoed lonely in the empty car park.

This time the policeman moaned.

"I don't think he's going to be any help, seriously," Jayden said. He grabbed Sophie's arm and dragged her towards the stairs again. There was a sudden crash behind them.

Jayden spun around with his eyes wide and his breath in his throat. The windows of the hatchback had been broken by something, two holes smashed through from one side of the car to the other. The policeman took another slow step.

"What the hell was that?" demanded Sophie.

"Who the fuck cares, run!" Jayden followed his own advice and sprinted for the stairs. He heard Sophie's feet slapping on the concrete not far behind him but he didn't pay it much mind. All he thought about were the stairs ahead of him, and how they were getting closer, step by step.

After far too many strides, with panic rising in his chest to grip his lungs, Jayden's feet landed on the first of the stairs. Only then did he turn, chest heaving, to see what had happened behind him. Sophie reached him almost instantly, worry creasing her forehead. She leaned over a little to catch her breath. Jayden put his hand on her shoulder, but looked across the car park.

The policeman seemed to be in roughly the same place, far from the hatchback, still creeping towards them one laborious step at a time.

"We need to find a weapon or something."

"Jayden, that's ridiculous! We can't attack a–"

"For fuck's sake you fucking idiot, there is something seriously fucking wrong going on here! Last night we watched as a psychopath ripped people apart in a movie theatre down the road from here! Then we watched police and your boyfriend try to help people who had been hurt by that guy and they got slaughtered. The police have blocked off this area, the news says something bad is happening. Get it through your fucking head! That cop doesn't seem to be fucking human anymore!"

Sophie stared at him. Jayden could tell his cheeks were red with anger. He took a deep breath and tried to calm down.

"Look, I know it's really hard for you. And I wish it was all a bad dream. I was hoping that it was a bad dream when I came down here to find you. But face the facts! Look at this!" He waved a hand towards the officer shuffling through the car park. "We need to find some way to get past this guy and back to your place so we can drive the fuck away from all of this. I was going to suggest we go to Kanuka Creek, it's far away from everything."

Sophie's face was as still as a porcelain doll's, and just as pale. "Oh right, you just want to run back to Mia? At least you're beginning to think about other people for a change."

"It's not about going back to Mia, but Kanuka Creek is the middle of nowhere, that's got to be a better-"

"It's absolutely about going back to Mia." Sophie nodded and pursed her lips, then shook her head a little. She peered into Jayden's eyes. "I just don't know if you want to go back to her because you are worried about her, or because you wish you had her back." She reached forward and put a hand on his upper arm. He looked down and swallowed heavily. "There's a reason you guys split up Jay. There's a reason you came down here. It's been two years, there's no reason to go back there."

"Sophie? We can't talk about me right now." Jayden pointed across the car park, ignoring the cold hand that had clutched his heart as she spoke.

Sophie nodded very slowly. "Okay." She clenched her fists and started striding up the stairs. "Okay, I'll give you my keys in a second. Let's find a way around this guy."

Thank fuck for that, thought Jayden as he followed her up to the next level of the car park.

Jayden and Sophie slowed down at the top of the stairs, taking the time to check around the heavy wooden two-way doors for any danger. The second floor of the car park seemed to be totally deserted. The downstairs had been spotted with a few cars, possibly abandoned, but at this level there didn't seem to be any.

"Good, it's safe." Jayden began to walk carefully across the car park, looking for another set of stairs.

"Where are you going?"

Jayden turned around to face Sophie. "What do you mean? I'm getting out of here."

"But you're looking for stairs aren't you?"

"Yes." He nodded slowly, with wide eyes and an exaggerated enunciation of each syllable as he added "So that we can go up again." He pointed to the next floor.

Sophie shook her head and laughed softly. "Jay, you doofus. Eventually there will be no more upstairs and you won't be able to go any further. Didn't you think of that?"

Jayden felt heat spread across his cheeks again in embarrassment. He scowled and turned away. "What exactly do you propose then, Miss Let's-walk-into-a-fucking-minefield?"

"I don't know. Let's head to the edges of the car park and maybe there'll be something we can use to get down." There was a thud from the level below them and they both jumped. Jayden peeked through the small wire-grilled windows in the doors, but he couldn't see anything on the stairs yet.

"Okay," he nodded his head. "But we do it quickly."

"Agreed." They began jogging across the smooth grey concrete floor, keeping their distance from the heavy rectangular columns that held up the roof just in case something was waiting for them behind one. Neither of them spoke to the other.

At the far edge of the car park, they grabbed onto the thick concrete railing and looked out onto the quiet street.

"James!" shrieked Sophie.

Jayden stared. On the far side of the street, and almost a block to their right, stood a figure that looked for all the world like James. He had on the same shirt, the same pants. Jayden couldn't believe what he was seeing. *He's alive? He's actually alive?*

"I told you! I fucking told you Jay!" said Sophie in voice somewhere between a sob and a scream. He could see her legs begin to buckle beneath her, and he reached out to make sure she didn't fall over. Her could hear her murmuring, "He's okay, he's okay, he's okay" over and over to herself.

He looked back over the railing, ready to call out to James. Then another figure walked onto the street.

"Oh shit."

"What?" Sophie pushed herself up to the railing and looked out at the scene.

"I think it's a cop," said Jayden. The second figure seemed to be in a blue uniform. It held up a hand at James.

"A cop? A cop like the one behind us?"

Jayden shivered. "Fuck, I hope not." He glanced back over his shoulder. *We are going to need to get the fuck out of here soon too,* he reminded himself.

He turned back to look at the distant figures just in time to see thin black lines burst from James and stab into the uniformed figure in front of him.

"What the fuck!?" yelled Sophie.

James leapt forward at the uniformed person, bearing them to the ground. James' arms pinned the other person to the pavement, as dark shapes like massive insect legs unfolded from him and began jabbing rapidly at the person below. It was like watching a sewing machine, but with blood blossoming out from the two figures. James' head tilted back and turned. Now, even at this distance, Jayden could recognise his friend's face clearly.

"Jesus," cried Jayden, and he grabbed Sophie's arm and pulled her back towards the thick grey columns of the carpark behind them. He dragged her with him as he ran back through the car park, trying to figure out how they could get away from the things that had once been James and once been a cop. Sophie and Jayden burst out from the columns at another railing over a street. Mercifully, this one was empty. The murmur of distant morning traffic still echoed through the buildings to them. Jayden ran a hand through his hair and breathed out heavily before swallowing. Sophie was leaning on the concrete railing with a furrowed brow and pursed lips.

"Alright," she said.

Jayden winced. She hadn't lowered her voice at all, and it sounded shockingly loud. He whispered when he replied. "Alright what?"

"Alright, that's enough."

Jayden glanced at the void between them and the street. The footpath looked very hard and unwelcoming below. "Yup, I'm sick of running around too. You think we can get down here?"

"No. I mean, I can't do it." Sophie turned to face him, grabbing him by the shoulders. Jayden flinched away from her eyes, red with blood vessels and surrounded by dark blue skin. Sophie looked drained and exhausted, as though she hadn't slept in weeks and hadn't eaten in longer. "Without James, there's no point."

"Wait, what do you–"

"Here." Sophie dug in her pocket for the keys. "I parked by the Korean Restaurant on Victoria Street. You get out of here."

"What?!" Jayden stared at the keys dangling from her hand. There were about five or six of them, of various sizes. The morning light seemed to make them glow. There was a plastic square with a picture of a floral arrangement attached to the keyring. Jayden could just read the tag as he began to reach out for the keys in her hand. It was one of those Name Meaning tags. It said "One who understands."

"Sophie, what are you talking about? You don't need to-"

There was a bang from back in the depths of the car park. The doors to the stairwell had been thrown open hard, slamming against the walls on either side. The policeman was trudging his way closer, inch by inch.

"Thanks for coming to me Jay. I'm sorry it was a waste of your time. Now, Run!" Sophie smiled at him and then, before he could respond, she started sprinting towards the policeman. Jayden watched her racing away with the keys dangling from his finger-tips. His head felt as though it had been drained of blood, and he felt dizzy. He wanted to call out to her that he hadn't come into the city for her. *I'm not chasing you,* he thought. *I didn't come back to Wellington for you Sophie. Mia and I had broken up, I just needed a place to stay while I figured things out.*

He felt unsteady, and wasn't sure if he would be able to remain standing as she ran away from him. Her hair lifted like a halo.

I mean, it's not like she was single when I came back, and James is a decent guy, why would I want to get in the way of that? I couldn't get in the way of that, I'm was a wreck when I came back. I'm still a wreck at the moment! Could he call to her, reassure her that he knew how terrible he had been? His mouth felt as though it was stuffed with sand.

No, the only reason I'm down here at all is for those keys. I just need these keys. He lifted them up in front of his face, as though they might vanish if he stopped looking at them.

On reflection, he probably should have tried to find another way to leave when he realised that she had come into this area, roped off from the real world. This place was going to kill them both, he was sure.

He started running alongside the railing that over-looked the street, hoping that the columns between him and the officer would make it difficult for the other man to be sure where he was going. He knew that was unlikely, but it was all he had. He heard his breath rushing through his throat like a gale, the sound filling his ears with each gasp. His chest felt tight and his heart felt like a tumbling boulder, jarring against his ribs. He glanced to his right, wondering if he would see Sophie. He immediately wished he hadn't.

Sophie was still running towards the officer but, as Jayden looked, something erupted from beneath the policeman's shirt. The buttons mustn't have been done up, because the shirt billowed to either side as something long and thin shot forwards towards Sophie. A slithering rope of dark fleshy brown and pink material slammed against Sophie's stomach like a harpoon, piercing through her entire body, and she faltered in her sprint towards the officer, knocked backwards. She didn't collapse to the ground though. The tentacle remained impaled through her belly, impossibly holding her up in the air. Then, it recoiled, dragging her towards the officer.

Jayden looked away and pushed his legs harder, ran faster. Her scream pierced the stillness of the car park, ringing and echoing off the gray featureless surfaces back and forwards, over and over and over.

And then suddenly, her voice ceased, though the echoes burned into his ears. Jayden gritted his teeth and kept forcing his feet to move, as fast as he could. They felt stiff and solid, like marble posts instead of functioning legs. He wanted to scream, he wanted to cry, but he knew that he couldn't stop, not yet. Columns blurred past him on either side and a terrible deep moan rattled across the car park, like the gurgle that would be heard if the ocean slipped away down some monstrous plughole.

Fucking impulsive woman, he thought as he ran. *What the hell did she do that for? We could have made it! Jesus Christ what the fuck WAS that!?*

As Jayden tumbled past yet another pillar he saw that he had reached the far side of the car park. He fell against the railing, looking down on another street. He had never looked back as he ran and so had no idea where the policeman was. The thing could have been following directly behind him and the idea rattled through his skull like a bell, drowning out all other thoughts. He decided that it didn't matter, he would just run as far and as fast as he could without looking back. That thing wouldn't stop trying to kill him if he knew where it was, and looking back was a great way to miss what was coming up ahead of you. Besides, that tentacle thing would probably be able to kill him before he even knew what was happening. No, better to just move.

He bit his lower lip to keep from laughing or crying, he wasn't sure which. There, not three meters off to the right, hidden from anyone further inside the car park by all the pillars and columns, was a skypath. It was narrow and straight, but the covered walkway stretched across a small lane from the car park and into what looked like a multi-story department store or mall. Jayden dashed for the entrance.

CHAPTER SEVEN

J ayden thudded across the skyway in a nervous
jog. Nothing had smashed into him from behind
yet, and so he assumed that he was still far
enough away from the creature wearing a police
uniform.

But now he wondered, what was waiting on the
other side of this arch? Perhaps there were more of
these things in the store, hiding among the mannequins or behind the racks of CDs? He'd never find
out if he didn't get moving, and he knew that there
was definitely one behind him. Every step felt like he
was pulling his feet out of thick mud, or as though his
legs were filled with lead. His lungs were burning.
Why didn't I go to the gym, he panted. As he passed the
halfway point of the bridge the light from outside
made him realise that it was still early in the morning.
So much had happened that he would have not been
surprised to discover that it was late afternoon already, but morning sun was glaring directly off the
building he was heading for, making the windows
shine like molten gold. The light also made it impossible to make any further guesses about what would
be awaiting him over there.

Inside, the store was dark, even with the sunlight

bathing the building from outside. Like so many stores that want their customers to lose connection with reality, all the windows were covered with displays, posters, or simply walled over. With the police keeping people away from the area, no one had come in to turn on the lights this morning either. Jayden moved slowly between the racks, trying to figure out how to get downstairs and out. Again, the designers of the store were working against him, having made the paths and displays loop around on each other worse than a tangled knot of hair blocking a shower drain.

Finally he found the escalators, though they were turned off, and he scrambled down the steps as quickly as he could. He squeezed Sophie's keys in his pocket as he reached the bottom and looked around. Suddenly he was gasping for breath, with tears pricking at his eyes. He doubled over and panted, his throat clenched tight. After a minute, the panic passed and he was able to raise himself to stand upright again. A moan sounded from somewhere upstairs, distant and echoing. *Run*, he told himself.

Legs aching, Jayden began to jog through the downstairs part of the store, searching for a way out. He passed a rack of brightly coloured toddler toys and then realised he was passing it again. The moan rattled down the escalators again, closer and clearer. *Shit!* Jayden spun on the spot wondering what the hell he could do to get out before the thing that had been a policeman came flopping down the frozen black stairs. A ray of sunlight sliced across the darkness.

Jayden strode over to it and pulled at the heavy vinyl poster that was keeping the sunlight beyond from filling the store. Behind the poster he discovered a window display filled with half-dressed mannequins contorted into positions that no one would ever think of getting into by themselves. Outside,

Jayden could see the street. He felt laughter shaking his chest, and he put a hand on his chest to try and calm his nerves and stay silent.

Maybe I could use one of these things to smash the glass, he began to wonder, before a movement outside caught his eye.

The buildings across the road seemed to be a block of apartments, five or six stories high. Jayden could see lonely potted plants on each balcony, desperately trying to make the narrow spaces feel hospitable. They clustered beneath clothes racks where laundry waved, drying in the wind. A figure shuffled away from him on the footpath in front of them. The sight of the figure made Jayden's mouth dry.

Two thick tentacles connected the figure to a window in an apartment far above the street, like a marionette to its puppeteer. Jayden watched as the figure seemed to be pushed along the street in front of the dangling lengths, each step wobbling and uncertain. There was a muffled crash and another figure plummeted from a window far above, only to be caught up moments before hitting the ground, held hovering a few inches over the concrete by another pair of tentacles, each a twisted cable of red and white flesh-like threads. Something dripped from them to the footpath below the figure as it was lowered until its feet made contact with the ground. It began to move in the opposite direction to the first one.

What are these things, Jayden asked himself again, hearing the desperation in his own thoughts, echoing through his skull. *There's no way I can break out here now,* he realised and he began to crawl backwards out of the window, hoping that he might find another exit. Then the moan of the policeman somewhere behind him made him jump, banging his head on the knee of a mannequin wearing a long red dress and a wide brimmed hat. It wobbled back and forth on its metal base and Jayden held his breath. *Don't you dare, you fucking son of a bitch,* he swore to himself, reaching out to try and grab the mannequin before it fell. He was too late.

The mannequin thunked into the broad glass of the window, the impact resounding like a gong or church bell, reverberations echoing on and on in the air. The moan behind him raised to a screech, and sent a wave of fear down his spine. Deep inside the store racks of clothes and cheap metal interlocking shelves crashed and rattled on the linoleum floor as the thing that used to be a policeman began shoving them aside. Jayden scrambled forward into the display window, panting in panic and hoping that the thing wouldn't notice him behind the thin material of the poster. He glanced up at the window.

A spear of flesh and bone and gristle burst through the glass, missing his face by millimetres, spraying him with fragments and shards. He felt them bite at his cheeks and exposed hands, but thankfully none struck his eyes. Drops of black liquid, thick and gooey, splattered him as well. He retched and heaved, the smell of raw meat flooding his nostrils. The tentacle pulled itself back through the window, gashing itself open on the edges of the broken pane seemingly without a care.

Outside Jayden saw the two figures turning and groaning towards him. They moved quickly, but awkwardly, hanging from the tentacles that connected them to the upper apartments of the block. Another noise, this one more a shriek than anything else, echoed through the store behind him. A second tentacle came shooting toward him from the figures on the street outside, and he managed to duck aside enough to avoid it penetrating his body. *I'm fucked either way,* he thought. *May as well run!*

Jayden shoved aside one of the mannequins that stood before him, using its stiff figure to clear as many of the jagged triangles of broken glass from the frame in front of him as he could, and then lying it on top of the rest. He ducked under the tentacles hanging in the window frame, leapt through to the footpath, and began running as hard as he had ever run in his life. He ran in loops and zags, changing direction constantly. The rear window of a green car a metre or two to his right was smashed as he avoided a harpoon-like appendage again. His eyes were full of water making it hard to see, and he didn't know if it was from the wind in his face or if they were tears of fear. An alley to his right had lights shining at the end of it, red and blue lights. He spun sideways and pounded down its narrow width. At the other end of the alley was another police car, sitting with its lights spinning but the doors closed. No one was in it.

Jayden burst from the end of the alley and recognised the street. Before he could actually get his bearings a few observers with serious expressions on their faces turned to try and speak to him, reaching their hands out. He spun and ducked to avoid their grasp. A young woman with a blue suit tried to call out to him, the camera guy behind her turning to get him in shot. Jayden didn't pause, bolting further into the city in a desperate attempt to get other people between himself and the things that he had seen.

Jayden elbowed people aside as he ran further and further into the city, jumping out onto the roads to cross in front of buses and cars that blared their horns at him. Eventually he began to make sense of his surroundings, of the people wandering through the streets and staring at him, and he began to slow down. He couldn't bring himself to walk slowly though. He had to move his feet fast, striding along the footpath.

He found Victoria Street and began to look for Sophie's car. His stomach clenched hard and he bent over to lean on a bus stop.

"You okay man?"

Jayden didn't even look at the figure that came over to him, shaking his head as he stood up and moved on.

By the time he had located the car and began driving out of the city, there were more sirens in the air. People on the footpaths were glued to their phones, and talking to one another in hushed voices, unclear what was going on. Some were nervously looking up and down the streets, but Jayden ignored them all and began driving out of town. He turned towards the Wairarapa and pressed his foot down on the accelerator. *Idiots,* he sneered as he saw traffic heading into the city. *Haven't you been paying attention at all?* He drove in the opposite direction, out of the city on a motorway that was nearly empty.

The sun was nearing its peak as he headed towards the hills. He rubbed the skin under his nose and set his right arm on the window, enjoying the feeling of wind blasting against his face as he drove. "They don't have a clue what they're getting into."

He considered shouting a warning to the occupants of the cars, just as he had considered putting up notices in the windows of the car, or texting someone. James would have put up notices. Jayden sniffed and kept his lip pulled into a semi-sneer as he considered James.

The stupid bastard always thought he was a knight in fucking shining armour. Shit. Jayden began to wonder what it was that made James act that way. He had used to assume that James just wanted to look good, that the man had wanted admiration from others. Jayden had always figured that was why James kept Jayden around, for the contrast.

Did James even know that he was getting himself into a dangerous situation? Was he used to stepping up and being the hero in situations that weren't so dangerous, and so he didn't even consider what he was doing?

Because the stupid fucker sure is dead now. Jayden drove on, his face falling as he kept thinking about his friend. *Maybe James really was like that. Maybe he was just a good person, helping others.* Jayden's shoulders hunched lower as he drove. The thought sat in his brain like a toad on a dinner table, unavoidable and unwelcome.

Wellington disappeared behind the hills as Jayden kept driving towards Lower Hutt. Jayden pressed his foot against the accelerator and tried not to look into the rear view mirror.

ON EITHER SIDE of the road rose the hills and mountains of the Tararua ranges. The sun was high overhead, leaving the world shadowless and outlined in bright colour. Jayden drove without paying attention, trying to think of nothing more than his hands on the steering wheel and his feet on the pedals. At first, he had let the radio play, letting the random and mindless music of the pop station wash over him without requiring any thought or engagement. But that left him open to the annoyingly high-pitched voices of the presenters, and they were discussing the news out of Wellington.

"... to understand what is being reported, I mean, the police seem very confused."

"They do, they do! But I have to respect it, they're keeping people out of the area, so it must be pretty dangerous. I wouldn't want to do that job!"

"Right?"

"Yeah," grumbled Jayden. "We were all expecting you to leap out of your comfortable chair and declare that you wouldn't stay in your cushy job where you just talk about nothing for hours at a time, just so that you could sign up to be a cop. What a moron."

"But I did see some interesting photos coming out of Facebook, have you seen these?"

"No! There are photos? Wow, that seems morbid."

"Oh there's nothing gross, it's actually quite hard to tell what's in the photo. So, the clearest one shows an empty street, all at a strange angle, because the person has had to lean around a corner or something, you know? And so all that's all that you can see, right?"

"Right."

"All that you can really see, is some guy standing in the road!"

"Just standing there?"

"Yup!"

"That doesn't sound that scary. I was thinking it was, like, a terrorist or something!"

"I know, it all makes it seem really boring. I wonder why they are keeping everyone out though?"

"You two don't have a fucking clue," Jayden growled, wishing that the two idiots on the radio could hear him. "It's a fucking nightmare what's happening there, and anyone with any sense would be getting the fuck out! Leaning around a corner to take a photo, what idiot does that?"

"Actually, the guy in the road might be a terrorist, I'm just seeing now that the photographer might be in the hospital!"

"What did I tell you!" crowed Jayden.

"Oh wow, oh that's terrible! What happened, do we know?"

"No, it doesn't look like we know much. Apparently leaning around the corner to get a photo was more dangerous than they thought!"

Jayden thought of the thick meaty tentacles that

had smashed through the glass window of the store, piercing the thick plastic of the mannequins, remembering the rush of wind as the hideously sharp cartilaginous material had shot by within a hair's-breadth of his head. He remembered how Katie's head had looked when another of the tentacles hadn't missed her. He tried to forget the sound Sophie had made when the tentacles reached her.

"Yeah. It's real fucking dangerous."

The conversation was dragging Jayden back into memories that he did not want to relive, and so he tried to ignore them, but the presenters' inane babble was piercing and he couldn't shut them out. They knew nothing, they had nothing to add, but the speculation was so numbing that Jayden growled to himself and turned off the radio. It was better to drive in silence.

Hours passed. The sun began its slow journey towards the horizon. Jayden stopped to refill the petrol tank of the small car. He sat in the driver's seat, breathing deeply, as he mustered up the conviction to open the door. His fingers rested on the latch for a full minute before he swore beneath his breath, pulled the latch, and shoved the door open as quickly as he could. He tumbled out and raced to the back of the car, swearing again as he realised that he hadn't released the petrol cap. He paused, thinking about how he must look from the outside. He glanced over his shoulder.

Around him the station was quiet. The canopy sat overhead, shading customers from the early afternoon sun, and a loose plastic panel thumped periodically as the wind caught it. A woman stood filling her car two pumps away, watching him with a bemused expression. A Tūī was singing in the trees at the end of the forecourt.

"Are you alright sir?" called the attendant from the

door to the station shop. She was leaning against the doorframe and brushing wisps of long black hair out of her eyes with her hand.

"Yup, fine, don't mind me," called Jayden before he stalked back to release the petrol cap and got on with filling the car. *Don't be such an idiot,* he told himself. *You're far away from that carnage. You're fine. No one else is, but at least you are.* He coughed to clear his throat and sniffed, then breathed out deeply.

As he filled up, he noticed a smear on the rear tyre. It looked as though the tyre had run through a roast dinner. Chunks of solid brown and white were wedged between the rubber treads, and a dark gravy-brown liquid smeared across the surface. *Well that's fucking gross. When did that happen?* He nudged a piece with his shoe, and gagged as it slithered free from the rubber.

Jayden walked inside, ignoring the way the attendant at the door watched him go past, like he was some alien intruder or carnival attraction.

"Just the petrol is it?"

Jayden caught himself before he snapped "Do you see me carrying anything else?" at the other attendant standing behind the counter inside. *She's just doing her job,* he told himself. *You're just feeling exhausted by everything that's happened.* He tried to tell himself that, tried to make himself smile. He felt the corners of his mouth spread apart, but from the way the attendant leaned away, the effect must have been much more unsettling than he intended. He stopped trying to appear pleasant and held up his bank card.

"Do you have a rewards card?" asked the girl.

"No, if I had a bloody rewards card, I'd have got it out already, wouldn't I? Do you think I'm an imbecile who doesn't know how to buy things?"

The girl blinked and her mouth began to open. Then she clenched her jaw and pressed a button on the screen in front of her. The card reader beeped at Jayden, and he swiped his card, looking down so he didn't have to look at the girl. As the word "accepted" appeared on the display, he turned without saying anything and walked straight into the woman who had been watching him outside. She was shorter than him, and he instinctively reached out as they collided, which had the effect of pushing her in the shoulder with his elbow. She yelled and tripped over.

"Why the hell were you standing right there, you stupid woman!?"

Immediately Jayden saw anger and confusion pass over the woman's face. He shook his head, there was never any point in trying to explain what had happened. No one wanted to hear about the shit going through his head. It was always easier to just get away.

He stepped over the top of the woman and began walking out of the station shop.

"You're not even going to help me up? No apology?" The woman's voice was firm and incredulous.

"Watch where you're standing next time," he replied. "Don't expect me to have to watch out for you." In moments he was striding across the forecourt, climbing back into his car, and driving away.

CHAPTER EIGHT

He passed over a long bridge that slipped low over a broad brown river. The water rippled as it meandered through the wide riverbanks and Jayden appreciated the way it made him feel like a hawk swooping low over the water. That feeling of freedom, of movement, helped compensate for the panic he had been pushing through for hours. The low bridge and its low railings made the green grass fields that surrounded him seem endless.

Jayden drove along the final stretch to Kanuka Creek, and he could feel the tension evaporating from his shoulders with every minute that passed. He sat taller in the driver's seat, and he felt his grip on the steering wheel lessen. *I just need a good sleep,* he thought. *I'll get settled in and just get a good sleep and then I'll be ready to figure out what I do next in the morning.*

The road curved around a steep outcrop of rock, alongside the river that wound around its base. An orchard of apple trees grew on the other side of the river. At least, Jayden supposed that they could be apple trees. They seemed to have red fruit growing in the branches but, honestly, they could have been watermelon trees for all he knew.

The road climbed to meet the crest of the out-crop. Jayden breathed deeply. He was nearly there. All of this would be some strange nightmarish memory soon. Without warning, a figure burst over the rise of the hill in front of him, a person running directly to-wards him on the road. Jayden swore and spun the steering wheel sideways, planting his foot on the brake pedal as hard as he could. *How did they get here so fast? Where else are they?*

As the car spun and the wheels screamed in protest, rubber scraping across the asphalt, Jayden re-alised that stopping was probably the worst thing he could do in this situation. He tried to spin the steering wheel back into a sensible position, to regain control before he slammed into the rocky wall beside him, exclaiming "fuckfuckfuckfuckfuck" as he did. He tried to temper the accelerator, so that the car would be able to take off again as soon as he was facing the right way.

Should I keep going or try to turn around, he thought frantically. *Maybe I should try to run the bloody thing down?* He flicked his eyes across the road, trying to find the figure again.

It was standing motionless in the centre of the road, still at the crest of the hill. Now, as the car came under control again and he was less surprised, Jayden was able to focus and actually take in what he had seen. It was a young child, a girl if he went by the evi-dence of her long black hair. She was frozen in place, her face a grimace of shock and fear. He figured she was about seven years old. But she stood normally on the ground, and her expression seemed human. Jayden grimaced and wound down the window.

"Why the fuck are you standing in the middle of the goddamn road, you silly bloody child?" he yelled.

"It's, it's, it's-" spluttered the girl, her voice catching in the back of her throat.

Jayden rolled his eyes. "Oh spit it out already."

"It's the cross country," finished the young girl, turning to point back along the road the way she had come. Jayden raised his eyes and felt his shoulders fall as he leaned back into his seat.

"Shit."

Pounding up the road was a horde of tiny children, dressed in identical tee shirts and shorts, with a few teachers towering between them. The closest teacher came jogging up to the car and leaned her hand on the roof, bending lower to address Jayden through the window.

"Excuse me, did I just hear you swearing at this child?" she asked, a wide smile trying to seem polite beneath furious eyes. Jayden groaned.

"You know, you shouldn't even be on this road, we closed the whole thing off for the cross country." The woman shook her head slightly, rustling her straw-like hair beneath a ludicrous red floppy bucket hat. She leaned in closer. "Are you sure I didn't hear what I thought I heard?"

"I didn't see any fucking signs or anything," muttered Jayden, his eyes staring straight ahead through his windscreen.

"I'm sorry?" snapped the woman. Jayden rolled his eyes and turned to look at her now. She was skinny, with short blonde hair in a bob around her chin. She was wearing a baggy tee shirt herself, with a logo that seemed to be a stylised windmill and mountains design.

"Ah fuck this," he said, and he wound up all his windows and flicked the lock for the doors. He waited as the woman knocked on the window a few times, and pretended he couldn't hear her as she tried to get his attention. Children swarmed around the car, peering in at him curiously as they passed, until hurried along by other teachers. Eventually the woman gave up and ran off with the last of the children, but not before she took a photo on her phone, of him sitting behind the steering wheel with his arms crossed. Jayden snorted in satisfaction as he recognised the way her mouth shaped around the words she was using as she left. *I thought it was naughty to use language like that.* He nibbled on his lower lip and restarted the car.

Fuck. It was only children. Jayden tried not to think about the thoughts that had flashed through his mind just before he had recognised the girl. What would that woman have done if he had hit the girl with his car? Even if it was an accident, and he simply hadn't noticed her in time, that would have been bad. But if he had panicked and deliberately swung the massive metal vehicle at the tiny child... What would he have done to himself? Jayden began to push on the accelerator, driving the car out into the road, around the corner, and heading into Kanuka Creek, ignoring the acid bubbling in his gut.

Ah, Kanuka Creek, he thought as he rolled past a large beaten up corrugated iron shed, as tall as a large house, and probably wider. The mechanic's sign that was attached over the shed's huge double door was rusted and beginning to fall apart. *But why fix it,* thought Jayden. *After all, no one would possibly risk going to some other mechanic and getting the glares and anger reserved for traitors by the locals, every time they went to the pub. Who cares if they take a month to fix a bloody wing mirror? Who cares if they charge you three times what the guy in the next town charges? You've got to be loyal!*

He drove past small wooden homes, often with overgrown front yards full of waving stands of grass and weeds. Bees thronged the air around those homes. A small butcher's shop was on the left, a blue and white awning shading the footpath directly outside, though the fabric was beginning to wear thin and some holes were beginning to show in it. In the window sat a massive leg of ham on ice. Something about the barren cold surroundings of the leg made it seem small and unappetising.

Further into Kanuka Creek, the main street was brighter and less unkempt. The shop-fronts were well painted, and there were even one or two people sitting and chatting in the wiry metal chairs set outside in the sun. The dairy, the petrol station, the local fire station, all of them had people bustling inside, completing menial tasks and ensuring that the mediocrity of their lives would continue apace.

He drove past the Kanuka Creek Bar and Motel. The building was a solid white wall that towered over the footpath, with only a few tall thin windows interrupting its flat monstrosity. As he went past he remembered walking through the door at the other side, into the bar through thick clouds of smoke from the old men sitting at wooden benches outside, their heavy glasses of beer seated next to them, faces as wrinkled as old apples. He thought of the heat inside the bar. Its heavy dark wood furniture and velvet lined seats managed to exude heat, until he had pulled off his jacket and hung it over a chair next to the pool table. He remembered her eyes watching him from the far side of the pool table.

Bet you can't sink the red ball this shot!

Oh, I think I can. I think I could sink anything I wanted right now.

You'd like that wouldn't you?

I think you'd like it too.

Jayden felt as though the car was being crushed around him, as though the world was shrinking. He was reminded of the scenes in underwater action movies where the submarine would collapse under the pressure of the depths of the ocean, crushing in on the heroes with a violent self-contained implosion. That was what this small town did to him. He couldn't breathe.

He turned onto the main street and then left again almost immediately, driving past the large fire station on the corner. It was a broad and low brick building, with a double doored garage space for two engines. Firefighters were standing around the engines in their weird oversized trousers, laughing together.

"Better stay on task guys, wouldn't want anything to burn down while you're on the job," murmured Jayden. He sneered. "Or maybe you'd be glad of the entertainment."

A few twists and turns later, winding past fields of flowers and strawberries, Jayden spotted the letterbox he was looking for. It was a very ordinary letterbox, except that it had been painted to look like a white chicken, with the head attached to the door so that it would look as though it was pecking the ground when opened.

Jayden shook his head at the sight, but couldn't stop himself smiling a little. "You and your chickens."

Down the dusty dirt driveway sat a small house with a green corrugated iron roof, nestled under a broad limbed tree. Jayden parked next to a small hatchback and then leaned back in his seat. *What are you doing here,* he asked himself. *Is this really the best idea you can come up with? This shitty little town that you hated when you lived here. Why would you think this is the best place to hide? When things go to hell and you don't know what's going on and there's fucking monsters killing people; you come running straight to your ex? What does that say about you man?*

Then she walked out of the front door.

Mia was looking well. Her blonde hair was pulled

back in a low ponytail, and she had speckled blue fabric wrapped around her like a harness. There was a small bump in the harness in front of her. *That'll be the kid,* Jayden realised. He'd heard that she had had a baby with her new partner through the grapevine in Wellington. Somehow, it had never felt real to him, but now there they were.

She was obviously surprised to see a car in the driveway as she walked outside. He could tell by the way she paused when she saw it and then lifted a hand to shield her eyes from the sun, so that she could squint through the windshield to see who was in it. Jayden lifted his own hand to wave at her and then lowered it again as her face froze. *Ah shit.*

Mia was a good person. She must be, because even though she recognised that it was Jayden in the car, her ex fiancé, who she had broken up with under acrimonious circumstances, she still recovered enough to smile at him and make her way down the front steps to greet him at the car as he got out.

"Jay! It's been so long! How are you? What are you doing here?" She stepped up to him and opened her arms, catching him in an awkward semi-sideways hug to avoid squashing the young child who was strapped into the fabric around her. Jayden returned the squeeze, noticing that her hair smelt of flowers.

"Things have been fucking bizarre in the city, I needed to get out."

"But why did you come *here*?" She tilted her head slightly as she looked into his eyes, like a sparrow on a cafe table.

"I just..." Jayden tried to think of an answer that wouldn't sound like he was pathetically trying to recapture their past. He hoped that he wasn't trying to do that. "You guys are the only people I know that are close enough to drive to, I guess."

"Aren't your folks in Palmerston North? Could you

have gone to them?" Mia's question came quickly, but she still used a friendly tone.

"No, they moved further north a few months ago." Jayden impressed himself with how quickly the lie came to his lips.

"I hadn't heard that. Well, I suppose you should come inside and tell me about it. Cup of tea?"

Jayden nodded and followed Mia into the house. A dark cat shot out between their legs as they walked through the door.

It was a small house, with two small bedrooms right next to the front entrance, and a cosy lounge just beyond. He could see through an open door into the kitchen. Rugs, clothes and small brightly coloured plastic toys littered the ground, forcing him to step carefully and sweep objects off a seat before he could sit down.

Mia spoke to him from the kitchen as she made the tea. "So, what was so bizarre in the big city?"

"Have you been paying attention to the news today?"

"No, why?" The kettle began to bubble from the other room.

"There's been some sort of... Well... I guess you could say it was a terrorist attack?"

"What?!" Mia swung back into the lounge. "I thought you meant you were struggling with your job, or friends, or something!" Her eyes were wide and her face had paled. "What happened?"

"The police have had to close off a couple of blocks since last night. Someone's killed some people." Jayden felt as though he were reading out loud from a script he had never seen before. The words were written by someone else, and had no meaning as he said them. He stared at a large photo next to the TV in the lounge. Mia and her partner were standing together in it, his arms around her shoulders and his hands cupping her heavily pregnant belly. Her smile shone.

"Jesus, that's horrific," Mia said as she came the rest of the way into the lounge and looked around, picking up toys and bibs and tossing them aside.

"What are you doing?"

"Looking for the remote. Surely there'll be some live coverage if this is happening now?"

Jayden got up and began looking too. He was surprised at the way Mia seemed completely unaware of the child still strapped to her. It wobbled back and forth as she searched. Eventually she pulled a black plastic remote from beneath one of the couch cushions and turned on the TV, flipping through channels to look for a news broadcast.

A slightly round man with lashings of product in his hair was staring seriously into the camera and speaking in very sombre tones. "- unclear what has occurred in Wellington over the last 12 hours. Police are warning people to get out of the city centre, as they say that they are worried about how safe the area is. The Police Commissioner is meeting with members of parliament and has said that there have been some deaths so far in their attempts to contain the threat. We have many reports from family members of missing persons, but so far have been unable to verify any of these reports. If you fear that someone you know has been affected, the city council is preparing a website to check in and to try to coordinate efforts to identify those affected."

The screen changed to a view of the city from above, moving slowly and panning across empty streets. The man's serious voice continued.

"Here you can see the streets where initial reports claimed someone or possibly multiple people have been chasing and killing members of the public. As you can see, it is quiet out there at the moment, but the police insist that no-one is to go into the area."

Jayden's breathing had gone shallow and he was feeling light headed.

On the screen, a tiny figure appeared, walking out of a building and along the road.

"Oh thank god, someone is alive," breathed Mia.

"I don't think so."

Mia turned to stare at Jayden, her brow creasing in confusion. He shook his head and kept watching the screen. The serious voice had reached the same conclusion as Mia, but as it spoke, a second figure appeared further down the street. It wore a blue police officer's uniform that glowed in the afternoon light. Before anyone could respond, something burst out of the first figure, a pair of barely visible threads from this distance. The officer staggered and spun, but did not fall.

"What was that?" Mia yelped.

The screen cut back to the round man whose eyes were wide and whose mouth was gaping like a fish in the air.

"What was..." he caught himself and coughed. "Well, you saw something happen there. We will try and get more information and let you know what is going on as soon as we can. As we said earlier, police are advising people to stay very clear of the area."

Jayden felt his stomach clenching and bile rise in the back of his throat. He reached out and took the remote out of Mia's hands, though his hands were shaking so much that he had to try three times before he got the TV to turn off. He leaned forward on the TV cabinet with both arms and his head bowed until the nausea passed.

"You were there?" Mia's voice was soft. When Jayden looked up, she was looking at him with compassion, and it made him feel like a child. He squeezed his eyes shut for a moment, relishing the darkness.

"Yes." He straightened up and frowned. "I saw..." He didn't know how to explain the chaos he had witnessed over the last night and that morning. "I saw them close up."

"What are they? That didn't look like a terrorist, or even like a gun. What is happening there?"

"They were like... monsters... They were people, but they dangled like puppets on strings, even when they walked. And they have some sort of... Tentacle thing... that they can shoot at people and it..." He leaned forward again as his throat closed.

"Did... did you see anyone...?" Mia couldn't finish the question.

Jayden just nodded.

"Oh my god," she breathed. "Can I ask who?"

"James." Jayden stared at the worn carpet beneath his shoes, flinching at Mia's gasp. "Sophie too."

The lounge was silent as they sat, thinking about the friends who had died.

Mia took Jayden to the baby's room, explaining that she would take the baby into her room for the evening while they tried to find out what was happening and what he would do the next day. It was only while she collected some clothes, nappies and bottles that he thought to ask about the child.

"Her name is Estelle," smiled Mia. "She's a treasure. She's only waking up two times most nights now, so I'm feeling pretty good these days."

Jayden didn't know what to make of that statement and so he just nodded.

"And how is..." he trailed off, having completely forgotten her new partner's name.

"Hayden. He's well." Mia walked out of the room with her arms full, calling over her shoulder as she carried it all into her room. "He's been getting plenty of work building new homes, and doing renovations. Kanuka Creek has been growing!"

Jayden bit his lip and tried not to laugh. "Hayden?" he asked.

"Yes, that's right," she called back to him.

"So you went from Jayden to Hayden."

"Oh my god." Her voice was slightly high pitched. "I never thought of that! Jesus."

She brought him a glass of water and a simple peanut butter sandwich as she came back into the small pastel decorated room.

"Sorry I don't have much else to offer. I'm sure you could use a bit of time to try and relax after what you've been through. Why don't you lie down for a while?"

Jayden agreed with this idea more than any other he had ever heard.

While he lay down on the couch in the semi-guest room, Mia spent almost an hour on the phone to her new partner. He tried to sleep, but every time he was on the edge of drifting out he would suddenly find himself reliving the memory of the car park, hearing Sophie's instruction to run, and remembering the way her scream had suddenly cut off. It replayed over and over until he resigned himself to staring at the ceiling.

This house was safe and quiet, a far cry from the tiny room in a flat that he had been stuck in for the last two years. It made him wonder what he had been trying to prove, bouncing between jobs that he couldn't stand, hanging out with people who only infuriated him. Why hadn't he just stayed here in Kanuka Creek? Maybe he and Mia could have found a place like this for themselves?

She walked past the door and he saw that she had removed Estelle from the wrap of fabric, and was cradling her in her arms, breastfeeding her, with her cell phone pinched between her chin and shoulder.

She smiled through the doorway and continued her pacing.

He would have stayed if he could have. But he had ruined that himself. He couldn't blame her for sending him away.

CHAPTER NINE

Jayden was jolted awake by the sound of an engine grumbling closer to the house. He hadn't realised that he had even managed to get to sleep. He tried to sit up, frowning at the thick taste that smeared through his mouth. He squeezed his forehead and sat on the edge of the bed. Footsteps rose from inside the house and he glanced up just in time to see Mia pass and go out the front door. A car door slammed.

"Thank god you're home babe," Mia's voice echoed back into the house.

"I know, have you heard the news?" That must be Hayden. Jayden judged the voice. *Too rough,* he thought. *Sounds like a Neanderthal. Probably some guy that chugs beer by the can and plays rugby all weekend.*

The couple came back inside.

"This is Jay," said Mia, bringing Hayden to the guest room. "He was in Wellington last night."

"Oh shit, really?" Hayden was a tall man, but thin. Jayden's gaze was drawn to the man's Adam's apple, which seemed overly bulbous, like he had stopped halfway through swallowing a whole lemon. "So, you were there when this all happened? Fuck, that's brutal man." Hayden stepped into the room and held out his hand. Jayden stood up to shake hands with his host. Hayden's grip was firm and Jayden tried to remove his hand as soon as possible. "I wondered whose car that was out front."

"That's not actually my car, it belongs to my friend Sophie." Jayden spoke before he thought and instantly pictured her in his mind again, standing alone on the pale concrete of the car park. "I mean. It... it was."

"Oh my god," Hayden's face was pale, and his eyes opened wider. "Was that... Did she..."

Jayden sighed, feeling tightness pull across his shoulders. "This morning."

"Shit man. Do you need a beer?"

There it is, thought Jayden.

The three of them moved into the lounge, and Hayden went on to the kitchen and returned with three squat brown bottles of beer. There was an image of goblin on the label and Jayden turned it around to try and read what is said.

"Oh, this is my favourite, it's an ale brewed some-where in the south island. Troll's Head." Hayden twisted the top off and took a sip, sighing happily. "Nice and dark, but not too heavy. Really helps settle the nerves after a rough day."

Mia took a sip and smiled.

"I thought you didn't like beer," said Jayden, be-fore he took a sip himself. *Damn it. That's not bad.*

"I usually prefer a pinot," answered Mia with a small frown. Estelle gurgled from her baby bouncer on the floor. "But I'll enjoy a beer from time to time. Today seems like a reasonable time."

Hayden lay down on the floor next to the baby bouncer and leaned on one elbow as he took another sip of his beer. He reached over to tickle his daugh-ter's sides, and was rewarded with a tinkling laugh.

"So, Jay, how do you know Mia?"

Jayden turned his eyes to Mia, not sure how to respond. Her face was suddenly tight.

"Jay and I are old friends," she said then took a large mouthful of beer.

"Of course, but how did you become friends." Hayden's smile was easy, and he was watching Estelle as he spoke. *Does he really not know? Didn't she ever tell him?*

"We were engaged." Jayden's voice was loud, even to himself. "Until about two years ago."

Hayden turned to look at them both and raised his eyebrows. "You two were *engaged?* You were going to get married? How close to getting married were you?" His voice was beginning to rise.

"I mean, it was serious, but it was a long time ago babe," Mia began trying to explain.

"We were two months out from the day. Invites were sent. I think we lost all our deposits, right?"

Mia bit her lip and nodded once, shortly. Her eyes never left her new partner. Jayden sighed.

"It's no big deal man, I wrecked things really thoroughly. She got rid of me as soon as she could."

"Wow, she did a great job of getting rid of you, here you are." Hayden's voice was mild, and he didn't look upset, but the smile that he had worn so easily earlier had slid from his face.

"Maybe you should go back to the other room Jay," murmured Mia.

"Yeah sure, whatever."

Jayden went back to the room he had slept in before, sat down on the couch and looked around. There wasn't much to look at, just a couple of framed paintings of characters from children's books, one a duck swimming in a pond while wearing denim overalls, the other a bulldozer with eyes and a hard hat. Jayden pulled out his cell phone, but he could make out some of what Mia and

Hayden were saying to each other before he un-locked the screen.

"... not tell me about this? You never even men-tioned this guy before, and you guys nearly got married?"

"I did mention him, I did!"

"When? When the hell did you tell me about your ex bloody fiancé?"

"I told you about the man I was with before I met you!"

"You told me that you were seeing a guy and he cheated on you and you broke up with him. You didn't tell me his name, and you certainly didn't tell me that you were engaged to the bugger!"

"Well, I'm sorry, I didn't want to relive painful memories."

"Oh, but having him stay in our daughter's room is totally okay? That won't relive any painful memories, or open up previously closed down bundles of emotions?"

"Of course not!" Mia sounded shocked.

Like an emergency alarm, Estelle started crying. Jayden had never heard anything like it. The baby's wail pierced the air and he actually touched the side of his head to check if his ears had begun bleeding. The voices from the other room stopped as the par-ents checked on their child.

Jayden went back to his phone, unlocking it and flicking through his social media feeds. There was a lot of speculation about the chaos in Wellington, but not a lot of solid news to refer to. It wasn't something he wanted to focus on anyway, so he skipped most of those posts, looking for funny pictures that had nothing to do with Wellington instead.

After a few minutes Jayden felt as though someone was watching him. He looked up to see Mia standing in the doorway with her arms crossed.

Jayden put down his phone and lifted his hands in a defensive gesture.

"Okay, I probably could have revealed all that better. I'm sorry, I shouldn't be causing trouble between you guys. But how was I supposed to know that you hadn't told the man you have had a child with about some fairly major elements of your past? I mean, how reliable is that foundation for a relationship, especially one that you're bringing children into?"

Mia rolled her eyes and held up her phone. She looked back at Jayden and raised her eyebrows. "I'm sure you know about community pages?"

"What?" Jayden didn't understand the change of topic.

"Community pages. Social media pages where people in a community can be in contact with each other online."

"Yeah, obviously?" Jayden shrugged.

"I saw this post just now, while Hayden was changing Estelle." She held up the screen, but from where he was sitting Jayden couldn't tell what was on the display. He shrugged again.

"It says that a strange man tried to run over the primary school children who were running in their annual cross country early this afternoon."

Jayden hunched his shoulders and turned to look at the wall beside him, pretending to study the duck's overalls. "Oh yeah?"

"Yeah. It says that this disaster of a human yelled swear words at the children, swore at a teacher who tried to stop him, and then completely ignored the school and didn't even offer any explanation or apology. What a prick, right?"

Jayden shrugged again. "Yeah, dickhead, right. What's this got to do with me?"

Mia stomped over and stuck her phone in his face. This time he could see the post clearly, with the attached photo of him sitting in the driver's seat and grimacing.

"Why don't you tell me?"

Jayden didn't say anything.

"Well? What the hell was this all about? And now you're causing problems between my partner and me? Jesus Jayden, you may have gone through something pretty awful in Wellington, but don't take it out on fucking children! What have they ever done to you?"

"It wasn't-"

"It wasn't what? What excuse could you possibly have?"

Jayden sighed. "I drove up the hill and nearly hit a kid, then I panicked and yelled at them because I thought they were running on the road like a little wild thing. There were no signs or anything. It wasn't until after that that I saw the rest of the school and realised what happened."

Mia was watching him with her lips pressed into a straight line.

"Then that fucking woman wouldn't let me get a word in edgewise and so I figured, why bother? So I waited them out with the windows shut."

Mia licked her lips and shook her head, looking down at the ground.

"I'm not saying it was good, I just... I didn't mean to attack the kid." Jayden cleared his throat. "I didn't mean to cause a problem with your guy either. I just ran and you were the closest person I thought might be able to help." He rubbed his face. "If you can put up with me overnight, I'll leave in the morning."

"No." Mia breathed out deeply. "You're still a dickhead, but it sounds like you'll need a place to stay for longer than that. Stop being such a pain in the arse though, okay?"

Jayden nodded.

"Dinner won't be far." And with that, Jayden was alone in the room again.

Jayden heard Hayden shut the back door at the other end of the house heavily and assumed the other man must have gone outside, but he waited a few minutes before daring to poke his head around the corner to find Mia.

"How's he taking it then?"

"He's pretty pissed off." Mia was sitting on the couch, breast feeding Estelle. She had her head laid back on the top of the couch, with her eyes closed. She didn't open them to reply to Jayden.

"Yeah, I figured." He sat down in one of the other chairs. "But, I kind of get it, I mean, you hadn't told him at all?"

Now she lifted her head to raise an eyebrow at him. Estelle burped and Mia rolled her eyes, then re-arranged her clothing and stood up to make sure the baby didn't have any more wind coming.

"Of course I didn't. What should I tell this lovely man that's asking me out for dinner? "Sorry, just thought you'd like to know, I was supposed to get married this weekend, but my fiancé was an absolute fucking pig and now I'm single?""

"That doesn't sound particularly attractive," admitted Jayden. "But surely you could have told him later?"

"It never seemed especially relevant once we were dating. He was the most important thing to me, and I hoped he felt the same about me. I didn't want to dwell on someone who didn't think I was important."

"I did think you were important," began Jayden, but Mia snorted and cut him off.

"If you thought I was important, you wouldn't have gone to the pub and slept with Pip, would you?"

Mia stood in front of him, her small daughter

resting with a head on her shoulder, bouncing slightly on her hip.

"Would you describe that as the actions of someone trying to show their fiancé just how important they are, or not?"

Jayden coughed. "No, it's not."

"Exactly. I'm going to try and get Estelle down for a nap."

Is she trying to avoid being around me now? He thought to himself. *Why not just ask me to leave? Fuck, why did I think this was a good idea?*

Jayden walked through to the kitchen and opened the fridge. Luckily, there was more beer, so he pulled one out and looked out of the window over the sink. Outside he could see Hayden was standing next to a wide silver barbeque and frowning. Jayden went out the kitchen door to join him.

Outside was a wide concrete pad that seemed to serve as a deck. He paused to look around, taking in wide green fields of grass that seemed to stretch endlessly around the house, peppered with cows. To his left, around the corner of the house, Jayden could see a washing line spinning gently. Between the pale sheets and clothes hanging from it he caught a glimpse of a work shed. Hayden was standing by the barbeque, to his right, beneath one of the lounge windows.

"Evening," he said by way of acknowledgement.

"Sorry to be so temperamental after all you've had to deal with man," said Hayden, poking at some sausages with his long barbeque fork. "I was caught a little off guard with that one. She never even mentioned having a friend named Jayden, let alone one she was about to marry!"

Never even mentioned my name? At first Jayden was insulted, and even felt a bit of anger rising, but he managed to purse his lips and hold it down. Mia was pissed off enough, and he really needed a quiet place to stay tonight.

"I probably could have suggested it a little less bluntly," said Jayden, putting the bottle down on one of the barbeque's wings.

"Not for me mate, I'm on duty tonight. One's probably pushing the rules as it is."

Jayden didn't say anything to that. *Oh, I probably should have brought one out for him. He said it was his favourite, didn't he?*

"Thanks though. Here," Hayden picked it up and flicked the top off with his fork. "You have it. You could probably use something a bit stronger after to-day, huh?"

"Yeah. It's all been overwhelming and I actually want to avoid talking about it if I can."

Hayden nodded. "Yeah, I think that's what Mia is doing right now. She didn't want to talk about this whole fiancé thing, and insisted on me making some dinner while she fed Estelle."

"Probably just worried."

"Yeah. And thanks for apologising about the whole bombshell, but it's really not your fault." Hayden poked at the sausages again.

I don't think I actually apologised, thought Jayden.

"What are you on duty for?" he asked, steering the conversation away from any hint of blaming him for the tension between Hayden and Mia.

"Volunteer firefighter. If you hear the klaxon go, I've got to drive into the station. It's been pretty quiet recently, but you never know of course."

Of course he's a bloody hero, groaned Jayden to himself.

"So, imagine that you are sitting in a crowded movie theatre," said Jayden, gesturing with the beer bottle to suggest the size of the space. "You see some-thing weird by the entrance. Within a moment, there is a scream, and something violent happens, and people start running, shouting, trying to see what's going on." He took another sip of the beer. "How would you react?"

Hayden sniffed and turned the sausages. "I think these are done," he began, then turned to face Jayden. His mouth had twisted slightly to one side as he considered the question. "How would I react? I think I'd probably have to head over and see if I could help. I'm not very good with first aid really, but I've had the training at least."

Jayden nodded and turned away from the man and his barbeque. Around them spread field after field of grass, dotted with cows. To the right, partially cut off by the house, was a low hill that seemed to run across the whole horizon. Behind him were the ranges in the distance, cold and tall. The sun was already dipping towards them.

How did he always seem to end up surrounded by these people, and their need to look like heroes? Couldn't they see that behaviour was just asking for trouble? He rolled his shoulders back and forward. They felt tight and tense. If these heroes would just admit that, really, underneath it all, they were scared and wanted to run away, that would be better. At least then they would be showing their real self. At least then they would be being honest.

"So, how are you holding up anyway?"

Jayden was surprised. "Is that really the question you want me to answer?"

"It really is," said Hayden. "If there is some unrequited or unresolved business that you've come here to sort out, my perspective on it is totally through Mia. I'll talk to her and work things out with her. You're just some stranger in my house for how much I'll tell you about that."

He began shifting sausages off the barbecue and

onto a yellow and blue dinner plate. "But you're my guest, you kind of count as an old friend of Mia's, and you've had a shit day. For that, I ask, how are you doing?"

"I'll be fine." Jayden felt resentful of Hayden even asking. *You wouldn't know anything about what I'm coping with right now. And why would I want to share any of it with you anyway? You're a stranger, not someone who I was going to share my life with.*

Before he could say anything, Mia came out of the house, swiping on her phone.

"Guys, listen to this. I turned on the TV to see what the news was saying, and the army has apparently told people to get out of Wellington."

"What?" Hayden dug his own phone out of his pocket, swiping and typing to see for himself. "Oh my god, you're not kidding."

Jayden moved closer so that he could look over Hayden's shoulder at the phone. The news website on the small screen got straight to the point, highlighting the army's instruction to get away from Wellington. There was a video clip embedded in the article also.

"What do they have to say about it?" asked Jayden. Hayden obligingly clicked on the video. A reporter with her hair pulled tight to the back of her head greeted the viewer and then outlined the events of the day. Police had struggled to isolate whoever was causing trouble, and indeed appeared to have lost multiple officers, including the rarely deployed armed response unit. Then the army had sent in some soldiers as the next level of response. Politicians were quoted as being very worried about the need to use soldiers in such a way, but the intense nature of the emergency was pushing matters forward quickly. Following a warning that violent scenes would be forthcoming, there was some footage of the soldiers positioned across a seemingly empty city street. As they watched the clip, gunfire erupted from the soldiers and strange blurry lines knocked some of them down. The reporter declared that losses had been high, and that minutes ago the army had asked everyone to get away from the city.

"At this stage it is impossible to tell where the perpetrators are, or how many of them are loose in the city. Please, stay safe." With that, the news summary video had finished. The three of them stood next to one another, staring at the tiny screen in Hayden's hand, an unspoken wish for more information hanging between them.

"Fuck, I guess we should go inside?" Hayden reached out to put one arm around Mia's shoulders. She leaned into him, resting her head on his shoulders.

"Wellington is a long way away," said Jayden.

"Yeah, but I just feel exposed standing out here surrounded by wide open space. There's no one around if something happens."

"You must be very glad that you got out before the crowds that will be trying to leave now."

Jayden stared at his ex. "Glad? Nothing about this fucking situation is making me glad! I watched two of my best friends, two of my only friends, die in front of me because they were dumb enough to go running into harm's way on the off chance they could make a difference. Not to mention one of their friends who I'd only just met."

He knew that he was ranting, waving his hands around in the air like an animal, but it was hard to bring them back down.

"Am I glad to have got away from the chaos? To have gone running to the only place I thought I might stand a chance of finding a friendly reception, and that's the home of the woman I was going to marry and her man. Can you understand how sad it is that in all this fucking island, this is the only place I had to go?"

With a great effort, Jayden pulled his hands down and picked up his beer. He managed to tone down his voice as he finished.

"I'm not fucking glad about any of this."

Hayden released Mia and stepped forward, placing his hands on Jayden's shoulders.

"It's all been really overwhelming. But I am glad you got out, and I'm glad that we are somewhere for you to run to, even if it makes you feel bad. Come on, let's go in and eat something. That'll help." He stepped back from Jayden, who was lost for words. He wanted to tell the man to fuck off, but also his throat was clenched tight and his stomach was rolling. Hayden picked up the plate of sausages and fried potato slices that were sitting by the barbeque and led the way back to the door. Jayden swallowed the last mouthful of his beer and resolved to drink at least one more once they went inside. *Let's see how friendly and understanding this prick is once I've drunk all his favourite beer.*

CHAPTER TEN

The sun had continued its slow setting as they had spoken, and the sky was becoming a deep dark blue, like the bottom of an ocean trench, filled with pinpricks of light. A few thick gold bands of light stabbed over the mountains behind them, but the fields were flooding with darkness. Hayden had a point. The land suddenly felt very empty and open and quiet. Standing in the backyard, under the outdoor lights, slapping mosquitoes away, left a person feeling rather on display.

"Shit, what's that babe?" said Mia just before they all went inside. The men turned to see where she was pointing. "Is it the Davies kids again?"

Far away across the paddocks to the left, only visible now due to the rapidly diminishing sunlight as it hid behind the ranges, Jayden could see some lights in a copse of trees. The lights seemed to be swinging around, as though chasing fireflies, and winking on and off.

"What the fuck are they doing?" he asked, trying not to let the panic that was beginning to close around his chest leak into his voice.

"Yeah, I reckon it'll be the Davies kids. They were at it only a weekend or two ago, weren't they?"

Hayden glanced at Jayden. "Some of the neighbour's teenagers like to go possum hunting some nights. Although, they seem to enjoy having a few beers along the way too. They got a bit too fucking close to the house last time." The crack of a gun firing rang through the still night air as clearly as someone knocking on the front door. Jayden flinched and hated himself for doing it.

"I better call their dad and make sure they stay away over there in the trees. Better we keep our possums than have some drunken boys shoot the bloody house!"

"Thanks love," said Mia and the pair stepped inside.

Jayden followed, seeing the golden glow from inside the house envelope them while he was still lingering outside in the shadows. He frowned.

Hayden and Mia set the food down at a square table that occupied an open space in the kitchen barely large enough to fit it. Mia pulled a very small chair out of the back laundry room and sat on it, gesturing for Jayden to sit in the slightly nicer chair next to her.

"Thanks," he mumbled. "Do you guys normally eat at this... this table?"

"No," she replied, serving some of the sausages and potatoes onto his plate. Hayden placed a large bowl with a very simple green salad tossed together in it on the table. "Normally we'd dish up and go into the lounge and watch TV while we ate from our laps. But, guests are guests, and we have been trying to be less media focused."

"It's hard not to just want to shut your brain off after you've been hard at it all day," added Hayden. "Whether that's hammering wooden frames, or changing a baby's nappy fifty fucking times and trying to clean the house. Wouldn't you agree mate?"

"I never want to shut my brain off," Jayden lied. "I mean, that just seems like a bit of a cop out, doesn't it? Surely we should all be trying to better ourselves?"

"Seems to me that you should probably be trying a bit harder then," said Hayden, with his eyes on his plate as he stuck a forkful of salad into his mouth.

"What was that?" Jayden tilted his head and glared at the other man.

Hayden looked up and rolled his eyes.

"Look, mate, you've been through a lot, and this is a weird place to find yourself looking for comfort. But you could keep some of these comments to yourself, you know? We're here to help, not to be your punching bag."

"If you can't be at least a little more polite, maybe you *should* go and find somewhere else to stay tonight," said Mia, with her arms crossed.

Jayden leaned back in his chair and blew air out through his lips. "Sure, whatever. Is Pip still in town?"

Mia pressed her lips into a straight line and glared at him. Hayden looked from his partner to his guest and shook his head. Jayden bent further over his plate and avoided looking at the people who had brought him into their home and fed him.

The rest of dinner passed in silence, though towards the end Estelle began crying in her room.

"That's strange, she normally lasts a lot longer at this time of night," said Mia. "I'd better see if she needs another feeding. If it's a nappy, this one's yours," she said, raising her eyebrows at Hayden, who snorted and nodded his head. She walked out of the kitchen and down to the other end of the house.

"Come on man, let's sort you out somewhere to sleep," said Hayden, standing and picking up most of the dishes. *He's still letting me stay?* Jayden was shocked. Hayden carried the dishes over to the kitchen bench and rinsed them in the sink before stacking them to be washed. Then he turned around and sighed when he saw Jayden standing by the table, just watching him. His shoulders slumped. "Any other person would have offered to bring over a few plates themselves," he said before coming back to gather more cutlery and crockery.

"Oh. Sorry." Jayden picked up the mostly empty plastic salad bowl and followed his host over to the bench again.

Once the dishes were stacked, Hayden led the way around a corner on the side of the kitchen that led into a small room, barely more than a hallway to another backdoor. The door itself was made of two large glass panes, with a translucent plastic cat flap in the bottom one. The frosted pattern in the glass and the dark night beyond made it impossible to see through the door.

This room was the laundry, with lots of baby clothes and a few tee shirts hanging from string over their heads, and a plastic basket full of tangled damp clothes waiting to be taken and hung up outside. A pre-packaged, build-it-yourself cupboard was also present, with the door hanging off one hinge at an angle and its back panel pulling itself off despite the thin staples intended to hold it on. Sheets and towels filled the cupboard.

Hayden stood for a moment, studying the folded material, reaching out towards a pile near the bottom of the cupboard before shaking his head slightly and murmuring something, then reaching up and grabbing a set of sheets that Jayden thought seemed pretty much identical to every other set in the cupboard.

"Right, here you are," Hayden said. "We could set you up on a couch in the lounge, or I think there was a fold-out bed in the baby's room? Did Mia say anything to you?"

"Yeah, she said I should just use the baby's room,"

said Jayden. *There's a fold-out bed in there? Does the couch turn into a bed? She didn't tell me that!*

Hayden didn't respond. He was looking over Jayden's shoulder with a slightly confused expression creasing his forehead.

"What?"

"It's nothing really, I just... I would have thought Mia would have let me know what was going on with Estelle by now. Can you hear her?"

Jayden cocked his head. "No."

The house seemed as quiet as a museum. A drip from the kitchen tap was the only sound to break the silence. A sudden gunshot from across the paddocks even made Hayden frown.

"That sounded like they might be getting closer, I need to call their dad before I-"

There was a crash from the other end of the house, a clattering of objects rolling and tumbling on wooden floors that seemed to go on and on and on.

"What the fuck?!" Hayden leapt to the kitchen doorway. Jayden instinctually stepped away from the noise and toward the glass panels leading outside. He stood with his hand on the handle and imagined how he looked to the others. Something had just happened to someone he used to care deeply about, and his first instinct was to try to get away. No one could blame him, surely? After what he had seen? He groaned and allowed his hand to slip off the handle, then turned to follow in the direction Hayden had gone.

As he turned into the lounge, a figure swung around from the bedroom and Jayden yelped. Then he realised that it was Mia, carrying Estelle in front of herself as the baby breastfed.

"Are you alright Jay?" she asked.

"Sure," panted Jayden as he leaned against the wall

for a moment. His heart was spasming. "Hayden seemed to think something was wrong?"

"Sort of," Mia smiled and shook her head. "I sat down to feed Estelle, but I didn't bother turning on a light. I thought that maybe I'd get her back to sleep that way. Then, when I heard that gunshot, I was so surprised that I went to stand up, even though Estelle was latched on. I knocked over a bucket of nappies, which knocked over some toys and..." Mia grinned ruefully. "I think I scared him, he looked pretty pale when he came charging into the room."

"It was a strange moment."

Behind Mia, Jayden saw Hayden leaned around the doorway from the hall to the bedroom, his cell phone held to his head. He rolled his eyes at the other two as he spoke quietly. "... damn close to the house. You know we've got a new-born in here... Yes, I know that they're good lads." He turned away and walked into the bedroom to finish the call. Another crack echoed through the quiet night. Mia shook her head to flick a strand of hair away from her nose.

"It's so frustrating when people don't take the time to think about who else is around them before they act. The boys are probably having a grand old time, but they don't care about how anxious it makes me about Estelle." She rocked the small babe gently.

"It's not that they don't care," said Jayden. "You're right, they didn't think first, but lots of people don't have the mental space to spare to think of every single possible impact of every single thing that they do. A lot of people are just trying to cope with the things directly in front of them, and that's all that they can manage. I mean," he ran a hand through his hair. "You don't know what's going on in their lives, maybe they have exams or something like that. Something that is stressing them out and they just want to try and blow off some steam."

Mia watched him with an odd look on her face.

"What?" he grumbled.

"You might be right," she answered slowly. "But what they do has real impact on others, and if they haven't thought of them, no matter how reasonable it is to think that they are coping with a lot, those impacts could still cause harm. I'm not going to pretend that they aren't causing trouble."

"Sure, I guess, but just... Just don't say that they don't care. Because they probably do. If someone told them what impact they were having, they'd feel bad, they'd try to avoid it in future. They just... might have more issues crowding that one out and forget." He was twisting a piece of paper that he had found in his pocket between his fingers. Sniffing and clearing his throat, he stuffed the piece of rubbish back into his pocket.

Mia was still looking at him with the strange expression. Her eyes were wide, almost staring, but there was a turn to them, a softness around the edges. Her mouth was a firm line though.

"I'll try not to assume that they're intentionally causing trouble," she said, shaking her head slightly. "But they are still causing harm, and if they can't change, I just..." she trailed off, looking away from Jayden and at her small daughter.

"Well, I don't know if he'll manage to get them back in tonight, but I think he took me seriously." Hayden said as he came back into the room. "I'll tidy up Estelle's room. Jay, could you go and get those sheets that I dropped. We'll get you set up. I, for one, want to get to sleep as soon as possible with all the horrible stuff that's happened today. See what the new dawn brings with it."

Jayden managed to help pull the sheets over the fold out couch and then lay down on it. It was much less comfortable now that it had been converted into a bed. He wished that they had left it as a couch. That had been alright for the afternoon nap he had ended up taking.

A MECHANICAL WHINE began to wail in the distance, winding up rapidly and then trailing off in a drone that seemed to never end. Jayden swung out of the bed and poked his head into the lounge. Hayden was standing at the doorway to the bathroom with a toothbrush stuck into his mouth.

"Ah fuh," he said, dripping bubbles onto the carpet. "At's uh ucking ire iren."

Jayden blinked. "What?"

Hayden walked back into the bathroom and spat into the sink, wiping his mouth with the back of his hand. "I said, that's the fucking fire siren. I'm heading in babe!" he finished by yelling to Mia who was still in their bedroom with Estelle.

"You're leaving?" asked Jayden, following the other man to the front door. "But, there's drunk kids shooting guns in the fields. All hell has broken loose in Wellington. Why the fuck are you leaving?"

Mia caught Jayden's arm and pulled him back a little from the door, then turned to give her partner a kiss. "You take care, love," she said.

"I will," he replied, gripping her in a quick hug. Then he looked at Jayden. "I know things are a bit wild out there. But it's my job to help out when something goes wrong. So, that's what I'm going to do. Hopefully I'll see you guys soon."

And with that he turned away into the darkness of the night and climbed into his truck. The engine roared into life and the headlights flashed on. Before Jayden could say anything else, the truck had spun around in the space next to the house and rumbled off down the long driveway and turned towards the lights of Kanuka Creek's main street. *God, when will you stop pretending to be Mr Perfect,* scowled Jayden in his head, as though he was talking to Hayden. *You have every reason to say "I don't want to do this" tonight!* He thought of the thin mattress he had been lying on the old springs of the fold-out couch. *And kick me out if you're angry at me! Stop pretending that it's okay if I stay!* The emptiness of the silent night was the only reply he received.

Mia turned to go back inside, but Jayden reached out and placed a hand on her shoulder. He was staring out into the darkness. She turned back, pulling her fluffy grey dressing gown tighter around herself.

"What?"

"Listen," Jayden said, cupping a hand by his ear and looking towards the sky.

Mia mimicked him for a minute then shook her head. "I don't hear anything."

"Exactly. Where've the boys gone?" He pointed out to the fields. "Can you see their lights?"

Around them the fields were soaked in the heavy black of night. The distant mountains behind the house were just barely visible as a ragged edge to the star filled sky, and to the opposite side of them it was hard to distinguish the wide rolling hill that bordered the paddocks from wisps of cloud that passed over it. Silver dots reflected light back at them from all around, similar to the stars, but they didn't shimmer. There were no waving beams from spotlights, no intermittent crack of guns going off.

"Hopefully their dad got in touch and they went home."

"Does that seem likely?" Jayden could feel the cool air creeping down the back of his neck.

"As likely as anything else. Why, what are you trying to say?" Mia suddenly turned to him with a condescending twist to her lips. "It took you hours to drive up here, are you worried that some bad guys have managed to hike this far in about the same amount of time?"

"I..." Jayden closed his mouth and thought. That was what he was worried about, but it was ridiculous. How would they possibly have come so far so quickly? "Sorry, you're right." He grimaced.

He blew through his lips and shivered down his shoulders. "Man, it got cold quick." He glanced around the fields again as they began to walk inside. "What are those bloody lights though?"

"What lights?" Mia scanned the area. "Oh, those silver lights?"

"Yeah. The dots in all the fields. They're creepy."

"It's just the cows. You know how cat's eyes glow in the dark? Well, it's the same thing, only their eyes are silver."

"I'm not a fan." Jayden looked along the driveway as he closed the door. Just before it banged into the frame, he could have sworn he saw something moving on the gravel driveway. He blinked, swallowed thickly, and then opened the door slightly, only opening it enough to peek through.

"What are you doing now?"

"I thought I saw something moving by the drive-way." There was nothing there now. He kept watching. Something landed on his shoulder and gripped onto him, making him gasp and lurch sideways. Mia shook her head and let go of him.

"Seriously, I think you are going to need some professional help to deal with this. You're paranoid."

Heart pounding, Jayden nodded. "I think you might be right." He didn't like admitting it, but he was having trouble reacting to normal everyday things appropriately. He probably would need help to un-tangle the mess of nerves that the events of the last day had made of his head. He closed the door again.

There was a crunch from outside, like a thick branch slowly being broken over a knee.

Jayden's muscles froze. "What do you think that was?"

Mia was frowning at the door. "I don't know. Maybe a cow stepped on something, or knocked over a fence?"

There was a second tearing noise. This time it dragged on much longer.

Mia stepped past Jayden, who struggled to relax his muscles enough that he could turn his head to watch her or even to step aside. Mia clicked the dead-bolt of the door into place.

"Turn off the lights in the house and then come back here," she said, moving into her bedroom as she spoke.

Jayden shoved his legs into motion, feeling his stomach bind itself into a tight ball as he moved through the lounge to the kitchen and then began turning off lights in each room as he returned through the house to the bedroom. Mia had turned off the light in there also, but he could see the temporary cot that she had set up for Estelle next to her bed. The baby's regular breathing in her sleep was the only sound Jayden could hear. Starlight outlined the objects in the room, passing through a wide but short curtainless window set high into one wall of the bedroom.

"Mia?" he whispered, moving into the room with his hands slightly ahead of himself to try and avoid a collision. Now he could see that she was standing to one side of the main bedroom window, holding the side of the curtain a centimetre or two aside from the frame, giving her a sliver of space to peer through to the fields in front of the house. She shushed him and pointed to the far side of the window. "What can you see?" she asked in hushed tones.

He mirrored her pose, pressing his body close to the wall to allow the maximum view through the smallest gap. With the house dark as well, he was able to see relatively clearly outside.

Down the driveway, some fence posts had been knocked down, tearing wires and rails off with them, and leaving some of the neighbouring posts leaning haphazardly. There were no other signs of movement or cows or any other explanation for what might have damaged the fence.

"What do you think–" began Jayden, but Mia shushed him again.

"Not just the fence, look down the driveway, in the paddock."

Jayden followed her instructions, looking further down the driveway. He stared into the darkness, squinting to try and see whatever it was that she had seen. Then, there was a blur, a shifting of space, as something he had assumed was part of the landscape rose up and strode across the field before settling down again. It was clearly humanoid, but distance and darkness hid any other features. He felt bile rise up his throat.

"What the fuck was that?" he managed to splutter.

"I don't care," said Mia. "If it's part of the trouble in Wellington, then we need to get the fuck out of here. If it's not then someone's being really creepy and weird and we need to get the fuck out of here." She turned away from the window. "Do you have anything in the house that you need to bring with you?"

"Not really. I didn't bring anything with me from home, I just ran."

"Good, then you can help me. I have a sports bag under the bed, and we'll need to throw a bunch of stuff for Estelle in it."

He pulled out the bag as Mia grabbed nappies,

wet wipes, bottles and dummies from a shelf by the cot. She jammed them all in and then began to grab some clothes and blankets.

"Can you go to the kitchen and get one or two of the instant formula tins?"

"I thought you were breast feeding?" Jayden was confused.

"Sometimes the formula is easier, and if we're running away from something then easier is probably helpful. Any other questions or critiques about my parenting now? Right now? Really?"

"Sorry." Jayden began to leave the room, and instinctively reached out to turn the lights on as he did. He caught himself with his hand millimetres off the switch. *If there's something out there, probably better not to give them clues to what we're doing by turning lights on and off,* he thought. *Best if they think we are asleep while we get out of here.*

CHAPTER ELEVEN

He moved carefully through the darkened lounge and kitchen. After opening three cupboards, he decided to risk using his cell phone's light as a torch, pointing it mostly at the floor to try and avoid letting anyone outside know where he was. Thankfully, it worked and he found two tins of formula, one nearly empty. He turned off his phone and took them back to the bedroom, where Mia was carefully tying Estelle into her harness.

"Thank you, that's perfect," she smiled. "But I did just think, it might be good if we had the axe."

"The axe?"

"You must have seen it? Hayden splits our firewood, and the axe is near the shed outside by the washing line?"

"Yeah, I think I saw it. Have you got everything you need?"

Mia stood up straight and bounced up and down on the balls of her feet, with her arms held around Estelle in case the wrap didn't hold. Then she nodded. "Yup, let's go."

"Do we have to go out the front door to the car? Maybe we should sneak out the back and around the side?" Jayden tried to pretend he wasn't trying to convince Mia to come with him to the back of the house, especially as she had a tiny baby. But the aching in his heart beneath his ribs told him that company was what he desperately wanted.

"No, I think you're right, it would be better to go out the back." Jayden blew out his breath and felt his shoulders relax. "We saw something at the front, and so if we move around the side of the house there's less chance that whoever or whatever it is will see us. And then, it also means we're by each other when you get the axe."

Jayden nodded and began to head back down to the kitchen. Mia followed, carrying the bag of baby supplies at her side. Jayden winced and paused as a floorboard creaked beneath his feet, and he waited to see if there was any response.

"Go on, go on," came the insistent whisper of Mia from behind him.

Jayden led the way towards the laundry door and paused as the cat door rattled slightly.

"Did you have a cat?" he whispered as loudly as he dared back to Mia.

"We do, her name is Aroha."

Jayden watched in the dark room as the cat flap was slowly pushed forward and the small figure of a brown and white mottled cat made its way inside. Her fur was a little scruffy, and she was walking with a limp. Just as Jayden was about to ask Mia what he should do about the cat, he noticed that the flap was being held open by a dark cord that extruded from between the cat's shoulder blades.

It raised its face to stare directly at him. Even in the darkness, Jayden could see that its eyes were milky white orbs. The cat stretched its lips back over its gums, revealing thin white teeth, and it hissed. As it hissed, parts of its legs and shoulders lifted out like insectile limbs or segmented tentacles, a cloud of sharp fingers that were pointed all directly at him, exposing the cat's red flesh as they peeled out.

Jayden stepped back, lifting his hands in defence, and looked at the clouded glass of the door. A deeper black shadow was outlined in it.

"Fuck!" he yelled and spun around. Glass exploded from the doorway as a spear of gristle burst through, missing Jayden by a hair's width and smashing into the wall. A cloud of dust and plasterboard blew over him, and his feet skidded as he bolted towards the side door, the door that they had used to get to the barbeque. As he ran he deliberately did not look towards the doorway to the lounge, where Mia would have been. He felt a shock of guilt at the idea that he might be abandoning a woman and her child to the thing that was following him, but he hoped that it would mean that the thing wouldn't know that she was there. The thought wasn't very comforting.

He grabbed the door and then threw himself sideways instead of opening it. Another spear of meat and bone crashed into the door, splitting the wood horizontally. Jayden didn't look back, but wrenched at the handle and was pleased to see the way that the broken wood tore at the limb when he swung it open, leaving oozing black gashes in its gnarled surface. He jumped out into the black night air and began running around the side of the house, ducking below the windows. As he turned past the corner of the house, he heard a heavy thud behind him as something fell out of the doorway onto the concrete pad.

In front of him stood the clothesline, pale cloth flapping from its wires in the light breeze of the night. He ran towards it, hoping that the movement of the clothes would help conceal him. Somewhere beyond it should be the shed that Mia was talking about, and his only chance of finding something that he might be able to defend himself with. However, he couldn't see an axe yet.

On the far side of the dangling clothes Jayden paused. His chest heaved as he panted for breath and he could feel his pulse pounding on the sides of his head. The thing couldn't be far behind him, but where was the fucking axe?

The moon must have come out from behind a cloud, because the shed in front of him was suddenly illuminated by a pale white glow. A heavy looking door was built into the left hand side of the roughly made shed. Corrugated iron lay angled on the roof. A large four paned window was on the right, with a hole smashed through the bottom left pane. And the axe was leaning next to the doorway. A thick slice of a log sat in front of the window, with a smaller hatchet wedged into it.

Jayden took in all of this in a moment then moved forward.

Just as his hand closed around the axe handle, a geometrically-patterned shift ripped from where it was pegged to the clothesline as a meaty tentacle tore through from behind the clothesline and continued on to break the shed window. The broken glass cut more jagged lines down the twisted flesh, from which black liquid began to run more freely. Jayden hefted the axe up over his shoulder as quickly as he could and then brought the heavy metal head down onto the thick length of meat.

He was surprised at how easily the tentacle fell apart under the axe. The surface was all gristle, and horrible meat, but as it split and tore apart, flakes of mouldering material fell from the wound, like a rain of dead wet leaves. The end leading back past the clothesline recoiled and slipped backwards out of his sight. He grabbed the hatchet and heaved, pulling it out of the circle of wood. With the hatchet held in front of him and the axe resting on his shoulder ready to swing, Jayden walked back towards the clothesline.

He had never felt his heart pound as hard as this in his life. He thought it was going to shake his ribcage apart. Clothes hanging on the line rubbed past his face and shoulders, their embrace making him feel surrounded and confined, but also hidden. He couldn't decide if he felt more or less safe as the sheets passed over his face. He stepped out of the clothes to find the monster was only standing a few feet away.

Fear makes one's senses work faster than usual, and Jayden was able to take in many details of this thing during his first flash of fear, the first of the creatures that he had seen up close. It had a human face, though the features hung loose, as though the flesh was beginning to fall off the bone underneath. Its eyes were the same milky white that the cat's had been, unfocused and staring. Its chest was exposed, the flesh twisting into a braided cord of meat and white tendon that dragged on the ground in front of it, the end ragged and oozing still. The sight gave Jayden a brief flush of pride, having managed to wound the thing. Its clothes were still well made, and if not for the eyes, the horrific tentacle, and the strange way the thing held itself lightly, as though it might gently float off the ground, he might have thought it was just another person.

All of this flashed into his mind in the same moment that he yelled and dragged the axe from his shoulder and thumped it directly into the thing's face.

Again, he was surprised at how easily the thing collapsed under the impact of the axe. The face crumpled like a paper mask and, again, a flood of damp leaves seemed to pour from behind it. The thing lifted its arms but fell backwards from the momentum of the axe, and Jayden let go of the handle as it was pulled along. The thing lay on the ground shuddering and spasming, but scrambling with its arms as though it was hoping to pull itself up again. Jayden wondered if it could still see him or sense him in some way. The face was ruined, to such an extent that it no longer existed, so it had no eyes to see him. Did that matter?

As the thing twisted on the ground, the axe fell away and Jayden saw something hard and black and round inside the head, half covered by whatever the flaky material contained within the broken shell was. The round object glistened like an oil spill.

"Fuck this," muttered Jayden, and he swung the hatchet directly into the dark orb. It was much more solid than the tentacle or face had been and the hatchet barely left a scratch on its surface even though he managed to hit it square and hard. The thing froze for a second, then thrashed around again, managing to turn onto its stomach.

"Oh, you don't like that huh? Let's see what we can do then." Jayden swung the hatchet at the thing's neck, and was relieved to find that it separated from the body with the same ease that he had noticed with the tentacle and the face. The body immediately fell still and the head bounced and rolled on the ground. The damaged black ball began to unroll and pull itself out of the wreckage, looking like some disgusting giant bug from what Jayden could see. He retched but swung the hatchet at the bug. This time the strike was enough to pierce its shell and the bug was cut into two pieces. Each piece twitched, with their numerous tiny legs waving, but Jayden slammed the hatchet blade into each piece over and over, dicing them into small greasy chunks.

Jayden knelt on the ground next to the body, panting for breath and trying to ease his pounding heart. An evening breeze cooled his brow and rustled the laundry hanging on the line behind him. His teeth were chattering, and he was overwhelmed with a sudden pressure in his stomach. He was suddenly intensely aware that he was kneeling on the grass next to a human body, with a human head that he had severed. He leaned forward and threw up onto the ground by the remains of the creature, unable to restrain himself before his stomach had emptied.

After a few fruitless convulsions ensured that there was nothing left behind, he managed to sit back on his knees in the short grass. He smacked his mouth at the foul taste and roughly wiped the back of his arm across his lips. Wet black leaves spilled from the corpse, not blood. The body seemed hollow except for the strange jumble of litter, and the edges of the wounds that Jayden had managed to inflict were sharp and thin, like a broken bowl. It was as though the whole creature was a porcelain doll that he had smashed part of.

"I wonder who that was," he said to himself, shuddering.

There was a soft noise from the house and he whipped his head up, hefting the hatchet desperately, ready to heave it into anything that was coming. Mia was standing at the corner of the house, with her hands over her mouth. From the clothesline, in the night, he could not tell what colour her eyes were. *Did the thing get her before it came after me,* he wondered. A more terrifying thought clutched at him. *Were there two of them?*

He rose to his full height, keeping the hatchet in front of him, despite how empty and unsteady his legs felt.

"Jayden?"

Mia's voice was as quiet as the whimper of a puppy after the madness of the last few minutes. Or was it seconds? He felt as though it had taken an hour. For now though, all that mattered was that she sounded like a regular person, not some weird dead ceramic-skinned thing. Although, her tone of voice was the sound of a regular person walking closer to the edge of a cliff into insanity.

He staggered over to her, giddy relief washing through him as he could see that she appeared un-harmed, and Estelle was still wrapped in her harness. The sensation lifted his limbs, all weight and exhaus-tion forgotten. The baby had woken, but Mia had managed to latch her to a breast to keep her from crying out.

"Are you both okay?" he said.

Mia nodded slowly. "I guess so. But Aroha..." Mia turned to look at the wrecked doorway to the laundry, shoved into the house and leaning in pieces on the wall. Inside the broken glass, Jayden could see a dark lump that he assumed must be what was left of the cat.

"The thing dropped her when it came after me, I guess," he said. He glanced back at Mia. "I know you might not like the idea but, maybe I should, you know..." He bounced the axe on his shoulder.

Mia shook her head. "It's finished. The... the..." She licked her lips and ran her fingers through Es-telle's short hair. "It stormed through after you and I peeked into the laundry and Aroha was just..." Mia bit her lip and looked at the ground.

"Okay, okay." Jayden began to reach out to her, but his hands were full. "Come on, let's get to the car. I don't want to stay here, even if I did manage to kill one."

They moved around the side of the house quietly and climbed into Sophie's car, Jayden putting the weapons into the front passenger seat, and Mia climbing into the back with Estelle still in the harness.

"Is that safe? Do you need a baby seat?"

Mia turned innocently wide eyes on Jayden where he sat in the driver's seat, with his body twisted around to address her, his hand on the back of the passenger seat. "Oh yes, I'm so sorry for making a decision about the safety of my child, when there was a childless man known for his selfishness who could correct me on that decision available. You just wait here while I spend time battering a car seat out of the other car and into this one. I'm sure that if there are any more fucking monsters in the fields, they'll just wait!"

Jayden sucked his lower lip between his teeth and nodded.

"I'll just drive, shall I?"

"Sounds like a clever fucking idea."

The engine started easily and Jayden began to roll the car backwards so that he could turn it to face down the driveway. He left the headlights off as long as possible, hoping that the lack of illumination would help keep any other of these monsters away from the car for a few precious seconds longer. The gravel crunching beneath the tyres made him wince, and he stared intently into the black rear-view mirror trying to guess how far the car was from the fence. Then, as they began to roll forward between the fences that lined the driveway on its long rutted path to the main road, he twisted the knob to turn the headlights on.

The driveway was blessedly clear before them, but next to the broken section of fence falling into it was a pile of red that Jayden couldn't tear his eyes from. It wasn't moving, and it seemed small enough that it wouldn't be hiding anything. Jayden sped up as they moved down the driveway past it.

"What do you think it is?" he asked, before pulling his attention forward.

"I think it used to be a cow," answered Mia. He could hear the grimace in her tone of voice. They pulled up to the end of the gravel driveway where it met the asphalt of the road.

"Okay. Which way should we go? Where's your nearest family?" Jayden knew his nearest reliable family was all the way in Auckland, many many hours distant. He hoped Mia didn't mention his parents in Palmerston North again. Mia had to have better and closer options.

"Turn right."

Jayden spun the wheel and they began to drive out onto the road.

"Who's along here? How far is it?"

"Just the fire station in town. Take the left."

Jayden let the car slow down, then half turned in the seat, peering back over his shoulder at her while trying to keep an eye on the road. "In town? You mean, you just want to go into town? The town that's, like, five minutes away? If those things are here, then they'll be there too!"

"What's your point?"

Jayden was gobsmacked. "My point? My point is, why the hell are we using this time to just find somewhere that's likely to be as dangerous as here? We could drive far away! Fast!"

"Jay, you used to be someone who had at least some compassion. I know that you found it hard to understand why people did the things they did and said the things they said, but you used to try. I wish you'd try to be more like that Jay again."

"That Jay is dead," he growled and hunched his shoulders.

"And so is this one, drive!" Mia screamed as a figure stepped out onto the road in front of them. Under the harsh light of the headlights, it was possible to make out the thick dark liquid that streamed down the figure's shoulders, and the strange limping stagger that brought it haltingly forward.

Jayden stomped onto the accelerator and the car leapt forward, the engine whining under the strain.

"Do I hit it?" Jayden yelled, his fingers gripping the wheel so hard they turned white. He was trying to duck below the windshield and watch the road at the same time.

"Just go!" Mia shouted in response and within a second Jayden's instincts took control. He turned the wheel a little to try and avoid the thing, but felt a judder as the side of the car clipped the figure and sent it reeling. He concentrated on pressing the accelerator down and sending the car shooting like a firework towards the main streets of Kanuka Creek.

"Did you see what happened to it? It wasn't a real person was it?" He called over his shoulder. The air in the car felt thick and stuffy. He wanted to open the window but the idea horrified him in ways he didn't expect. He felt the same breath-restricting panic that he had felt when he was a small child hiding under the blankets in his bed, terrified of allowing a hand or foot to be exposed in case the monsters in the night found him. The air beneath the blankets felt just like this, hot and heavy, but he couldn't risk even a small opening to allow fresh air in.

"No, I saw it, sort of!" Mia's reply came back quickly, raised over the sound of the engine working harder than it had ever been required to before. "It looked like a cloud of leaves falling down around it. I think you might have broken its arm off."

"Sounds good to me."

CHAPTER TWELVE

The streets in Kanuka Creek seemed deathly quiet. Each storefront was a black and empty window beneath a dimmed sign. Even the lights inside the shop at the petrol station were off, though the forecourt was still lit up like a signal fire. Jayden tried to remember if the station closed overnight or if there should have been a night shift worker in there. He doubted he had known even when he lived here.

"Where do I go?" he asked.

"It's just up there," said Mia, pointing over the seat and jutting her hand past his face. Jayden was driving much slower now that he was in the closed in streets, surrounded by buildings.

"Why are you going so slow?" asked Mia.

"I just don't want the car to rev too loudly." Jayden breathed out softly. "I mean, we can't see what's around any of these corners, there's so many places to hide. It looks so dead on these streets... " He let his voice trail off, hoping that the explanation would be enough.

"I suppose that kind've makes sense. Although, these streets have always been dead." Mia began giggling at her joke, but the laughter went on much longer and louder than Jayden thought was reasonable.

"Are you okay?" he asked.

"You don't care," sniffed Mia, her laughter cutting off as though struck by a cleaver, and she refused to respond to any further questions.

Moments later Jayden was able to see the fire station a short distance ahead of them. It was made of brick, barely one storey tall and not very wide. Most of the building was taken up with the massive double-doored garage for the fire engines themselves. As they approached, it was clear that at least one side of the garage was empty, illuminated by a few flickering fluorescent bulbs. Jayden felt his shoulders lift and a smile managed to establish a foothold in his cheeks.

However, as the car crawled to a stop outside the station along the curb, Jayden was able to see that there was another engine parked inside. His shoulders slumped again.

He heard a sigh of relief from the seats behind him.

"We made it."

Jayden screwed up his face. "Did we though?"

"What do you mean?"

"Well, we don't know if it's any safer here. We did have the option to drive *away* from the source of the monsters, but here we are having driven *towards* them. Seems to me that we don't know whether we made it or not yet."

There was silence from the back seat. The car was silent and the headlights were off. Jayden tried not to steal a glance out of the rear-view mirror. Nothing moved on the street. Jayden grimaced, steeling himself to break the silence.

"Why did you swerve?" said Mia before he had a chance.

"What? Swerve?" Jayden's head jerked in surprise.

"Yes. When we left my house, one of those things came out onto the road. You could have smashed it, but you swerved."

Jayden rolled his shoulder uncomfortably. He felt as though he was wearing a tee shirt that was a few sizes too small. His mouth opened to reply, but he had nothing to say for a few moments.

"I just... sort of... realised that it might have been... might have been a normal person..."

The silence rolled over them again. Jayden tried not to remember a body lying face down on the grass, its severed head rolling back and forward on the grass nearby. A small rhythmic sucking noise became noticeable.

"What's that?"

"Estelle has her dummy in, so that she won't cry."

"That's good. It'd be pretty awful if she let them know where we are."

"Thanks for that cheery thought."

Jayden looked along the dark and empty street. The light from the fire station garage seemed to spread much further than he would have thought possible, but every other yard and house down the street seemed as empty and unlit as a tomb. Was that something small pushing at the white fence of the house three or four further down the road?

"Come on, let's get inside this place," said Mia.

The pair loaded themselves up with their supplies before pushing the doors of the car open as fast as they could and jumping out. Jayden winced as the doors reached the extent of their swing, and bounced back to slam shut with a resounding bang. Mia didn't look twice, but started jogging up to the station. Jayden hefted the weapons in his hands and jogged after her.

They reached the front door to the office and reception area of the station and tried the handle. The door was locked, and didn't budge at all. Mia spun around and swung her gaze across the station, searching for somewhere to go.

"Can't we just knock?"

"If we knock loud enough to wake someone or get their attention from the other end of the station, we'd probably be almost as loud as those car doors," snapped Mia. "I'd prefer not to bring more attention down on us at the moment actually."

"Try the garage then?"

They strode along the brick wall, peering into the dark windows that they passed. Curtains and blinds blocked their view in most cases, and the rooms seemed still and empty when they were able to steal a better view.

At the garage doors they leaned against the glass and looked around inside.

"I wonder why they've left these lights on, when everything else is so dark?" asked Jayden. "It really makes the place stand out."

"Will the doors open?"

Jayden pushed and pulled at the large doors and looked around to see if there was any smaller way inside. "Doesn't look like it."

"Shit. What are we going to do now?" Mia turned to look out at the small town around them, with her hands cradling Estelle in the harness on her chest.

Jayden squeezed the strong wooden handles of the implements he had in both of his hands. They were a confidence boosting weight to his arms. "I'll smash a window," he decided.

"Oh Jay don't be an arse. If you do that, then there's a hole into the building. Do you want an easy way for one of those things to get in?"

Jayden flinched at the thought of it. "I... I won't smash a window."

"Good."

Thin wisps of cloud slid past the moon above them, and Kanuka Creek lay silent around them. It was as though the buildings were holding their breath.

"I really don't like this," said Jayden. "I know this town is small, and people don't have much to do in the middle of the night, but I feel like this place is dead."

Mia nodded. "It's quieter than usual. But if that's the case, where are the monsters?"

Jayden opened his eyes wide and stared at her. "Why would you say something like that? Do you actually *want* hideous dead things to come firing tentacles at us?"

"No!" Mia started giggling again. "I just don't know what we do now!"

"I say that we get out of here." Jayden looked to his right down the street, back towards the main road of Kanuka Creek. There was a soft glow into the black sky from the petrol station sign. "We get back in the car and find some other relatives of yours to shelter with. Can you call someone?"

"Yes!" Mia's excited cry seemed far louder than Jayden was comfortable with, but then he realised that she was actually only speaking in a normal talking volume. The dark sky seemed to be sucking away any hint of noise in the town.

"Good," he said, and began walking back towards the car. *The doors would be unlocked, and the key was in his pocket so-*

"No, I mean, I can call someone."

"I know, that's what I suggested. Are they near Taupō or what?"

"They're in here hopefully!" Mia dug her phone out of her pocket and began swiping on the screen to unlock it and find her contacts. "Here we go." She poked the button and held the phone to her ear.

Jayden walked back in time to hear the faint buzz of a voice answer at the other end. If he really focused, he could make out some of their part of the conversation.

"Babe! Is that you?" crackled the voice.

"Yes," breathed Mia. "We're outside the station right now, where are you?"

"Outside the station?" yelped the voice. "Jesus, don't you know what's been going on? You can't be out there!"

"We know, we got attacked at home," said Mia, with a hint of iron entering her voice. "Where are *you*?"

"I'm right here, hold on." The phone fell silent. Mia looked into Jayden's eyes.

"I think Hayden is here. Hold on a moment."

Jayden turned slowly, looking around the street again. His neck prickled with the feeling that someone was watching him. He was pretty sure that he really didn't want anything in this town to be able to see him at the moment. The axe and hatchet in his hands were reassuringly solid, but the street was open and empty. If anything was coming, those extending limbs seemed to be able to stretch a very long way, and he would be a sitting duck while he stood illuminated on the driveway to the station.

His attention was dragged back to the white fence that had caught his attention earlier. It reflected the starlight from its location in front of a small cottage, not much further down the road. Was there something behind the fence?

"Thank god," said Mia and Jayden turned back. Inside the garage Hayden had just appeared from the internal door. His eyes were wide and flicked constantly around as though he was unable to look at any one object for more than a moment. His mouth was pulled down into a grimace. With wild arm movements he gestured for Jayden and Mia to move further around the building. As they followed his directions, Jayden realised there was a small external door on the side of the garage, a normal person-sized door. Hayden slid behind the one engine parked inside and along to the door, watching them through the glass as they walked to the corner. Mia went by first and Jayden followed.

Just as he turned the corner, close enough that he accidentally clinked the red bricks with the hatchet in his hand, he glanced back up the street again. There were no streetlights on anywhere in Kanuka Creek, and all the houses seemed to be dim. But the moon was bright, and so he was sure that he saw something moving over the fence at the house down the way. Whatever it was, it was mostly pale, and after it tumbled across the fence it stood up straight, to the full height of a person, before beginning to wobble towards the fire station.

"Shitshitshit," Jayden began hyperventilating and pressed closely behind Mia.

"Hey-" she began to complain, but Jayden lifted the hand holding the hatchet to his face and used one finger to shush her, half closing his eyes in terrified anticipation of being caught by whatever it was. He hurried her to the door, where she knocked extremely gently. The click of the lock shifting sounded like someone knocking an ornamental vase to smash on the floor of a massive marble museum in Jayden's mind but he followed Mia in as quickly as he could.

"What's the-" began Hayden, stepping back from Jayden's harried expression.

"I saw one, I saw another one, have you actually seen them here, because one's coming, it was just down the road and I saw it and I think that maybe it saw us, I saw it coming, it's coming, oh fuck what the fuck do we do now?"

"Shit, one's coming here?"

Jayden nodded, all his muscles clenched tight. His knuckles were snow white where he clenched his fists around the axe and hatchet hafts.

"None of them have figured out that we are in here, the last fucking thing that we need is one finding us. Come this way, quick!"

Hayden turned the lock again and then led the pair to the back of the fire engine. There he helped Mia climb up onto a space on the back of the engine, so that her legs wouldn't be visible to anyone peering beneath the engine from outside. She settled into a corner between the chassis and a railing, then Jayden hopped up as well. He had to move carefully so that he managed to hold onto his weapons and also so that he didn't jab anybody else with them, and then he crouched down beside Mia. Hayden was the last up, motioning for Jayden to hand over the axe as he did so. Jayden's first impulse was to pull the wooden handle closer to his body instead, but then he pursed his lips and slowly offered the axe to the other man.

"Cheers man," whispered Hayden. "We've scrounged together a few things to try and defend ourselves with, but I didn't think of bringing something with me right now. Pretty fucking dumb, right?" He grinned, and the sight of someone smiling in the midst of this terrifying night of monsters and death nearly made Jayden double up in hysterics. *What the hell is he smiling for? His partner and her child were nearly killed! For all this idiot knows, we're all about to die right now!*

There was a strange, scraping, squeaking noise. It dragged on for a while then stopped. Then, after an odd pause, it started again, but for less time now. The sound continued that way, on and off, for about a minute.

"They've come by the station a few times so far,"

breathed Hayden, staring up from his position straight into the rear wall of the garage. He clutched the axe diagonally across himself. The metal head glinted as Hayden's slow deep breaths lifted it in and out of line with the fluorescent lights above. Mia had one hand reaching out to lay on his calf, and her other arm was hooked by the elbow through a handle on the railing. She was gently stroking Estelle's wispy hair. The baby slept in her harness, slowly sucking on the dummy in her mouth.

"Oh good, I'm glad we came here then. Sounds safe as houses," answered Jayden as quietly as he could. The squeaking sound echoed across the small concrete space. It sounded as though it was coming from right next to his head, vibrating down through his ears to his spine. Jayden imagined one of those things in the garage, walking alongside the engine, right up next to him, watching him from an angle that he would never see, its milky eyes turning to examine his skull and then that dripping horrific appendage rising at its chest and-

"They don't seem to go inside buildings unless they are chasing something," said Hayden. "I don't think they're very smart."

"Have you seen what they can do? I don't think they need to be smart."

"You said we," interrupted Mia. "Who else is here? And how come you aren't out at the call?"

"There's a few of us. We've been laying low in the bunkroom. It's easy enough to stay out of sight that way."

Hayden turned his head. There was no noise anymore.

"I think it's probably gone. They don't seem to be very cunning, so I don't think it's trying to trick us. Come on, come to the bunkroom and we can catch up. I want to know what happened at home to get you guys rushing out here as well!"

Hayden was right that the thing seemed to have passed them by and kept moving, although mustering the strength to expose his quivering legs to anything that might be watching through the huge glass doors took every drop of Jayden's willpower. The trio moved quietly across the floor, watching the doors closely for any hint of movement. From in here, the world outside the glass garage doors seemed much more intimidating. The shadows seemed deeper and darker and full of unseen threats. The only light came from those small fluorescents in the garage, and the pool of light that they emptied onto the street in front of the station was small and surrounded by the black of night. Then, without Jayden quite believing that it was real, they passed into the darkness of an unlit hallway and were out of sight of the door.

As Hayden led the way through the small dark space, Jayden felt a question rise in his mind.

"It seems like a bad idea to leave those lights on, why didn't you turn them off? Everywhere else is totally blacked out."

"Yeah, that was part of how people knew something had gone wrong. The power to most of the town went down at once. Terina said she thought she saw a big flash over by the hills just before it happened."

"A flash?" Mia's voice seemed loud in the small space. Hayden paused and turned to face them, though it was impossible to actually make out his expressions in the darkness.

"Yeah, like that time a possum shorted out some part of the relays or whatever it was? There was that massive flash and then a blackout?"

"I remember. People thought it was hilarious that a possum could cause such a big problem!"

"I know right?" Hayden laughed softly. "But anyway, maybe something did that again. I actually thought that it might have been someone crashing into a power-pole and that was, you know, why the alarm sounded?"

"Why *did* the alarm sound?" asked Mia.

"No wait," Jayden felt his mind tangling into knots. "Why are the lights on if there's a blackout?"

"Okay, maybe I should start at the beginning. Come in here." Hayden pointed at a door on the left of the hall and the others walked in before him.

CHAPTER THIRTEEN

Inside Jayden discovered a small room full of solid wooden bunks built into spaces in the walls. A single short and wide window was set into the top of the far wall, which explained why Hayden said that the bunkroom was easy enough for them to hide in. Nothing would be able to see them through that unless it already knew that they might be inside and was climbing up to get a peek.

That thing that scraped by the doors a minute or so earlier might know there's someone inside the building, thought Jayden. He swallowed heavily, his gut twisting.

Seated on the bunks around the room was a small group of people. From the faint moonlight that eked in the tiny window, Jayden could just about make out their faces.

"Hey everyone, this is my partner Mia and my daughter Estelle. Something happened to them back home, but they managed to get here, thank god."

There was a murmur of congratulations at the good news of this family being reunited.

"And this is her... friend, Jay. He was in Wellington when all this shit started."

"Wow," said the woman sitting nearest Jayden on the right. She was older than him, with short curly hair. "That's pretty intense. My name's Terina. How are you doing?" She extended a hand towards him.

"I guess I'm alright," said Jayden. He gingerly took her hand and shook it.

"Did you see any of it?"

"Yes." Jayden spoke as quickly as he could to avoid any memories flashing across his eyes. The darkness made it much easier to recall and picture those moments. They hung in the air before like cinema projections. He shivered, closed his eyes, and twitched his head to one side, dislodging the visions.

Hayden was leading Mia around the other bunks and introducing the people sitting on them, so Jayden moved over to meet the people he was going to be stuck with for a few hours.

"This is Jack and Stacy." The couple were clearly very young and they were cuddled together deep against the wall on a lower bunk. It was hard to make out more than that in the darkness below the upper bunk. "They joined up to be volunteers about three months ago. Stacy's been out on quite a few jobs, her first aid is top notch. Jack's not made it to as many, but he's a good lad." The couple nodded. The whites of their wide eyes glowed from the back of the bunk.

"Next we have Mike." Mike was a large round man, with a large round head completely devoid of hair. He also held out a hand to shake with Mia and Jayden.

"Glad you made it in here," he said. His voice was scratchy and rough. "I'm not sure what's going on out there right now, but I'm hoping we can all make it to daybreak and then get some help."

"Thank you," answered Mia.

Jayden grunted.

"And lastly we have Pip."

"Oh for fuck's sake," said Jayden.

"Pippa Clarke." Mia's voice was flat, and much louder than anyone else's had been.

"Quietly," urged Hayden, but he turned his head from his partner to Jayden to the woman sitting on the edge of the bunk. "You guys all know each other?"

"Quite well in fact," said Pip. She sighed. "Of all the fucking people," she muttered to no one in particular before she lay down on the bunk.

"Jay had an affair with Pip. She's the reason we broke up."

"Oh fuck you Mia," said Pip from her position stretched out on the mattress.

"I wouldn't say that it was an affair," began Jayden. "I mean, it wasn't like we were in love, going behind your back, or-"

"Oh, you weren't going behind my back? So, when I went to my hospital appointments and you went around to her place to shag, that wasn't behind my back?" Mia's voice was dangerously loud now. Hayden gently put his hands on her shoulders, but even in the gloom Jayden could see the glare that was directed at him.

"Um," he began, hoping that he would be able to think of a way to sooth Mia's temper as he spoke. "Well..."

"We didn't plan it." Pip's voice slipped between them, like a shark between swimmers at a crowded beach. "Yes, it kinda counts as behind your back I guess, because you didn't know and all. But he just came round to hang out. We watched Wayne's World and had a few beers."

"That's not all you had!"

"No, it wasn't. As far as I'm concerned, it was a silly mistake and I'm sorry it upset you."

Jayden bit his lower lip. *Would that be enough to smooth things over?*

"I thought you were a friend of ours." Mia shook

her head, bouncing Estelle gently to try and keep her asleep. Her angry voice escaped in a hiss. "That's not how a friend behaves. And you!" Mia jabbed one finger towards Jayden. "It is certainly not how a fiancé behaves when his partner has had a miscarriage!"

Jayden knew that everyone else in the small room was able to hear the conversation between the three of them. The room had been full of that extra quiet silence that implied all ears had been pricked up as they spoke; giving the absence of sound a strange, almost physical presence. But it was still galling to hear the gasps and soft whistles of inrushing breath as the others took in what Mia had just said.

"I know." He shook his head and walked away, climbing onto the top bunk above Terina. He could see her head shaking at him as he climbed, the whites of her disappointed eyes following him in the dark room. *Yeah yeah,* he thought. *Now you all know Jayden is this awful man who did something really terrible. He is totally irredeemable and worthless, why would we even want someone like that here with us? Let's all judge him.* He lay down on the thin mattress, hearing the cheap sheet crackle as it shifted underneath him. *Get in line.*

Back at the other end of the room, Hayden sat Mia down on a bunk, clearly the one he had been sitting on, and began to explain what had happened after he left the house after the siren.

"The drive into Kanuka Creek was straight forward, there was no one else on the roads. As I pulled up, the first engine was just leaving with a load of volunteers who had made it here faster. I even waved them off. I figured I'd go inside and see if anyone knew what had happened before I came home.

Terina was here and then Jack and Stacy showed up just after me. Terina said that it was a traffic accident on the highway south."

"Yup, I was here when the call came in," she added.

"Then why weren't you on the engine when it left?" Pip's voice sounded harsh to Jayden's ears, like scraping ceramic dinner plates together. He wondered if that image had come to mind simply because he expected her to ruin everything again.

"Someone has to stay and let the stragglers know what happened." Terina's casual denigration of Hayden and the others seemed like a joke, but it did make Jayden wonder if being late for the siren was frowned upon.

"South you say," he said. "So, closer to Wellington? Do you think it has anything to do with these things?"

There was a pause as the various others around the room considered whether or not to answer him. *Awesome, I'm the fucking pariah again. Great.*

"I suppose it could, but there's no real reason to think so. Traffic accidents happen, we get called out to do what we can. That's just as likely," Terina explained in a sullen voice. She clearly would have rather left his question unanswered.

"Anyway, it was just after Terina had told me and the others that, when there was the flash from over by the hills."

"The possum in the equipment," added Mia.

"Yeah, or whatever it actually was," laughed Hayden.

"I reckon it was one of those things," said a new voice. Jayden searched around in the shadows to try and figure out who was speaking now. The voice was small and light, as fragile as a cobweb.

"Do you really think so Stace?" asked Hayden.

"Yup. They're so awful. I reckon that they must've smashed the power because they knew it would make it easier to get us."

"It's alright babe, we'll be okay here," said another new voice, a little deeper but just as fragile. Jayden assumed this must be Stacy's boyfriend Jack.

"Maybe," she murmured.

"So, the power went out," prompted Mia.

"Yeah, the power was out," Hayden picked up his story again. "Luckily the generators went on, because the station has a lot of emergency backups."

"That's why I came here," added Pip.

"Good for you," snapped Mia.

"Hey Mia," said Hayden, placing a hand on her shoulder. "You guys might have some serious issues from the past, but there are bigger problems out there tonight."

Mia snorted, but didn't say anything else.

"Anyway, we could see that the rest of the town had gone black, but we didn't really think much of it until they arrived."

"I saw them first," said Mike. "I was outside when I saw one pass by the intersection of the main street."

"Yeah, why don't you explain what you saw," said Hayden, stepping back to allow the others to focus on Mike.

"Just... just try not to be too graphic please?" asked Stacy.

"I'll try. The one I saw was kind of limping along the road. At first, I thought it might have been someone who was hurt. But then it... shot... like, a whip? Or a tentacle? Whatever it was, it seemed to shoot straight out of the guy's chest. I saw it hit someone else at the other side of the road and they..." Mike trailed off. "Even in the darkness, even watching from way down here to the intersection, it was not nice at all."

There was a pause.

"Is that all you saw? And that's why you guys hid in here?" Jayden asked, trying not to sound sarcastic, but he didn't think he managed to conceal his in-credulity. There was a small sound, like multiple people grunting in displeasure at the question. Jayden lowered his head back down onto the mattress so that he didn't have to imagine them all glaring at him.

"No, that is not all that I saw. Another one came along the street, and this one casually flipped a car over. Another one appeared down one of the side streets, closer to the station. I saw a guy on his front doorstep having a smoke, and he bolted inside when he realised that these things were so close to him. The thing chased him inside."

"It chased him? I never noticed these things moving quickly."

"Oh, and you'd know all about them would you?" Mike growled, clearly growing angry at the constant questions Jayden was asking.

"Actually, he does." Mia's voice was soft, and the reluctant admission from her carried more weight than any bluster Jayden could have offered. "He was caught in a cinema crowd with one, then one chased him through a car park. He was right in the middle when it started."

"Oh. Well." Mike paused as he considered Mia's point. He cleared his throat. "Anyway, it didn't move very quickly, no, but it also didn't stop. It tumbled over a fence and then just rose up as though it was being pulled by wires. The guy came back out the door, carrying his rifle."

Jayden blinked and nodded. "A gun, fantastic. I didn't get to see how well a gun might help in this sit-uation. Do we happen to have one in here anywhere?"

"No, no guns in the station," answered Hayden. "Go on Mike."

"Cheers. The guy lifted the rifle, pointed it at the thing, and blasted it."

"Probably a .22, am I right?" asked Jayden.

"Yeah, probably. It hit the thing in the shoulder, I saw it spin and nearly fall. But then it straightened up and kept coming. Pieces of its arm were dangling off like Christmas decorations, and something was falling from the wound, though it didn't seem to be liquid, like you would expect blood to be.

I think the guy went into shock, because he didn't fire again, and then it wrapped its good arm around the gun and threw it away. And I do mean it wrapped its arm, as though there was no elbow or anything."

There was a groan from the blackness deep in the lower bunk.

"You alright Stace?" asked Mia.

"I'll be fine, but please get to the end of this," replied the younger woman.

"Yup, I'm nearly there. The thing killed the guy, and in deference to Stace I'm not going to explain exactly what happened, but it sounds like you can imagine it for yourself. Then, before it had a chance to turn around, I ran back into the station and started shutting doors."

"Me and Stace were in the kitchen, and bolted in here when Mike said to," offered Jack.

"Me and Terina ducked back in quick smart ourselves," added Hayden.

"And are you a volunteer too?" Jayden asked Pip. She snorted.

"God no. I don't think these guys would have accepted me even if I *had* volunteered."

"I don't think that's true Pip, we're always keen to get anyone involved with the fire service-"

"Shush Hayden," interrupted Mia. Jayden could practically hear the fire burning from her eyes, staring across the dim room at the other woman.

"When my power went out, I glanced outside to see if it was just my fuses or something bigger. You know, something affecting the whole street maybe?

That's when I saw the one down the street shove its arms into a guy and make him pop."

There was another retch from the gloomy bunks.

"Thanks for nothing Pip!" snapped Jack.

Pip laughed once. "And that was all I needed to see. I considered staying in my flat, but it's falling apart anyway, the walls are made of fucking cardboard. So I decided to come over to the station. At least it still had some lights on."

"Yeah, I was asking about that before," said Jayden. "Why don't you shut those off? Then you could all hunker down in the dark until morning. That'd be much less likely to catch their attention, like the one that nearly saw us coming in."

"We could I suppose." Hayden's voice sounded surprised. He clearly had never even considered the idea. "I suppose we figured making sure we didn't lose power would be a good thing. I don't know if there is even a switch to turn them off without turning off the emergency generators."

"As long as we stay out of sight, we should be fine. They don't seem to come in unless they are following someone," chipped in Terina.

"Your funeral, I guess," said Jayden. There was yet another gasp from Stacy. "Oh for fuck's sake, there's some ridiculous bloody shit happening tonight Stacy, if you keep gasping and gawping every time something violent happens, you'll die of asphyxiation before any of these monsters manage to rip you in half."

"Jesus Jay," muttered Terina from the bunk below him. "That's hardly necessary."

"Oh whatever. Wake me up in the morning, and don't let me get killed in my sleep." He rolled over and squeezed himself into the corner where the wall met the thin mattress. With his eyes closed, and his heart pumping heavily, Jayden tried to shut out the murmured conversation that followed his outburst.

But why should he have to soften things for someone who could barely understand what was going on? Why should she be allowed to not have to face up to the death that had happened? Jayden had watched his best fucking friends die, he had had to pull himself together and swing an axe into what appeared to be another human, hoping that he was not wrong and killing some innocent who was just freaking out.

He wondered about the others in the room with him. Was there really any way to know what kind of people they were? Would they be useful during this nightmare, or would they all crack, just like Stacy had? Mike seemed pretty stern and no nonsense, but what if he just screamed and pissed himself when one of those beasts broke in? Jayden curled tighter around himself. There's no way to know what the real Mike would be like once those things stripped away his bluster and bravado. There was no way to know what any of them would really be like.

He heard the sounds of Estelle whimpering over the top of Stacy's sobs, and burrowed his head further into the corner. Mia seemed happy now, her life had gone well. *I mean,* he thought, *right up until the moment that weird dead people had lurched across the farm fields and bashed their way into her home.* There was no reason for Jayden to keep blaming himself for her anger or her sorrow, was there? Anything he had done to ruin her life had been passed over by the arrival of Hayden and Estelle, right? Jayden should just forget the past entirely.

He thought about what Pip had said earlier about them watching a movie together the night that Mia had gone into the hospital. He had told Mia about them going to the pub that night. He knew that there had been a night at the pub; a night that had led to drunken kissing in the car park, staggering through the park to Pip's house, and all the foolishness that

followed. Until she had spoken tonight, he had forgotten the night he had gone around to watch a
DVD. Other occasions were floating to the surface in
the bog of his memory. Now he was realising that, as
much as Mia hated him for what she knew, it probably wasn't hatred enough to cover the parts of the
story that she didn't know.

As a much delayed sleep slowly overrode the
adrenaline and panic that had washed through his
body during the evening, Jayden knew that his past
was not undone in any way.

CHAPTER FOURTEEN

J ayden rolled over and nearly fell off the edge of the bunk and into the middle of the floor of the room. Soft snores rose around him as he jerked to wakefulness in time to stop himself plummeting over the edge. He spluttered and smacked his lips, trying to clear away the sticky taste of sleep. As he pushed himself back into the centre of his mattress, he realised that he could still hear the sounds of Stacy's weeping, but it was not coming from the shadowed lower bunk opposite him. The murmuring sound was echoing from somewhere outside the bunkroom entirely.

Jayden lay on his mattress and stared at the darkness of the ceiling. A faint light from the moonlight outside stole in through the small gap of the window to the room, but Kanuka Creek seemed to be still and silent outside.

Fuck it, thought Jayden. *Maybe I should check on the girl. I mean, if she doesn't shut up one of those things will probably hear her anyway.* So he swung his legs over the side and climbed down to the ground. *I wonder if Jack is awake with her? You'd bloody hope so, wouldn't you?*

He peeked around the doorframe into the hallway. The dim glow from the lights in the garage of the station illuminated the hallway, but Jayden could see nothing but stillness and a glimpse of the remaining engine there, its chrome metal attachments and nozzles shining even in the low blue fluorescence. In the other direction, where the sounds were coming from, there was less light. But not none.

Jayden wondered where the light was coming from as he moved down the hallway. Were there other emergency lights?

It turned out that, no, there were no other emergency lights. What there were, were large windows in the kitchen, through which the light of the moon and stars were shining. Jayden felt his eyes widen and his pulse quicken as he looked out through the windows. The streets and houses that surrounded the station were easily visible beyond the glass, and Jayden's throat began to clench. *Shit, anything could see us through those! Is she in here? Why the fuck is she in here!?*

The sounds were coming from the far side of the room, near the fridge, which was humming. There was a tall cupboard set against the wall there also, which Jayden assumed must be a makeshift pantry.

Between the two tall objects, Jayden made out a figure, limbs tangled and thrashing. The crying and sobbing suddenly shifted in his perception, turning into gasps of panicked breath. *Oh fuck!* Jayden realised with a sinking heart that he was carrying no weapons with him and that he could do nothing to rescue the girl. *Do I run?*

As he stood frozen in the doorway, the figure turned in the silvery light and became clearer. Jayden relaxed. Although he had never seen either Stacy or Jack properly, he was fairly sure that the two young people wrapped around one another on the other side of the kitchen, with their faces mashed together and their hands running across each other's bodies, would be those two of his fellow refugees.

He realised for the second time that the cries he had heard were not what he had initially thought. He felt his cheeks flush and he began to step backward, to leave the couple to themselves. His eyes darted away from the couple, trying not to intrude on their private moment.

They settled immediately on the pale face of a woman standing outside the station.

The woman's face was slack and her jaw hung open. It was impossible to make out her eyes, due to the fact that she was facing inside and the only pale light came from behind her. Jayden felt his own mouth fall open and then hissed "Guys!"

Jack and Stacy separated and glanced around in confusion. "What? Who's there?" said Jack.

"Who's the pervert spying on us?" Stacy began to ask, but then her voice rose to a shriek as the woman shoved a hand into the window and the glass bent and shattered.

The woman stepped forward, gripping onto the ragged edges of glass that remained in the frame so hard that one of her fingers was sheared off and fell to the floor. Jayden watched the single digit drop, tumbling through the air, until it reached the tiles of white linoleum, where it smashed. And smashed was the word. There was no splatter of blood, no wet thwack of flesh as the finger struck down. Instead, the edges chipped and spun away like shards of a dropped teacup.

Jayden heard a voice yelling for help, and he wanted to try to calm them down, quieten them, before they attracted more of the creatures to the station. As he turned, firstly to run from the thing that was still only halfway through pulling itself in the window and secondly to try and spot whoever was making so much noise, he realised that it was himself. With a great strength of will, he managed to force his mouth closed, muffling the noise, but he was unable to cease the sobbing panting shrieks that bubbled up from his chest.

Jack spun Stacy behind his body, trying to do up the zip of his jeans with one hand and holding up the other in some semblance of defence. Jayden was looking down the hallway now, and felt a wave of relief pass over him as Mike came pounding out of the bunkroom like a medieval knight, galloping himself towards the kitchen. Jayden threw himself to one side and slumped to the floor as Mike sped past.

"Holy fuck!" came the cry from the big man as he saw the thing. It had clattered to the ground as it tumbled through the window and now began to stand up, its head twisted sideways to keep Jack in sight. It rose unnaturally, as though pulled by the shoulders on ropes. From where he was panting and wheezing on the floor, Jayden could almost have sworn that the thing left the ground completely for a second, just completely lifted off the surface before hovering and floating softly back down.

The thing turned its head to Mike now that he had entered the room, its attention split. There was no expression on the slack pale face, but the way it began to sway from one man to the other implied that it was unsure what to do next.

"We've got no chance," wailed Jack. He had finished doing up his pants, freeing up his other arm, but they were still held up as an ineffectual barrier in front of him. "I can't do anything to it!" His face was falling and tears were slicking a shining surface over his eyes and cheeks.

"Fuck that and fuck that thing too!" Mike reached out and snatched up the shitty hollow-metal-framed chair that was sitting by the doorway. It was beginning to rust, and the cushion covers were beginning to tear, but now Mike was holding a length of metal, with multiple prongs. He waved it in front of himself. "Maybe it can rip me apart, but I'm gonna fucking hit it on the way out."

The chair seemed to be a deciding factor for the thing, and it lurched itself around to face Mike squarely. Jayden couldn't think of the thing as a she, even though it was wearing a formal short brown skirt, and a tasteful sleeveless blouse. It had long blonde hair that hung in waves, but the milky eyes and gaping mouth drew the eye inevitably to its face.

Without a flicker of emotion on that face, a length of cartilage and flesh splashed forward from beneath its shoulder, slamming into the chair that Mike was holding and tearing it from his hands. The spear of flesh carried the chair away, all the way to the wall of the kitchen. Jayden noticed two things about this. One, the appendage seemed to actually erupt from beneath the thing's skin, in the shoulder region in this case, ripping the skin apart. However, there was no blood, and the thing didn't seem to display any pain. Two, and this was probably more immediately useful, the thing struck at the chair that Mike had been waving, slightly to his side. From the look on the large man's face, a mixture of shocked terror and gleeful relief; he had been hoping that the thing would take the feint, though he had underestimated the strength of its strike.

"I'm not having that," he yelled and he darted back to where the tentacle was stapling the chair and wall together. He grabbed one of the chair legs and heaved. Jayden was amazed to see the twisted metal snap and a piece of it rip into the flesh with amazing effect. A ragged slash was torn in the surface, leaking black liquid. The cord whipped back and disappeared inside the torso of the thing, which took another strangely light-footed step closer.

Mike swung the twisted chair-leg back and forth

and then held it up by his shoulder like a softball bat. "Come on you fucking waterlily, I'll show you what's fucking what!" He stepped towards the thing too.

There was a sudden roar from Jack, who dove forward and swung a heavy black iron frying pan onto the thing's shoulder, which cracked. The thing stumbled and twisted as though it were a clumsy human that had been stung by a bee.

Jack and Mike both stood by the thing as it twisted at the waist, its flesh pulling like dough. One of its hands raised up and touched its shoulder where the pan had hit. The shoulder looked like a car door that had been hit by a large rock, dented and crumpled, but rigid. Small cracks spidered across the surface. *What the hell are these things made of,* wondered Jayden. *Were they ever real people?*

Faster than he could respond, the thing flung a hand towards Jack, the limb stretching and whipping out as it flew through the air. It bowled him aside like a toy, flinging him up and onto the stainless steel kitchen bench behind him. Stacy cowered and shrieked as her boyfriend passed over the top of her.

Mike lunged forward with his chair leg, smacking the thing in the back of the head, leaving another cracked dent. The thing spun back, both arms outstretched, and caught Mike on his own shoulder, knocking him to the ground.

Jayden began to push himself backwards down the hallway, shaking his head and gasping for breath. Bright specks of white light seemed to be swimming across his vision. Stacy dropped to the floor and crawled beneath the thin table sitting in the middle of the room. Jack lay on the bench, groaning. His arm dangled off the edge. Jayden could see the frying pan on the floor by the fridge, still spinning gently on its rim, rocking to a rest. Mike pushed himself up off the floor. He had struck the floor with force, and there was blood dripping from his lip. He touched his lip gingerly, examining the red stain left on his fingertips, and stretched his jaw carefully. His gaze slid sideways and met Jayden's. Then the thing kicked him in the side.

Mike actually came off the ground and rose into mid-air, which was astounding given his size. He slid along the tiles until he crashed into the wall by the door. Jayden felt as though he was about to throw up.

As the thing took a step closer to Mike, Stacy appeared by its feet and swung the frying pan as hard as she could into its legs. Shockingly, the thin side of the pan tore through the monster's ankle completely, severing the foot. A burst of black wet leaves seemed to erupt from the wound, and then the creature stumbled and dropped to the floor. Thrashing wildly, it caught Stacy with a flailing arm and knocked her aside, the pan spinning away into the corner of the room again.

But the distraction had given Mike time to catch his breath and grab a piece of the discarded chair.

"Fuck you!" He yelled as he ran towards it, dropping the length of metal like an anvil onto the thing's shoulder. Like the pan had done to the leg, the metal rod tore through the shoulder, nearly severing one arm. It dangled to the side of the creature's body as Jack rolled off the bench and staggered to retrieve the pan.

"We can cut it up," shouted Mike, the shock carrying clearly in his voice. "It's soft, we can cut it-"

A thick tentacle burst from the chest of the thing, stabbing into Mike's shoulder and lifting him in the air. His scream was long and deep, pulling every breath of air from his lungs and converting it into pain and fear. His body lurched by inches, jerking down the protrusion as he was pulled by gravity, his blood pouring along the twisted gristle. Jayden saw the tip pierce through Mike's body and begin to push out from the back of his clothes.

"No! Mike!" shouted Jack, who ran forward swinging the pan like an axe. He managed to smash off part of the thing's other arm. *Like an axe?* Jayden's thoughts were drifting like clouds of fog, grey and heavy fog that concealed worrying shadows. *An axe would be helpful,* he thought. *Didn't I have an axe?*

The limb recoiled, unpinning Mike and dropping him on the floor. He grimaced and tried to lift himself, but the effort only sent further waves of blood gushing from his shoulder. As the thing turned to Jack, Mike managed to shove himself forward, kicking the monster's dangling arm so that it came off completely. He stomped at its legs, cracking the knee of one, and allowed his whole body to career into it, carrying it to the ground.

"Chop its bloody head off man!" he yelled as he tried to wrestle himself aside from it, while not allowing it enough purchase to climb off the ground. The thing began to rise slowly from the ground, shoulders first, carrying Mike with it as though he were a small child.

Jack swung again, and the pan tore gratifyingly through the neck of the thing. Black leaves fell and the head bounced away. The body dropped back to the floor and lay still.

The silence that crowded in on top of them was overwhelming. Jayden became aware of the sound of his blood rushing through his ears, roaring like a hurricane. He tried to will his heart to stop racing, just to reduce the noise. Slowly, the awareness of sound came back, the drip of blood onto the floor, the rasping breath of the humans in the room.

"Stace!" yelped Jack, and he dropped the pan with a flinchingly loud bang as he hurried to her side. Her desperate sobs grew louder as she became more convinced of her safety.

"I can't believe we killed that thing," murmured Mike. His voice was tight with pain. "Fuck me, but we did it." He groaned again, with one hand pressed to the wound in his shoulder. "I don't even want to look at this. Where's the first aid kit?"

"I think there's one in–"

A cluster of tiny strands, a dozen thin spears of red and black and white, burst out of the shadows in the corner of the kitchen and planted themselves in a line of needles up Mike's side and head, thin strands linking him to the dark corner. He yelled like a wounded dog and tried to pull them off, but the thing's head came flying towards him, pulling itself along the threads by sucking them back into its gaping jaw. When it reached him, it latched on, human teeth biting into Mike's shoulder. The tentacles began to retract and then stabbed at him, opening a multitude of tiny wounds.

"There's some weird black thing in the head," Jayden called. "You've got to crush it Jack!"

Jack grabbed the frying pan and swung it like a tennis racquet into the head, fracturing it badly and sending it flying off Mike. The big man's skin and flesh tore away with the head. Jack rushed over to where the head had dropped to the floor and smashed the flat of the pan down on it, crushing the whole head. Warily he lifted the pan, and examined the remains of the head. Shards of curved solid skin lay fragmented on the linoleum. In the middle, revealed as he nudged pieces aside with the toe of his shoe, were the remains of something black and slimy and organic. Just to be sure, Jack crushed those pieces even more. A thick yellow goop squished out from beneath the heavy black metal of the pan and Jack retched.

"Jack, is Mike..." Jayden was still unable to move his body enough to stand, but Mike was lying in the middle of the kitchen now, as still as a stone. Even from the low angle, Jayden could see the pool of dark red liquid spreading out across the floor beneath him.

Stacy was panting and gasping, both her hands held tightly at her stomach. She tremulously stepped closer to Mike and then her gasping got faster and a low whine began to rise from her throat.

"Shit, Stacy, calm down," Jayden began to say. He had managed to push himself against the hallway wall and use the leverage to stand up, but his muscles still felt weak and watery. His thigh was shivering uncontrollably. He waved his hands at the young woman, while keeping his head bowed and breathing deeply. "The last thing we need is another one to come by and hear us. Please Stacy, for the love of god, shut up."

"You're gonna get the rest of us killed you bloody idiot," snarled Jack at Stacy, grabbing her by the upper arm and dragging her towards the hallway. He was still holding the frying pan in his other hand. It dripped gobs of yellow ooze on the floor as he pulled her back towards the doorway to the bunks. "Stop being such a fucking loose unit."

Jayden coughed in shock and began spluttering, wanting to tell Jack off for his cruel words, but couldn't think of anything to say as the couple moved past him and into the dark bunkroom. Hayden stood in the doorway, with one arm on the doorframe and one held to his chest. The monster had rampaged through the kitchen so quickly that he hadn't been able to come forward to help any other way. He watched the two youngsters move past him, frowning at the back of Jack's head, then turning back to watch Jayden. He moved up the hall and put an arm across Jayden's shoulders.

"Are you okay man? I only saw some of that but... Shit, it looked nasty. I guess Mike..." Hayden left the question unspoken.

"Oh, Mike's fucking dead man." Jayden spat the words out like sour milk, scraping his tongue against his teeth to try and remove the foul taste of them from his mouth.

"Yeah, that's what I figured." Jayden could feel Hayden nodding beside him. "And now that window is just hanging around being all open to anything from outside. That won't be a problem for us in this situation, I'm sure."

Jayden wasn't used to hearing sarcasm from the overly chipper man, and the comment made him blink and turn to stare at him. Hayden raised an eyebrow.

"Well, if I didn't laugh about it I'd have to cry, and we certainly don't need two Stacys to calm down. Come on."

With Hayden's support, Jayden managed to walk back into the bunkroom, where they closed the door behind them. The moon and stars shone down on empty streets and dark houses. A scratching noise echoed through the still kitchen.

CHAPTER FIFTEEN

In the bunkroom a restrained and low volume hubbub was underway.

"... the right to talk to her like that?"

"She's my girlfriend!"

"If I was your girlfriend, I'd have smacked you one for that!"

"Oh fuck off, she's being a huge liability. Besides, I'd like to see you try."

"If I wasn't caring for this baby..."

"Lady, the baby's probably as dead as the rest of us anyway."

The stunned silence swelled like a wave before multiple voices crashed down in angry whispers.

"Jack you're going way too far, pull your head in."

"Jesus man, why don't you let it all out? Holding stuff in causes ulcers."

"You fucking asshole, I should flatten you now!"

"Hey hey, alright alright, calm down everyone!" Hayden strode to the middle of the room with his arms raised, leaving Jayden holding onto the frame of the upper bunk. "Yes, I heard the way Jack was talking, and I agree that he's probably said some things that he shouldn't have."

"Probably!?" snapped Mia.

I know, right, thought Jayden. *If I had said anything halfway as nasty as that, you would have all said that you always knew I was an asshole.* But the way the others reacted to Jack made Jayden wonder. Was this the real Jack, a dickhead who treated his own girlfriend terribly? Was this the Jack that had been hidden by the soft spoken youth who volunteered to be a fire fighter? Or was that the real Jack, who had now been hidden behind layers of fear and shock? Was this shitty guy just a facade to try and get through the night, to protect the real Jack who had been left behind?

And either way, what did that mean the real Jayden was? The one who had met Mia so many years ago? The one who had fled from the nightmare of a miscarriage with no thought of his partner? The one who had come back and killed one of these monsters tonight? How was anyone supposed to know who the real Jayden was? How was he supposed to know who he really was?

"Anyway, he's just had to try and fight one of those monsters with only a frying pan and he had to deal with the fact that Mike didn't make it. We can forgive him for being stressed out and snapping right now."

"Mike... didn't make it?" Terina's voice was slighter higher than usual, the question ringing out clear.

"No."

"Are... Are you sure? Sometimes first aid can seem hopeless, but you just have to-"

"Mike's dead," said Jayden, cutting off the older woman. "Hopes and dreams might be nice for kids, but let's deal with what's real. Bad stuff happens in the real world."

He could see Terina staring in his direction, but really, what was the point in discussing what might have been, or wishing that the world was not the way it was? Didn't that just waste time, didn't it just train a person to try and ignore what was right in front of their face?

"You know, when bad stuff happens, normal people might discuss how it affected them," contributed Mia, a blade hidden beneath the surface of her voice. "Instead of running off and just trying to dig themselves into a bigger hole."

Jayden felt his cheeks grow warm, and he shrugged.

"Anyway, the fighting smashed a window in the kitchen, so this door is now the only thing between us and the world beyond the station."

The background of sobbing that Stacy had been providing pitched upwards for a moment before returning to its steady sniffling.

"Shit. I suppose from the racket and all, I should have realised that something had broken in, but still, I'm surprised." Terina sounded flat.

"And so this door is all that we have now?" asked Mia.

"Exactly," said Hayden.

"I know that it's stupid, but I don't feel like that door is enough. I mean, the windows were probably even easier to break, especially if something saw us, but a single normal door." She shook her head and bounced Estelle gently in her harness, stroking the baby's head. "At least with the windows there were multiple hurdles. That felt a bit safer."

"I know what you mean," said Hayden. He put his hands on his hips. "So I was wondering if maybe we should try to find somewhere else to hide? I know the station had an emergency generator, but maybe somewhere else would be more secure?"

"The school could be good," came Jack's gruff voice. "Especially if we can get any equipment from the groundskeeper's rooms or staff areas, or something."

In the dim room Jayden could just make out Hayden nodding.

"Yeah, I think that's a good call. It's only around the corner."

"I can go check it out," said Terina.

"Are you sure that's a good idea?" said Hayden.

"Why wouldn't it be?" she asked.

"Yeah, and also, what right do you have to stop her?" asked Jayden.

"Jay, could you just stay out of this?" said Mia.

"No, he has a point," added Pip. "Why does Hayden get to make the decisions about everything? It's not like he was a higher ranking volunteer than the others, was he? And some of us aren't even part of that anyway, so why should we listen to him at all?"

"Oh yeah, of course you have something to say too. You two fucking people and your indignation about everything. Just for once can't you think about other people? Can't you just try to think about what would be best for someone else?"

"I am thinking about what's best for other people, Mee-Ah." Pip emphasised the name, making the other woman twitch. "Have you considered that maybe Hayden being the one calling the shots isn't actually what's best for everyone? I mean, I know that he's your precious darling man at the moment, but we all know that your record doesn't show that you choose men who are the most considerate of others."

"Hey!" Jayden tried to sound upset at the implied insult, but it was hard to disagree with Pip's assessment. She glanced at him and raised an eyebrow, though she was smiling as she did it.

"Um, you still haven't explained why I shouldn't go check out the school?" Terina was getting some emotion back in her voice, after her numbed response to the news about Mike. Unfortunately it sounded like that emotion might be anger.

"Okay, I get it, you don't have to do things my way!" Hayden raised his hands to try and bring some order to the bunkroom. "I don't mind! But maybe we should discuss our options, and agree on a plan or vote on it or something?"

The others looked around the gloom at each other. Jayden was glad for the darkness, it made it nearly impossible to actually see each other's eyes. There was some nodding.

"Okay, let's see what ideas we can bring to the table."

As the others spoke in urgent murmurs, considering what locations around Kanuka Creek might be able to conceal them, and how they could move a group so large through the streets safely, Jayden was stuck contemplating what the others had said about him. Mia had said that he ran off to make his life even worse when bad things happened. Pip had said that he was inconsiderate. James and Sophie had said that he drove people away and didn't appreciate their friendship. He knew that all of them were right, he had done the things that they said. So, was he really a bad person, was he just a worthless human being? Most of the time, he would probably have said yes. But something about this evening made him resent their judgments of him.

He had managed to kill one of the monster things at Mia's house, saving both her and her young child. And he had told Jack what to do to kill the thing in the kitchen. He had been very useful! Surely that showed that he could think about other people? Unless, maybe they saw those actions as just him taking care of himself. Maybe they figured it was a coincidence that others were helped by his actions. Was that the truth? What kind of person was he really? Was he what they saw, or what he felt? And exactly how *did* he feel?

He missed James and Sophie. They had challenged him when he complained, they had told him off for his behaviour, the same as Mia was, but they had done it in a way that showed him that they were still his friends. Mia wasn't able to do that, and really, that was only to be expected. She shouldn't be his friend. He knew that. But it did make it harder to accept if she was going to criticize him.

God, Mike was dead. Somehow that had been passed over already. Jayden wondered how the group would deal with that, or when. As he considered their situation, Jayden came to realise that Stacy was actually reacting appropriately to everything that had happened. She was annoying, and possibly so loud that they would be discovered, but at least she was reacting to what was happening. Sometimes he wondered if he even had emotions anymore.

He compared himself to the monsters. From everything he had seen about them close up, they were filled with rotten flaking material on the inside and that foul collection was concealed by a human-like shell, a fragile surface that was presented to the world, but that could be dented and cracked remarkably easily, exposing the gross layer inside. *Wasn't that the same as himself? Isn't that exactly like Jack?* They presented a human-like face to others too, grumpy cynicism from Jayden, a cheerful facade from Jack, but circumstances didn't have to change much before Jayden's selfishness and cowardice came to the surface, or Jack's anger rose.

And somewhere inside our ugliness, deep under the layers that seemed to provide some padding and protection, is a hard little ball that drives us on. Hard and armoured and kept well away from prying eyes, that was what people really were. Jayden wondered what that hard little ball was inside him. Was the Jayden that fell down in a hallway and couldn't even run away the real Jayden? Was the Jack that yelled at his girlfriend when she was overwhelmed by terror the real Jack? The real Sophie had been calm, and quiet. The real Sophie, the deep inside Sophie, had been a woman who ran towards danger just to give her friend, her awful selfish dickhead of a friend, a chance to survive. A friend who took advantage of their relationship, and complained about everything that she did.

The real James had been the same, running towards the danger. The people in harm's way hadn't even been his friends, he did it to give total strangers a chance. Those two had been real heroes.

What would be the real face of the people in this bunk room? And would they be able to help each other get out of this nightmare, or would they fall apart?

"What do you think Jay?" Hayden's question burst the reflective bubble that Jayden had been in.

"What?"

"God, he doesn't even pay attention to life threatening stuff. No wonder he didn't pay attention to me."

"Oh give over Mia. What do I think about what?"

"The plan Jay." Pip did not sound impressed either. "We just decided that Terina would go to see if she could check out a way to the school, and if it looks safe, because it should be easier for one person to do it while the others wait here."

"Oh. Sure, right, that's fine."

"You're not going to offer to go in my place?"

"No..." Jayden rubbed his face. *What did these people want from him?* "Should I have?"

"No, I'm happy to go, it's just that literally every other guy in the room offered."

"I offered too," said Pip.

"Yup, everyone except Stace and Mia offered."

There was a moment of silence in the room. Stacy's crying had subdued, and Estelle murmured in her sleep.

"Well, I'm sure that I believe that you *are* capable and careful. I don't doubt your ability to get the job done, like those guys did."

Terina snorted. "Okay man, whatever you say. Well, better get on with this I suppose! Does anyone have something I can take with me? I'd feel way more comfortable with a weapon."

"There's the frying pan. It seemed to do alright." Jack sounded much quieter than he had only a few minutes earlier in the evening.

"Sweet."

Without much fuss, Terina grabbed the pan and carefully opened the door. Hayden walked out with her, shutting the door softly behind them.

"So, what the fuck happened to you man?"

At first, Jayden assumed that Mia was talking to him, but then he realised she was directing her anger at Jack.

"What do you mean?"

"What's with the yelling at your own bloody girlfriend? She clearly is having a pretty fucking rough time of things, and you just decide to make it worse?"

"I was... I'd just had to... Look, I'm sorry alright?"

"First time you've said so. And you didn't even tell her, you told me."

"Stacy knows I'm sorry, she knows I love her. Why don't you just back off?"

"Oh, I know your type, boy. All sweetness and roses when you think it matters, but once the chips are down, in the dark and quiet, suddenly the monster comes out."

"You don't know anything about me!" Jack climbed out from his perch on the lower bunks, standing up and stepping closer to Mia. She refused to step back, looking up at his face. Both of their voices were rising beyond whispers now.

"I could make some guesses. Why don't you come and sit on this bunk with me Stacy, I'm sure you would love a chance to get away from this asshole."

Stacy's answer was punctuated with rattling breaths as she tried to talk through the desperation that overwhelmed her.

"He's never... been like... this before... It's okay... He's sorry..."

"See, now why don't you back the fuck off, like I said?"

Mia sniffed. "It's not fucking okay, and you just make sure you don't let him get away with it Stace, okay?"

The door swung open and Hayden walked back in.

"What's going on in here? I could hear voices from the hall, which is probably not a good thing."

"Mia thought that it was a good time to confront a young man whose temper gets away with him under extreme circumstances," answered Pip. "I think that maybe it's a good time to just be quiet, but maybe it's a mum thing."

"Oh." Hayden clearly didn't know whether to berate his partner, or support her.

"It's okay," said Jayden. "If something comes through the window after us, I'm sure they would put things aside for a few minutes while we get this all settled."

Pip giggled but before Mia could respond, Estelle wriggled in the harness, lifted her head, and began to cry. It wasn't a full throated scream, but it was long and loud, and sounded like a baby who was settling in to make noise as long as possible.

"Oh my god, they're going to hear us!" shrieked Stacy, before relapsing into an hysterical repetition of terrified phrases.

"Fuck not again," growled Jack. "Shut that baby up, for the love of god."

"Hey man, settle down," snapped Hayden. *Holy shit,* thought Jayden. *The decent caring man can actually get upset about some things. Maybe there are hidden not-so-sparkling depths to this guy.* Strangely enough, the thought made Jayden feel better.

"It's fine, it's fine," said Mia, unclipping Estelle from her front as quickly as possible. She swung the baby down to one of the lower bunks and ran her hands along the edges of the baby's night clothes. "I'm sure she just needs to change her nappy."

The changing was done quickly and efficiently. Mia was an expert, even in the dark.

"You're a good mum you know," said Pip.

Mia paused as she was pulling the sides of the new nappy into position. Then she hunched over closer to Estelle. "Thanks."

A few more moments of rustling clothes, then Mia was lifting Estelle back into her arms. "There! All good now!"

But it wasn't all good. Estelle was still crying, and Jayden couldn't tell if there was any difference in the noise now that the nappy had been changed.

"Does she need a feed babe?"

"She's been feeding most of the night," answered Mia, but she sat down on the edge of a bunk and re-arranged herself so she could cradle Estelle in position to feed. Estelle latched on and began to suck, but then spluttered and spat Mia out to continue crying.

"I didn't think so, but what the hell is wrong?"

"We're really gonna need to figure that out quickly," snapped Jayden.

"Thank you Mr Genius, I thought we would just leave the child to cry for the next few hours and hope for the best!"

"Did anyone else hear that?" asked Pip. She

stepped closer to Jayden as she spoke, reaching up to grab his shoulder over the edge of the bunk with one hand.

"Yes, we can all hear the bloody baby," sighed Jack.

"No, from outside the door."

"What? Shush!" instructed Hayden. He moved back to the door and leaned up against it, one hand raised to signal to the others to be as quiet as possible. Estelle was still crying as Mia bounced her on one leg and murmured in her ear, trying to calm her down. In addition to this, Stacy's crying and muttering hadn't stopped either. Jayden wondered if it would be possible for Hayden to hear anything over it all. But even through all of that commotion, Pip had thought that she heard something.

CHAPTER SIXTEEN

"I'm sure that's a footstep or something," Hayden frowned. "I'd better go check it out."

"I'm coming too," said Jayden. He blinked as everyone stared at him. "What? You all think I'm a selfish bastard, but you don't know me as well as you think you do." As he moved to get down from the bunk, Pip's eyes met his. They were wide with fear, but there seemed to be a hint of something else in the corner of them, something warmer. Jayden frowned then climbed down and joined Hayden at the door, picking up the axe from where it leaned against the wall next to the door.

"You brought an axe in." Jack's voice was light.

Jayden looked down at the implement in his hand. He looked back up at the bunks where Jack sat. "Yes? So?"

"Terina needed something to take with her."

Jayden felt his ears heating up and was glad for the darkness to hide his shame. "Well, I wasn't the only one who knew it was here, anyone could have mentioned it."

"You're right, I knew there was an axe, and I totally forgot. That's pretty shit, and I just hope that she is okay without it." Hayden clapped a hand onto

Jayden's shoulder and nodded at him. "Best leave the axe here, in case these guys need to defend themselves."

Then he pulled the door open and darted through. Jayden sucked in a gulp of air and followed, dropping the axe back against the wall.

The door banged as Jayden dragged it closed behind himself, which made him flinch. He turned to see where Hayden was, and saw the man hunching down with his arms out defensively. Jayden continued to turn and saw a dark figure at the kitchen end of the hall.

"M-Mike?"

"Run!" urged Hayden as he spun on his feet and shot down the hallway towards the garage of the station. Jayden was only moments behind, but he saw the figure begin swaying as it followed them.

"The door," panted Jayden, hoping that Hayden would understand the question behind it. *Did the Mike-thing remember that everyone else was hiding behind the door? Did they need to keep it from bursting through?* The pair skidded into the garage and turned, cutting off sight of the figure as they followed the benches around towards the front of the engine and the broad glass doors that looked outside. Hayden grabbed Jayden and hugged him close with one arm.

"It'll chase us, I'm sure. It doesn't know that there's anyone else here. And if you hear a door, we chase the bloody thing down."

"You told me to leave the axe."

Hayden blinked and stared at Jayden. "What?"

"It's just that... If we have to chase it down, I don't have an axe."

"This is a fire station. There will be something you can use." Hayden licked his lips then breathed deep and pulled Jayden further around the cab of the engine. "Come on. We need to see if it's come after us."

They moved quietly past the engine, past the door that Hayden had let Jayden and Mia in through. *How long ago did he let us in,* Jayden wondered. *The way exhaustion is dragging at my face and limbs, it must have been a week ago.*

There was rustling from the far side of the engine. Jayden felt as though his skin had been wiped down with a dirty sponge, leaving him clammy and with an urgent desire to scrub his face. Hayden paused and frowned, holding up a hand to halt Jayden. He gestured down, slowly crouching to peer beneath the engine. Jayden smacked his lips and bobbed down also, aware of how empty his mouth felt.

Under the engine they could see clear to the other side of the garage, where a pair of shoes were stepping in odd, out-of-time lurches across the floor. The feet moved in one direction and then the other. Jayden hoped that the thing wasn't sure where they had gone, or the best way to pursue them. He wished that they had opened and closed the back door. The noise might have convinced it to go outside.

"Hayden," he breathed. The other man turned his head slightly to acknowledge Jayden, but kept his eyes fixed on the feet that scuffed across the concrete floor.

"Hayden, is it Mike?" Jayden couldn't imagine that his eyes were correct. The figure had the same build as Mike. It had been dark in the hallway, and the figure had been silhouetted, but... He was sure that it had been Mike's face staring blankly down the hallway at them. Hayden shook his head.

"No."

"But, it looked like Mike. If it is Mike, how can we be sure it doesn't know where the others are?"

Hayden's head jerked and his eyes widened slightly.

"Mike's dead," was all he said, though Jayden could see that the doubt had been planted in him now. Hayden shook his head and grimaced. "But to be sure... We're going to have to kill it."

"Godammit, is there anything else we can do?" The idea of having to try to kill someone he knew, even though he knew Mike was gone, made Jayden feel cold and sick in his stomach. But it was too late, Hayden had begun moving towards the back of the engine, opposite to the direction that the thing seemed to be moving. Jayden followed, as quickly as he dared without making too much noise. He was trying to keep his breathing as quiet as possible, but panic was pushing him towards gasping.

At the rear of the engine, hidden by the machine on one side and protected by the rear wall of the garage on the other, Hayden tried to slowly ease open a hatch. Inside were a few pieces of equipment. *Of course,* Jayden thought. *It's a fire station, we can get some axes!* However, once the hatch had moved open a dozen or so centimetres, he could see that the hatch did not contain the types of weapons that he had been hoping for. Hayden reached in and pulled out a fire extinguisher. It looked very small in his hands, and awkward to handle.

Hayden nodded at the hatch, clearly expecting Jayden to get something. Jayden wanted to snap at the man that this was a waste of time, and why should he be expected to use something so ludicrous in his defence. However, right at that moment, the sound of something sharp scratching along metal came from the front of the engine. Jayden shook his head and swallowed down a sob, then reached into the hatch. He pulled out a heavy wooden broom, with a rectangular block of wood at the head, covered with dark green plastic bristles. He blew out through his lips. *I guess this is all I get,* he thought. *Maybe I can clean up this garage before I get torn to pieces.*

"Ready?" breathed Hayden, squaring his shoulders and hefting the extinguisher in his hands.

Jayden shuffled his hands along the broom's handle, spinning it so that the bristled head was hoisted up next to his own, like a large hammer resting on his shoulder. He shrugged. "I guess so, sure."

"Let's go."

Hayden burst from their hiding spot and tore across the garage floor, Jayden skipping and jogging behind him as he stumbled to keep up. The thought of being left beyond was too horrifying. The figure turned slowly, changing its direction with difficulty in the same way a cargo ship might struggle to change course. As the men ran closer, Hayden pressed the release on the extinguisher, unleashing a white cloud at the monster. Within a moment, it was hidden from sight behind the swirling fog. Hayden grinned and looked back at Jayden.

A thick cable shot up out of the fog and stabbed into the roof, cracking ceiling panels and shattering a light. Then, pulled up by the appendage, rising above the fog like a vision from a nightmare, rose the creature.

It *was* Mike, or it had been. That much was clear. Jayden could even still see the wounds on the side of his face where the other thing had attacked him with the tiny tentacles from its mouth. However, the small wounds were no longer bloodied or bleeding. Now the pocked skin looked pale and greasy, like the belly of a fish.

The Mike-thing dangled above them like a dead piñata, twisting its face to stare with white bulging eyes at them.

"Jesus," moaned Jayden. Hayden stepped back towards him, then pulled back and heaved the fire extinguisher into the air. It spun as it flew, and Hayden ran back to shove Jayden.

"Run!"

The movement propelled Jayden back a step and then he turned and ran back towards the hall. After two steps, he realised that racing back to the bunkroom would only lead the thing back to the others and so he planted his feet and shifted around to head towards the front of the fire engine instead. He turned past the front corner of the huge truck and leaned his back on the radiator grill. Biting down on his lower lip but trying not to break the skin, he peered back around into the main area of the garage.

The thing had sent another limb bursting out of Mike's stomach, wrapped around the red extinguisher. The device looked even smaller when wrapped in the dark red and glistening fleshy tentacle, jutting out into thin air from the main bulk of the monster. Hayden was nowhere to be seen. *Did he go back to the bunks? You fucking coward Hayden! I'm a piece of shit, but even I wouldn't endanger them all so directly.*

The thing seemed to be examining the extinguisher. Then, it tossed it aside, the bang and thud of the metal tube smacking into the concrete floor making Jayden flinch. He hoped that the others were trying to figure out how to get away after hearing all this commotion. The thing began to lower itself into the settling cloud. Once it was close to the ground, it began to swing its legs like a marionette, the feet tumbling forward and making only incidental contact with the ground. It moved towards the front of the engine. *Shit. It knows I'm here.* Jayden's throat clenched. *Now what can I fucking do?*

Jayden drew back from the edge he was looking around and began to move slowly towards the other side of the engine. *Maybe if I can get to that bloody door I can make a break for it.* The idea of bolting outside into the night and who knows what else, with one of these things directly behind him, did not fill him with pleasure. But it was the only idea he was able to come up with before the thing would lurch its dead form around the corner and kill him. *Alright,* he decided. *I run for it.*

He turned and took a few steps into the narrow space between the engine and wall, with the broom still clutched high. There was a bang from the engine and he turned and glanced up. The creature was planted on top of the engine staring down at him, Mike's blank face tilted to one side as it examined him.

Jayden swung forward with the broom, using its leverage to push himself backwards. He was just in time, as a tentacle pushed its way out of Mike's body like an earthworm creeping from the mud. It split the shell-like surface of Mike's stomach and lazily swung itself through the narrow space. The tip of the tentacle managed to catch Jayden in the shoulder, the foul end knocking him off his feet. He slapped his hand to his shoulder, checking the site of the injury, but the bony tip didn't seem to have broken the flesh.

Jayden dropped the broom as he threw himself back to the front of the truck. He reacted faster than he was able to think, diving to the floor and rolling under the engine. He hoped that the creature would be unsure where he had gone for at least a few moments, long enough that he could aim for a different escape route and bolt.

Jayden wiped at his nose with the back of his hand, trying to not even sniff in case the sound was enough to allow the thing to find him faster. He didn't have long anyway, and so he began to spin around on his stomach under the engine, trying to decide which way to run. That was when he saw Hayden at the far end of the space beneath the truck.

Hayden caught his eye and gestured, a series of grimaces and fingers jabbing. Jayden just shook his head in confusion, narrowing his eyes slightly as he tried to watch closely enough to figure out what Hayden was doing. Hayden grimaced and looked around. The thing didn't seem to have come down off the engine yet. Perhaps it was waiting to see where Jayden would run to next? Hayden began to crawl closer to Jayden, who tried to do the same.

"You go out the front," Hayden whispered as soon as he dared, as soon as the two men were close enough that there was a chance his breathy whisper might be heard. "I'll go out the back. It won't be able to go after us both. One of us can get out the door, and lure it away from the others."

Jayden hadn't considered that getting out the door would be a way to help protect the others. As far as he had been concerned, it was the only chance he stood of surviving himself. He hadn't considered what the others would do at all. His stomach felt like a ball of acid.

"So, one of us…"

"Is probably going to die when it sees us, yes." Hayden's face was stern, but his eyes stared back into Jayden's own, searching to see what kind of person Jayden really was. Jayden felt as though Hayden's gaze was peeling back layer upon layer of self-image and armour that he had developed over the years, through everything that had ever happened to him, until the real him was exposed beneath, vulnerable and small. Hayden nodded. Apparently he was satisfied by what he saw. *That just seems incredibly unlikely,* Jayden thought.

"Okay, back to your end, get out and run when I gesture three." Hayden began moving back to his original location at the far end of the fire engine. Jayden moved back to his own position, wondering if he would have the guts to be able to do this. It wasn't certain death, but it was damn close. Did it matter that he had wanted to do something like this anyway? Did that mean that it was still selfish?

Jayden flexed his fingers against the cold concrete of the garage floor. The engine creaked above him as weight shifted on it. *Don't jump down yet, don't jump down,* he silently begged the monster. *Or at least jump down somewhere I'm not.*

He looked behind himself, down past the length of his body, trying to quell the trembling in his legs. Beneath the far end of the engine, Hayden was looking back at him. The man held up one hand and made an over the top motion of lifting one finger. Then he waved his hand again slowly, lifting a second. Then, like it was moving through tar, he gestured with three fingers and began to lift himself off the ground. Jayden clenched his jaw and pushed himself forward too.

Jayden leapt from under the engine and turned as sharply as he could without tumbling into a roll. He refused to indulge his instinct to look backwards. There was either something there, about to kill him with a flick of its foul appendage, or there wasn't. Either way, his best chance was to run and get out that door. He raised himself into a crouch and felt something solid on the concrete beneath his hand. *The broom!* His fingers coiled around it and he continued to rise into a sprint towards the exit. As he ran down the side of the engine he saw the thing was standing at the far end looking down on Hayden who was running towards the door also. Jayden felt a burst of joy leap up his throat and he wanted to laugh. He could feel his cheeks pulling into a huge smile. *It didn't chase me!*

Hayden must have made a similar conclusion as Jayden, because his face drew tight and focused and he leaned forward as he kept running. A cord whipped down, faster than its bulky, fleshy appearance would seem capable of, slapping Hayden backwards. Jayden heard the air rush from the other man's lungs. Hayden coughed on the ground, and then managed to roll aside before the harpoon stabbed down into the position he had just been in. Despite appearing to be made of tendons and skinless meat, the white tip of the tentacle pierced the polished concrete floor of the garage, cracking the slab.

Jayden was at the door, hand on the handle, ready to swing it open. He looked back down the length of the fire engine as the cable drew up and stabbed down a second time. Hayden managed to roll aside again, but sweat covered his forehead.

"Go," he spluttered at Jayden.

Memories of Mia flashed through Jayden's mind. He recalled how young and happy she had been when they met, and how she had encouraged him to come out of himself. She had introduced him to many of the people who he would have counted as his truest friends, shown him places that he had never realised existed. It was Mia who had encouraged him to follow his dreams of research, leading him to study at the university over the hills from Kanuka Creek.

It was Mia who had sat, sobbing when they learned that she had miscarried. Jayden hadn't really understood what it meant at the time. And when she had gone to the hospital, he had told himself that going to the pub to 'numb his feelings' with beer was an appropriate response. It was Mia who had come out of hospital alone, while Jayden woke up in Pip's house.

It was Mia who had stayed in the small town. It was Mia who had found someone new in Hayden. It was Mia who had been gifted with Estelle, the child she had always wanted, and a man like Hayden who would actually support them both.

A man like Hayden who would come to check if a monster was standing in the hallway outside. A man like Hayden who would try to lead the monster away, knowing that he would likely die.

A man like Hayden who would tell a man like Jayden to run when he had the chance.

What kind of man was a man like Jayden?

Jayden ran towards Hayden, twisting his body with the broom, but wasn't fast enough to beat the tentacle as it stabbed down a third time and speared through Hayden's shoulder. Hayden screamed, and then Jayden was swinging the broom.

The heavy wooden head of the broom smacked into the cord, separating a wet chunk from it that slapped into the side of the engine and began to drip slowly down the metal. The thing made a squelching moan from above as the limb whipped back inside it, and then stepped forward. It dropped from the height with no attempt to land, simply stopping on the ground as though it had reached the end of a rope. It tilted its head at Jayden again, while Jayden tried to get a new grip on the broom and swing it around again. Before he could, the thing kicked Hayden in the face.

Hayden's head jerked back and blood spilled from a cut that opened up above his eyes. He screamed again. Jayden managed to move the broom, smashing it into the side of the thing's shoulder. Because he hadn't built up much momentum, the cracks were small and the arm stayed attached. The monster reached out for the broom, and Jayden nearly fell over as he tried to yank the brook backwards and keep it out of the creature's grasp. As he stumbled and righted himself, hauling the broom back for another swing, the thing's tentacle erupted out of its chest and smashed down into Hayden's. Its face still stared slackly at Jayden. Blood welled up and over the ruined sides of Hayden's chest, thick and dark, and blood began to bubble out of his mouth to join it.

"Fuck! I'm really sorry if there's anything left of you in there Mike." Jayden screwed up his face and let all his anger and frustration and horror fuel his strike. To get a good swing in the narrow space they occupied, the broom travelled up and over his shoulder, then came down on the thing's skull with the ponderous weight of an iceberg calving into the ocean. Black leaves exploded from inside its head, spilling out and over its chest and shoulders. Jayden hefted the broom and used it to shove the thing's chest, knocking it down. He stepped forward, poking at the twitching body with the broom.

"Where are you, you little piece of-"

A hard shelled black bulb, dripping with whatever moisture was soaking the leaves within the thing's surface, began to scuttle away from Jayden.

"No you fucking don't," he snapped, stabbing forward with the end of the broom and grinding the thing into the concrete even after he heard the squelch he was after.

Only then, with yellow-green fluid smeared across the head of the broom, did he turn around to see how Hayden was doing.

Jayden knelt down over Hayden's head, trying not to look at the bloody holes that pierced his body. The kick had left a wound across Hayden's forehead, and blood was bubbling out of his nose and mouth. He tried to talk, but there was no way Jayden could understand anything that the other man was trying to say; so Jayden sucked in a deep breath and reached out to put a hand on Hayden's shoulder.

"I got it. I got it, and they're safe." Jayden spoke

without much hope that Hayden would be able to hear him, but it was all he could think to do. For a moment he wondered if he should try some CPR, like he had seen in TV shows, but as soon as he shifted his hand to apply the mildest pressure to Hayden's chest, blood spilled out the edges again. He couldn't press there.

"I'm so sorry Hayden," Jayden whispered. "It shouldn't have been you. I shouldn't be the one to walk away from this, you were the one who deserved to get away." Jayden felt the memory of his thoughts, only moments earlier, that had wished for the thing to leave him alone. They burned in the back of his skull like coals. He was amazed that the world didn't begin to glow orange from the heat behind his eyes. "I wanted to survive, of course, but you deserve it much more than me. I'm sorry about how I treated Mia. You were exactly what she deserved too, and you both should get to enjoy each other for so many more years."

Hayden's hand twitched and Jayden reached down to hold it. There was the faintest squeeze, softer than rabbit fur.

"I'll do everything I can to keep them all safe. I promise."

The hand dropped aside. The bubbling in the blood ceased. Hayden drooped back against the floor. Jayden hadn't realised how much the man had been tensing, holding himself up. Now he slumped like a ragdoll.

Numb, and barely able to process what had happened, Jayden pulled himself up the side of the engine and began to trudge back towards the bunkroom.

CHAPTER SEVENTEEN

I n his overwhelmed and exhausted state of mind, Jayden didn't think to knock or say anything to let the remaining survivors inside know that it was him coming through the door. Because of this, an axe came whistling through the gloom towards him and it was only luck that sent the blow a little too high and to the side, the metal blade sinking into the door-frame and not his head.

"Holy shit!" he exclaimed as he shied away from the axe, sinking towards the floor.

"Jay?" Jack was pulling on the other end of the axe, trying to get it unwedged from the doorframe, but paused as he realised that there was no threat.

"Yes, 'Jay', you bastard! It's me, Jayden!"

"Oh Jesus, I'm sorry man!" Jack released his grip on the axe as though it was burning his hands. He began to step backwards with his hands up as though warding off Jayden's gaze. "I just... Something was just coming through the door, and I figured... Oh god, I could have killed you!"

"Yeah, yeah," nodded Jayden with his eyes wide and accusing. "You and every other fucking thing in the town tonight." He blew out a deep breath and began heaving himself up off the floor. "It's okay man,

I'm okay," he said, waving aside Jack's outstretched offer of a helping hand.

"Where's Hayden?" Mia's flat voice splashed like a bucket of ice over Jayden and Jack, and they both froze.

"Um," began Jayden, but then Mia was standing right in front of him, looking down at him with angry eyes.

"Where is he?"

"There was one of things in the hall, right? I'm sure you guys heard it. It looked like Mike, even though Mike died, but-"

"Where is Hayden?"

Jayden looked aside. "Hayden... Hayden didn't make it."

Mia didn't respond

"Mia?" Jayden began to walk forward, reaching out to his ex-partner. Estelle wasn't in the harness that hung loosely from around Mia's shoulders.

"Mia, are you-"

"What do you mean he didn't make it?" She stepped backwards and turned her head. It shook slightly, as if she couldn't believe that the question was real, as if she was denying that it needed to be asked at all.

"It had us trapped under the fire engine, and he came up with a plan for us to try and lead it away, but then it jumped on top of him, and..." Jayden trailed off. For a nauseating moment, the image of the thing stabbing down on top of Hayden flashed through his vision and his throat clenched.

"But you're here." The statement carried with it the weight of a coffin lid, slamming shut with its massive and final thud.

"Yes, I am." Jayden took another step forward.

"No!" Mia shoved him away and then wrapped her arms around herself. "No, that's impossible! How the hell can you be here, if he can't? Are you lying? Is he actually lying out there, waiting for us to go and help him? Is this your sick idea of a joke?"

"Mia, no, he's not there."

"That's impossible! Hayden was perfect!" Mia's cry echoed through the station, and Jayden wondered if he should try and quieten her before something outside heard.

"He was so kind, and giving, and he was always ready to help others." Mia's voice fell as she listed his qualities. "But you? You never really thought about anyone but yourself. You only did good things for others because you thought that they would owe you in return."

"Hey, I don't-"

"You left me alone! When I was at my most vulnerable and hurt, you abandoned me! And for what? Some goddamn slut at the local pub."

"Oh thank you so very much Mia, nice to see that there's no grudges held here." Pip stood up from the bunks nearby as she spoke, but she sounded more resigned than upset. Mia spun around and slapped her, the crack of palm on cheek making Jayden flinch away.

"Jesus woman!" snapped Pip. "Where the fuck did that come from?"

"Jay's an arsehole. He only cares about himself. No wonder he ran off. But my Hayden was better than that. How could he leave me?"

Jack stepped up behind Mia, reaching out his arms to her shoulders. As he tried to calm her, she spun around and buried her head in his shoulder, her deep sobs muffled by his chest. He rubbed her back awkwardly, watching the others over the top of her head. He shrugged a little as he rubbed her back, saying "There there" and "It'll be okay" over and over again.

Pip was rubbing her face, but she stepped closer to Jayden, reaching out to touch his shoulder. Jayden drew in a deep breath. He wanted to argue with Mia, but didn't know where to begin.

Was he trying to convince her that he wasn't as bad as she thought? Because, she really had a lot of evidence against him there. He doubted that anyone in the room would give him much slack in that. And, honestly, he wasn't sure that he didn't agree with that assessment of himself anyway.

But then why did he have this urge to confront her, to challenge what she was saying? Estelle gurgled from the nest of sheets and pillows that she had been settled into on one of the lower bunks.

"He was a good man Mia. You're right, he was better than me. It's not even a competition. And it's a total nightmare that he's gone. But he didn't run off and abandon you. Or Estelle. He tried everything he could to protect you, even going so far as dying in an attempt to keep that monster from finding you both."

Mia didn't stop crying, but the way her shoulders stopped shuddering and set in place made Jayden think that she was listening.

"I am sorry that I was the one that came back." And as he said it, Jayden felt the truth of the statement wash over him like a wave. "I wish I could have saved him. I wish it had come after me instead. But he didn't abandon you."

Jack nodded at him and kept patting Mia on the back as she hunched into him. Pip squeezed his shoulder and then stepped over to stand next to him, resting her head on his shoulder. Mia continued to cry, but Jayden hoped that he had managed to make at least a little difference.

. . .

THE FIVE OF them sat in silence on the bunks in the darkness. No one had anything else to say, and no one wanted to suggest a way of passing the time. Anything that they could have done would have felt disrespectful and dangerous. Sleep would have been gratefully accepted, if anyone in the room could relax enough to lie down and slow the rapid spinning of their thoughts, their unwanted memories and terrified predictions. The light from the moon through the small window slowly crept across the opposite wall of the room.

A hissing noise wound down the hallway. Jack and Jayden, who had been lying on the lower bunks nearest the door, sat up and looked across at each other.

"Did you hear that?"

Jayden nodded.

The noise came again, longer this time. It changed too irregularly to be a leak, shifting a little in volume and intensity. It had to be being made by someone or something.

"Terina?" asked Jack as he slid himself forward and off the bunk, reaching down to pick up the axe from where it lay on the floor.

"Maybe." Jayden followed, picking up the smaller hatchet. "Just, make sure of who it is before you swing that thing this time."

Jack grinned and shrugged. "Sorry man."

The pair quietly pulled the door open just far enough for each of them to slip through and then pulled it closed again behind them.

"Shouldn't we have left an axe for the others," whispered Jack, putting his mouth right up by Jayden's ear so he could be even quieter.

"Fuck, probably." Jayden swallowed and then chewed on his lower lip for a second. "Let's just go and get back as quick as we can."

They walked slowly together to the end of the hall, and looked into the kitchen.

On the other side of the room, framed by the shattered window and silhouetted by the light from the stars, they could see a figure standing outside.

"Terina?" called Jack carefully, trying to catch the attention of the figure, without being loud enough to actually alert them to his presence. It was a self-defeating way of doing things. Jayden shook his head.

"You'd better hope that it *is* her now," he muttered.

The figure raised an arm to shoulder height and waved quickly. It pointed toward the kitchen door.

"Shit, I think it is her!" Jack moved quickly into the kitchen, skirting the pool of dark liquid that covered much of the floor. Jayden followed but his attention was diverted by the blood. *Poor Mike.*

Jack reached the door a little after the outside figure, and then turned the lock as slowly as possible, cursing when the mechanism finally shifted with a loud thunk. He pulled open the door, and Terina stepped inside.

"Holy shit, it is you!" exclaimed Jack. "I was so sure that it was, but I was bloody worried too! Are you alright?"

"Yeah, yeah, I'm fine," Terina reassured him, smoothing down her jumper. "But it's pretty terrible out there. Had to hide a couple of times to avoid being seen by those things."

"Is the school a better spot than this?" asked Jayden.

"Well..." Terina shrugged and wobbled her head from side to side. "Kinda, I guess? I mean, there's probably more spots that we could hide in and lock up, which is better than this smashed fucking window."

"But?"

"But, it's a big distance between these places, and lots of houses are just as smashed as this. I dunno if one of those things would realise that we're in here, even with the broken window. Maybe we could just stay?"

"I thought the school was around the corner?" asked Jayden.

"It is!" said Jack, trying to communicate via his shoulders and head position a sense of confusion at Terina's statement. He shifted focus to her. "What do you mean it's a big distance?"

"I mean that it's dark and cold and those things are out there somewhere but how would we know–"

A dark spear shot through the window, as thick as a fencepost, glistening wetly in the low sliver light. It crashed into Terina's head, tearing her face apart and sending her body flying across the kitchen, before it speared into the far wall. The monster attached to the other end of the cable came flying into the kitchen after it, pulling itself along the tentacle like a bungee cord, tumbling over the broken glass of the window.

Jack swung the axe as Jayden spun around and dropped the hatchet on the floor. There was a damp smack as the metal head of the axe bit into some part of the thing, but Jayden was focused on wiping the blood and fragments of bone off his face. He held out his hands and stared at the residue that dripped off them. *My hands are shaking so much,* he realised. *Why are they shaking so much?*

There was another smack, like someone trying to chop down a tree. Jayden could hear a voice shouting.

"Hmmmm?" He turned his head to try and find out what the annoying buzzing sound was.

Jack was shouting backwards over his shoulder towards Jayden, but the voice sounded muffled, as though Jack had wrapped his head in thick blankets.

Jayden watched as the other man lifted the axe and swung it again, over and over, into the thrashing body of the creature.

A length of the appendage had been completely severed and writhed like a worm that had been split in half, flicking droplets of a translucent gel around the room. A drop hit Jayden in the lips and he wiped them with his fingers and tried to spit away the bitter taste.

"Mwum wum mwah wum wah."

"What?" Jack still wasn't making sense, though he seemed to have got into a real rhythm with his axe. Up, pause to gather strength, swing down. Smack. Heave the axe out, lift it up, pause again, swing. It was hypnotic. Something important needed to be said though. Jayden watched Jack for a bit longer. Jack had forgotten something.

"It will keep attacking and thrashing until you crush that black thing in its head. The bug thing, you know?"

Jack paused with the axe wedged into the cracked and leaking chest of the thing. An arm, half snapped off and covered in a spider web of fractures, was thrashing back and forth around the weapon, sending new black lines splintering across its surface whenever it struck the wooden shaft. Jack's eyes were wide, almost like a cartoon.

"Your eyes look like cartoon eyes," Jayden told him. His head felt very heavy and he wondered if maybe he should lay it against his shoulder. Maybe he should take a nap.

"What do you mean black thing? What bug?" It was strange that Jack's face looked so strained, when his voice was so quiet and distant. There were tendons stretched taut in his neck.

"You know, the one that attacked Mike. It had a little black thing in its head. You had to squash it with your frying pan." Jayden sat down on the kitchen chair. A nap, definitely.

Jack turned back around and began swinging the axe at the thing's head. Black leaves spat across the floor, in a mouldy smelling pile, as pale curved shards of the thing's hollow skin spun on the linoleum. A lumpen insect-like shape rolled away from the devastation, pushing aside the drifts of leaves, which stuck to its black shell, before Jack managed to slam the axe into it. Tiny yellow fountains sprayed out of the chitinous form, and then its sides fell over and remained still.

Jayden was lying his head on the table, watching all this sideways through unblinking eyes. His arms were crossed underneath, as a pillow. Jack leaned, panting, on the axe and wiped his forehead with the back of his arm. He looked back at Jayden, who lifted a hand and waved briefly, then tucked it back under his head. Jack shook his head and limped closer. Grimacing, he crouched down and grabbed the hatchet from where it lay on the floor. He groaned as his muscles and bruises complained. He hauled Jayden up onto his feet and shoved the hatchet into his hands. Jayden pushed ineffectually at the other man.

"Hey, quit it. I'm trying to have a nap."

"Come on, we have to get the others."

Jack hauled Jayden back down the hallway, calling out carefully as they approached the door.

"It's us! We're coming back in!"

Jack shoved the door open and hustled Jayden back into the bunkroom.

"You took the bloody axes, you idiots," began Pip as they came in, but Jack dropped the axe to one side and waved her to silence.

"We've got to get out of here now," he snapped.

"Jesus, I didn't mean-"

"Terina was just killed by another one that saw us

in the kitchen. Clearly this isn't a secure enough space anymore."

"Terina's dead?" Stacy whimpered.

"Oh god, we don't have time for this," cried Jack. "Just grab what you can and let's try and get to the school. Terina thought it seemed safe."

"And yet Jay made it through. Again." Mia gathered up her sleeping daughter and began fastening the harness around her. "How is it that cowards always seem to survive? Well, I answered my own question, didn't I," she sneered. "Rats that hide away and run from the problem always seem to find a way out of the shitheap."

Jayden frowned. Was she saying he was a rat? But he didn't get out of the shitheap, she was the one who had found a way out. He was left wallowing in his sad loneliness.

"Didn't Jay save you at your house?" asked Pip.

Mia ignored the other woman.

"And didn't he help save Jack and Stacy?"

"Just to try and keep himself safe," muttered Mia.

"And he went with Hayden when they thought that they heard something, didn't he?"

"And Hayden died!" yelled Mia.

"Jay didn't kill him!" yelled Pip back.

"He might as well have! He should have made sure that he died first, and kept Hayden alive!"

"I tried!" Jayden's cry was raw and he felt as though his throat was cutting itself apart. "I tried to get back to him, I tried to pull it off him, I wanted it to get me instead, but I was too late! Hayden was already... was already..."

Pip put her arm around Jayden's shoulders. He leaned into her. His eyes were burning, but he refused to let himself cry. Her free hand held his. "Come on. You did what you could. Now we need to go."

"She's not moving. I say we fucking go anyway."

Jack was crouched down beside the bunk where Stacy was. He straightened up. "She'd probably just be a fucking liability anyway."

"She's your fucking girlfriend Jack, what the hell is wrong with you?" Mia's voice was weary.

"Seriously man." Pip squeezed Jayden's shoulders, letting her fingers rest on him a long time. Then she moved over to the other bunk. "Come on Stace, we've got to go." She whispered as though she was trying to soothe a nervous puppy.

Slowly, like a hermit crab inching its way forward, and as nervous and jumpy as a kitten, Stacy crawled out of the lower bunk. Even in the gloom, Jayden could tell that her face was pale, blotchy and slick with tears. He wondered if she had managed to sleep at all while hidden in the tiny space.

"Come on." Pip held out a hand and helped Stacy climb off the bunks and stand up by the door. Jack snorted and picked up the axe again. Mia shuffled her shoulders in the harness, cradling Estelle close. That just left Jayden to stand up and draw a deep breath of cold night air. He picked up the hatchet and squeezed the wooden handle once or twice.

"Okay," he said. "Okay, let's go."

The group huddled together and moved out the door and followed Jack as he turned away from the garage

"Why do we have to go through this goddamn kitchen again?" Jayden moaned. Broken chunks of glass ground and crunched beneath their shoes. The light from outside was fractured and reflected by the small shards that covered the floor, sending up a rainbow-edged spray of spotlights. Blood and mucus left their smears across the walls and floors. Stacy's breath was coming fast and shallow, and Jayden assumed it would only be a few moments before she snapped.

"It's too late to change directions now man, just shut up already," growled Jack.

"Or what, you'll hit me with that axe? You were pretty fucking keen to hit me with it when I came in last time-"

"Give over Jay. Jack, let's just keep going shall we?" Mia's no nonsense tone kept them moving.

Pip stepped closer to Jayden as they approached the kitchen door. "Are you doing okay? It must be pretty hard to cope with all this." She gestured with one hand at the devastation that had been wrought on the small room, then placed the other on Jayden's. He felt an electric shock run along his arm as she did so. Where her fingertips touched his skin became warm. She turned back to look into his eyes, and drew closer to him.

"Fuck," gasped Mia. Jayden spun to find out what she had seen, shaking Pip off as he hefted the hatchet. Stacy began gabbling in a panicked stream of consciousness.

"What? What?!" hissed Jayden.

"It's okay, it's fine, I just..." Mia swallowed and breathed deeply, closing her eyes to help calm herself down. "I just saw Terina."

Jayden didn't look, but by the series of indrawn breaths that followed, the others had all punished themselves by investigating the body. He shook his head and moved up to follow Jack who was pulling open the kitchen door.

Outside Kanuka Creek lay in silver silence. There were no crickets, no distant grumble of cars or trucks. Even the wind seemed to have died in the small town.

"What time is it?" Jayden asked Jack as the others made their way to the door.

"Does it matter?" Jack replied.

"I guess not."

They all stared out into the shadowed houses and gardens.

"Alright, which way to this school then?" Jayden spoke with a bluster that he did not feel. He just wanted to keep moving. Stopping felt as though it would be the worst possible thing to do right now. He wanted to go somewhere safe and dark and small where he could feel like he was hidden away from the pandemonium of the world. A hole to hide in. *Maybe I really am the rat she thinks I am,* he thought.

"Stick with this one guys," said Mia. "When the rats flee the sinking ship, they may lead you to a new safe berth."

It's like she can hear my thoughts.

"This way," said Pip. She took Jayden by the hand, and they walked out of the kitchen and into the night together. The group crept out to the footpath and began their cautious progress towards the school. Above them, stars twinkled in the sky, looking as pretty as any poem or song had ever described them. Jayden felt as though this was insulting. It just went to show that the universe was dismissive and un-feeling towards humanity's woes. Surely the stars should have been boring down like the very tips of icicles, cold and threatening. At least that would have suited what was happening now.

Pip led the way down the path. The sound of all their feet clipping on the pavement was far too loud in Jayden's opinion, but they just kept moving forward. Pip squeezed Jayden's hand in her own, and then led them off the path and on to the grass. *She must have thought it was too loud as well.* Jayden wasn't sure if the rustling grass beneath their feet was any better.

CHAPTER EIGHTEEN

They moved along the street in a tight cluster, eyes darting around the gloomy houses and gardens, nervously scanning through the larger trees, desperately searching for something that they were praying to never find. Most of the houses were simply dark, sitting in their gardens as though sleeping, but some had broken windows, or smashed doors hanging in empty black frames. Gardens of flowers and well-tended hedges sat guarding homes that had clearly been visited by something terrible. But as they walked, they saw no bodies, no blood.

"I think we're going to be fine," said Jack from behind Jayden and Pip.

"What the hell are you doing?" groaned Jayden immediately, his shoulders slumping. "I mean seriously, is there any more perfect a way to guarantee that we aren't going to be fucking okay?"

"Oh grow up you dick, don't be so fucking pessimistic. It's quiet here, we can see down the streets, there's nothing around. The school ain't far, right Pippa?"

Pip pursed her lips, but nodded without looking around at him.

"See? Now let's just move our arses before something does show up!"

The group kept going. Stacy was whimpering and moaning, the same background groans that had filled the bunkroom on the edge of hearing, the same barely audible suffering that they had all grown numb to. Jayden glanced back once and saw that Mia had her arm hooked into Stacy's at the elbow, and was half-leading, half-dragging her forward.

From a house to their right, behind its low chain-link fence, one of the monsters burst through the front door, crumpling the wood like paper as it came. It moved its arms up and shook them around to wave aside the pieces of wood and metal that were collapsing around it.

"Run," shrieked Mia, holding her arms higher around Estelle and darting ahead.

"But I don't know where to go," screamed Jayden, his voice nearly as high as Mia's. He started to head directly away from the thing, into the road, then bobbed back and forwards, at first following Mia, then moving in the opposite direction. He could feel his lungs burning.

"Come with me!" Pip reached out to grab him and pulled him forward after Mia. As they pounded down the road, his heartbeat thudding in his ears and the cold night air turning his sweat to beads of ice on his face, Jayden was aware of Jack beside them. Jack slowed and turned his head, then stopped, gripping the axe tight in front of his chest, staring back down the road. Jayden paused and spun around.

"Come on man, what are you doing?!" he yelled at Jack.

"She can't run. She's overwhelmed." Jack said quietly, staring back at the shrouded figure of Stacy, still behind them. Jack began to walk back towards the house. Jayden could see the monster, a person shaped pool of darkness that strode across the garden and through the small wooden gate. Planks spun away from each resolute step. Jack began to run.

"Fucking move Stacy, what the fuck are you doing?" bellowed Jack, his voice echoing through the dead town. The noise made Stacy shriek again from where she was still standing, hunched over, in the middle of the footpath. Jayden stumbled back towards them and then stopped.

"Come on Jay, we can't do anything for them now," said Pip, tugging on his hand again. Jayden felt the heavy weight of the hatchet in his hand.

"Maybe I could..."

"You couldn't." Pip reached out her other hand and cupped Jayden's cheek, turning his face towards her. Her eyes reflected the starlight and Jayden became very conscious of how close her lips were. "We have to get out of here." Her breath brushed Jayden's face as she spoke. He licked his lips then nodded.

They kept running along the footpath towards the corner, where a squat plaster house had been built right up against the path, blocking their view beyond.

"Mia went that way," said Pip as they moved, gesturing around the corner. When they got to the corner, Jayden turned to look back at Jack and Stacy.

In the darkness it was hard to tell what was going on. The three figures blended together like pools of ink, thought the axe flashed like a distant lighthouse. Yells and shrieks carried on the still air to Jayden and Pip. Then one of the figures fell to the ground, vanishing in the shadows that clustered around the others' feet. Of the remaining figures, one was huddling down until it almost looked like a ball.

"I hope that was Jack killing that thing," muttered Jayden.

The second figure straightened up and then spun to face the other, rotating around a central point as though it was mounted on a pedestal. It didn't seem to move its legs. Then it swung one arm in a slow backhand, sending the first figure flying out and onto the asphalt of the road, where it lay still. Sobs rose in the night.

"It wasn't Jack," said Pip, and she pulled him by the shoulder and around the corner.

"Why are we even doing this?" asked Jayden as they jogged along the footpath. "These things are everywhere." He felt his head dropping, and he was finding it hard to keep his eyes open. "We're all awful people, we probably deserve this."

Pip spun around and slapped him. The crack of skin meeting skin was exceptionally loud, and she flinched. Then she leaned closer.

"You might think that you're an awful person, but I think I'm pretty decent. And you know what? I think you've got some good points too. So let's try and get through all this before we start all this introspective bullshit."

"Sure. But you said we should leave those two behind." *Isn't that about the worst thing that you could do? And I let you say it. I let you lead me away. James would have gone running back. Even Jack went running back, and he was an angry asshole. What does that make us?*

Pip bit her lip and rolled her eyes.

"Can we wait until we find somewhere safe, where that thing isn't going to see us as soon as it walks around the corner? Maybe then I will engage in your goddamn philosophical musings. Then again, maybe I won't."

"Fine."

Jayden watched the back of Pip's head as they ran. He began to realise that he had never really got to know her in the past. He would have said that Pip was a fun friend. The three of them, Mia and Jayden and Pippa, had spent a lot of good evenings at the pub, cracking jokes and playing pool. He would even have said that Pip was one of their best friends.

That's probably why Mia was so upset, he realised. *I didn't even just make a shitty decision with some random girl, I betrayed my fiancé's trust with someone else that she should have been able to trust.*

But even that night, he had thought that Pip was fun. That was why he had gone home with her, he had felt happy and light and free. That was what he was desperately trying to find as Mia was taken away from him into the hospital. He didn't want to think about the miscarriage. Even the word was dark and heavy in his mind.

The sight of Mia, crying and heart-broken on the floor, had left him numb and twisted with grief. He hated that he had been part of something that hurt her so much. And so, that night, he had run away from the pain, run away from the realities of what had to happen next. And he had run straight to the bed of a woman who was fun and smiling and who didn't have anything to do with pain and sorrow.

When he had woken up, he had known immediately that it was all over. The miscarriage had ended their excited dreams of family. His night with Pip had ended any future that they might have then shared. *Oh god, and I hadn't even had the guts to let Mia know it was over then. I had let it go on for weeks after that, let it happen again.* His stomach boiled.

But now? Pip's shoulder length hair whipped left and right behind her as they moved along the street. Now he realised that he hadn't known this woman at all. The reality of her, the inner Pippa, was someone who could look down a dark street at people she knew who were in danger, and could turn away.

What really made Jayden's stomach churn was the knowledge that he was that kind of person too.

They kept running down the street for a few hundred meters, and then Pip pulled him into a narrow path between two corrugated iron fences. A pair of metal tubes were bent over like gates in the path, blocking bikes from passing through, but Jayden and Pip were able to weave past with no trouble.

"Come on. The school's through here. Hopefully Mia stuck to the plan and ducked through here too."

"And hopefully it didn't see us come in here either."

"That too."

They kept moving as quickly as fast as they could without making noise. This path was even darker than the streets that they had just rushed through. It was a narrow space between the tall fences with no overhead lights to help them see their way. Trees and hedges poked over their heads like skeletal, grasping fingers. Jayden grew frustrated as he kept standing on dry leaves or discarded plastic wrappers from time to time, each crisp rustle sounding like a firecracker to his paranoid ears. The other end of the path came out on the edge of a rugby field, with four or five wide buildings sitting on the far side. A small figure seemed to be moving over there, outlined against the pale walls of the buildings.

"This is the school then?" asked Jayden.

"Of course. Come on." Pip began walking across the close cropped grass, turning her head from side to side, scanning for anything on the edges of the field.

"Um," began Jayden. Pip turned around. "Did... Did you not see that thing on the other side?" He pointed to where he had last seen the movement by the buildings. It seemed to have stopped, but he wasn't sure if that was because it had gone somewhere else, or if it was staying still. He squinted, trying to find it again. The pale walls of the distant buildings were like eyes staring back at him from a dark cave.

The thought reminded him of the milky eyes of the creatures they were running from and he shuddered.

"Wasn't that Mia?" asked Pip. Her brow creased and she turned to examine the buildings more closely herself. "I was going to follow her over there."

"Are you nuts? What if it wasn't her?"

"But what if it was? She is alone right now, with her baby. Weren't you the one saying we have to find her and help?"

"Since when did you care about Mia?"

"I'm not a monster Jay." Pip's shoulders were beginning to fall. "I'm exhausted. I'm just as overwhelmed and terrified as the rest of you. But just because I did things in my past that I'm not proud of, doesn't mean that I'm a terrible person. I can do better."

"And Jack? Was that an example of you doing better? That was only five minutes ago."

"Jesus Jay." Pip stood with her head bowed for long seconds, long enough for Jayden to begin chewing his lower lip nervously. "Jay, Jack and Stacy were dead. They might have been moving and making noises, but they were dead." She raised her head to face him, her eyes firm. "I know that movies and things say that the hero goes rushing back into danger, but that's only admirable if there is a chance that they can help. Otherwise it's just suicide." She pursed her lips and raised an eyebrow. "How likely is it that you and that little axe were going to be helpful to Jack and Stacy?"

Jayden shrugged. "I've killed a few of them tonight."

Pip nodded and stepped closer, lifting her arms to rest on his shoulders, her hands clutched behind his head. "You have. You have been really brave. Braver and more capable than Mia would have thought, and probably even more than you might have expected of yourself." Her eyes were wide and her breath on Jayden's face made his cheeks flood with warmth. He became very conscious of her body so close to his own.

"You've been... Well..." Jayden didn't know how to say that she had been flirting with him. Was he even right? Was this flirting? Or was he just imagining things? Maybe she was just wanting to feel close and safe given the madness that they had endured. "I mean, have you really been behaving appropriately with me tonight?"

She laughed softly and shook her head. "Oh my god. We were trapped in a tiny building, with fucking unreal monsters stalking around outside, and a guy who I had a fling with shows back up in my life. Before, he was with someone. It was a mistake for me to get involved with him. But now, he's not! Why not see if I can have a little comfort before I die?"

Jayden breathed in deeply through his nose. The smell of the mud and damp grass on the field filled his head.

"We're not going to die." He didn't even believe the words himself as he said them. He reached up and moved Pip's arms off his shoulders, taking her hands in his own. Pip smiled and squeezed his fingers in return.

"Whatever you say. But shall we go across the field and away from the things that we know for sure are behind us?" she asked. "We might get lucky and find Mia this way." Before Jayden could protest that he hadn't agreed that it was Mia that they had seen on the far side of the field, she had tugged him out onto the grass and began trailing along behind her.

They crossed the field without any further incident, which surprised Jayden. He absolutely expected another creature to come careening out of one of the houses or hedges that lined the field, but none did. He walked with Pip's hand in his own, and the warmth of her fingers was comforting. Even after everything he had seen tonight, it made him feel like smiling.

On the far side of the field, Pip and Jayden had to peer in through the windows to the classrooms. He wasn't sure what exactly they were looking for. Maybe to see if one of the monsters had broken in here and made it a death trap? Or perhaps they hoped to find Mia building some attempt at a barricaded hiding spot. Brightly coloured paintings hung from strings in each room, and long curtains shielded most of the rooms from view. They moved down the building, checking each room in turn. Jayden paused by a tiny fountain near the door of the first room. It was only a little taller than his knee, and he had to bend over double to get close enough to use it. His throat felt dry as stone. He took a quick drink, wincing at the sound of drops splattering to the concrete.

"She's not here."

He nodded. "I wasn't sure it was her anyway. So let's get out of here in case it was one of them. Back across the field." He began to turn around. "Maybe she didn't come down that path. Do you think she went to the main street?" He looked away from Pip down the fronts of the classrooms, back the way they had come.

"Does it matter?"

He turned back. Pip was standing with her arms held together in front of her, and her long hair draped forward, concealing her face. Jayden became extremely aware of Pip as she stood before him. He stepped closer to her, noticing how it felt to have her so close to him.

"Think about it. We thought there was something over here, but there wasn't. We know there is something back the way we came. Why not take advantage of these spaces?"

"But Mia could still be out there."

"I know, but she's not your wife or anything. We could just find somewhere safe to hide, just us. Maybe we could even try to escape by ourselves? We just need to keep moving forward, finding somewhere new to hide. We can't keep looking back over our shoulder all the time."

Jayden just stared. It was hard to process his thoughts right now. When had he last really slept, instead of running and reacting and operating without decision making? Now he had time to actually make a decision about what happened next. Hadn't she argued that it was Mia they had seen and that they had to come after her, only seconds earlier? Why was she changing her mind now?

"We don't even know which way she went," he said slowly.

"Exactly," agreed Pip. She brushed some hair back from her face. Her eyes shone as they looked over his face. "We could spend the rest of the night wandering through this school and never figure out where she went. We might run into another of those monsters. Maybe it *was* one that you saw, in which case we had better hide soon."

"She had her baby with her," said Jayden, his voice trailing off. He hadn't wanted to come over here in the first place, when she had said that she saw Mia and Estelle here. Why did he want to find them?

"Yes." Pip pursed her lips. "That's a terrible possibility, I know. But she's not your fiancé anymore. It isn't your baby. You don't have to take care of it."

"I didn't take care of her last time." Jayden's voice was fading, little more than a whisper.

Pip stepped forward and put her arms around him. She held him close against her, pressed their bodies together. Her soft voice carried just far enough to reach his ears, faint as the wingbeat of a moth.

"Who took care of you though?"

Jayden allowed his arms to wrap around her. He felt the tension leech out of his shoulders as she squeezed, and he felt like digging his fingers into her back, pulling her closer to him. He closed his eyes and shuddered.

Then he let her go and sighed, stepping backwards. He shook his head.

"I wasn't there when she needed me. I'm going to try and be there for her at the moment. It might not make up for what happened, but I don't want to be that person anymore."

As he spoke, he knew it was true. He had spent so long loathing himself for what he had done, sabotaging any other view of himself that others might have had. He had turned his self-hatred into habit, into a mask that others believed in too.

But the real Jayden was somewhere beneath those layers and layers of grime and regret. Somewhere inside, coiled up hard, there was a Jayden that wished he had stayed by Mia's side, and felt appalled at himself for going out with Pip that night.

"I need to find her if I can."

Pip sighed as well, but nodded. "Alright. I suppose-"

A scream pierced the air, ringing and echoing off the broad windows of the classroom beside them.

"Where did that-"

"Which way was-"

Jayden and Pip both jumped and exclaimed at the same time, clutching at each other.

"Come on!" Jayden reached out and pulled Pip with him, sprinting to the end of the classroom block. They darted around the corner and then looked through the shadows on the other side. Footsteps clattered down the narrow gaps and alleys behind the classes.

"Dammit, where should we go?"

"We could split up," suggested Pip. "That way at least one of us might find them?"

"Yes, that's probably..." Jayden shook his head. "Wait, what? No, we're not splitting the fuck up, I'll just die myself or be ruined with guilt because I let someone else die! That's what happened to Hayden! We stay together. Come on!" He grabbed her hand and led her to the right. Another scream rose in the night, then cut off.

"Shit!"

The pair burst from the passage behind the classrooms into a large concrete courtyard at the end of the long building. Small netball hoops poked up from the ground, and a bewildering network of painted lines covered its surface to create game courts. Opposite the last classroom, on the far side of the court, sat a small shed. Backed up against its corrugated iron roller door was Mia, hunched over Estelle who was still strapped securely to her front.

Standing in the middle of the courtyard, lumbering towards the small shed, was one of the monsters.

CHAPTER NINETEEN

Mia was panting and staring back at the thing. The shed door was torn and ripped, looking for all the world like a sheet of paper that a finger had poked through. Similar tears were ripped in the grass of the field nearby.

"Mia!" yelled Jayden. The thing ponderously turned to look over its shoulder at the newcomers. Its bulging white eyes made Jayden gag.

"Jay! Help!"

The monster swung its arm backwards, and a group of thin whip-like appendages lashed out from its fingers, growing and splitting as they swung. Jayden dove sideways and Pip shrieked as dozens of threads raked through the air, their tips slashing across her shoulder.

"Are you alright?"

"I guess," replied Pip, clutching at her shoulder, where a patch of red was beginning to grow already. "What the hell do we do now?"

On the other side of the courtyard, Mia was sobbing on her knees, with her hands clutching Estelle close. "I tried to get away, but this thing was behind the classes and I've been running so long and I'm so tired."

The thing began to lift its head towards her again.

"Fuck off you dick!" Jayden heaved his hatchet towards the creature, from where he was, huddled low to the ground. The weapon spun and wobbled in the air, but Jayden was amazed to see that he had aimed well. It struck the thing in the leg. The blade didn't bite, but the weight of the hatchet cracked the monster's calf and made it lurch sideways.

A bubbling groan leaked from it and it shuffled around to face Jayden more directly. Black ooze leaked from its mouth, painting its chin and chest.

"Nicely done," said Pip. "You distracted it and saved the mother and child." Jayden felt a small blossom of pride open in his chest and he held his head higher, even though he was still crouched on the ground. "Only, what are you going to use to hit it with now?"

A nauseating cold sensation dropped down Jayden's throat. In the middle of the courtyard, the thing tensed. Jayden pushed as hard as he could, rolling backwards towards the classroom. The rough concrete scraped his head as he rolled, and he scuffed his fingers on the surface. A thick cord of gristle crunched into the concrete where he had been laying, and the thing stepped closer.

"Let's try splitting up now?" asked Jayden as he scrambled to his feet.

"Why not" shrugged Pip. "Mia! I know you're exhausted. But fucking run!"

The three of them summoned their deepest reserves, forcing their legs to move once more, to power them away from the thing and around the corners of the buildings. Pip went back down the passage that she and Jayden had first come from. Mia managed to stagger to the left side of the shed, where low concrete walls contained a garden stuffed with flax bushes and short leafy trees. Jayden ran to the front of the classroom, where its windows faced out onto the field.

Then he stopped, turned around, and ran back across the courtyard. His temples pounded as he yelled, "Here I am you bastard!" with his head tilted back so that he faced the sky.

He didn't pause as he shot past the courtyard and banged into the other side of the small shed that Mia had been crouched beside. He grabbed on to the wooden planks and sucked air into his lungs. Each breath rattled in his chest and it was hard to suck down enough air. If he hadn't been standing on grass under a starry sky, he would have sworn that he was drowning. As he risked peeking back to see if the thing had followed him he felt his lower lip trembling.

A blur of dark and light smashed off a corner of the shed in front of his face, and he felt a shower of wooden splinters bounce off his face. Jayden began spluttering, trying to remove tiny fragments from his lips. He turned and ran again.

Jayden paused on the edge of the rugby field, looking around for an escape route. The flat feature-less expanse of the field stared back at him, silently mocking.

"Now what, you stupid fucking hero?" he whined at himself.

There was a crash as the creature pushed its way past the corner of the shed, dislodging more of the wall. Glass shattered from the shed's windows and the structure bent and swayed.

"There's no point in staying out here," he grum-bled, and he spun around and started sprinting as hard as he could back to the relative shelter of the classrooms. He was horribly aware that this meant he was running towards the creature, and its lumbering presence in the corner of his vision was worse than seeing the body of his friend lying in the garage of a fire station. At least there, the worst had already happened. Now he had to run in dread of what may come.

Jayden zigged and zagged as he headed round the other side of the shed, praying that the tiny movements would keep him alive.

He crouched beside the shed, looking out at the courtyard. In the middle of the concrete, sitting framed by the painted lines that divided up the flat space, the hatchet lay reflecting starlight to the sky. *If I can just get that,* he thought to himself, barely able to hear his own thoughts over the pounding pulse in his ears. *Then I could-*

Wood erupted beside him as one of the thick fleshy appendages smashed all the way through the shed from the far side. It thrashed sideways, bowling him over and knocking him further from the building. His shoulder throbbed, but he clasped his hand to it and felt no torn skin, no wetness of blood. *Thank Christ,* he thought, before staggering upright and looking at the wreckage around him. Broken wooden planks from the shed covered the concrete and grass, and a few rubber balls were bouncing and rolling away. He looked back at the shed as the limb began to slither back through it. *It's the Sports Shed.*

Jayden jumped back to the wall and leaned into the hole that remained. The inside of the shed was almost pitch black, and he was extremely conscious of the brutal thing that had smashed through it only moments before, but he leaned in and reached around to try and find something that he could use as a weapon. His fingers curled around a solid shaft and he tugged it out with a rattle as he withdrew his head from the hole in the wall.

A heartbeat later and the appendage burst into the shed again. Jayden swore and began to run towards the gardens to his right. *Okay, I couldn't get the hatchet, but I managed to get something.* His thighs burned as he ran and he looked at the new weapon he was carrying. It was a softball bat made of a silvery metal, and with coarse cloth tape wound around the handle.

As he ran around the curves of the concrete wall that enclosed the garden, with its tall bushes of flax and dangling branches, Jayden found Mia.

She had her back to the wall and she was hunched forward over Estelle. Her shoulders shook as she cried, but she was desperately holding in her fear and trying not to make any noise. She didn't even look up as his footsteps came around the corner.

"Mia! Why are you just sitting there?" Jayden was shocked to find her. He had hoped that she would have taken the opportunity to run much further than this, or to find a better hiding spot. Sitting on the ground, she was completely exposed.

She didn't look up, and Jayden had to strain to catch her ragged answer. "I stepped funny on that bloody gutter," she began, nodding her head towards a small indent in the concrete near a drinking fountain beside them. "Nearly dropped Estelle, right onto this concrete."

"Hey, she's alright though, let's just–"

"I think I've twisted my ankle. Hope I didn't break it." Now she did lift her head, wisps of her hair dangling to either side of a face that was screwed up in sorrow. Her damp cheeks glistened under the starlight. "I can't move Jay. I can't even stand up. There's no way I'm going to get out of any of this alive."

"Oh Mia, don't–"

"I'm already dead." She hung her head again, stroking Estelle's face gently. "You're going to need to take Estelle for me."

Jayden flinched and stepped backwards, lifting his hands palm out. "Oh, I don't think that's necces-"

"You need to take her!"

"Shhh!"

Jayden tried to force his ears to hear more, but could not tell where the creature was anymore. The school grounds were still. "Look, I have this bat, I'm sure we can get you somewhere safe."

A branch in the garden over Mia's head cracked.

Jayden swung the bat up to his shoulder and hunched over, praying that he would be able to swing fast and hard enough to incapacitate the thing before it broke every bone in his body. Mia curled ever tighter over her daughter.

Squinting into the thick criss-crossed branches, Jayden made out a figure. It ducked under branches and tripped over roots as it pushed closer to them.

"I don't think that's one of them," he murmured. "They'd just smash the tree down, right?"

A second later, Pip managed to break through the flax and trees, and then hopped down from the wall. Jayden sagged, wincing as the bat clonked on the ground.

"Oh thank fuck it's only you."

"Yeah yeah," frowned Pip. She drew a deep breath and brushed leaves from her shoulders. "Where do we go now, we haven't got long."

"We can't go anywhere." Jayden waved at Mia. "Mia twisted her ankle, and now I'm going to have to stay here and watch her."

"Stay here?" Pip's nose wrinkled and she leaned back in shock. "There's nothing here! We're literally standing in the middle of an open field, asking a monster to fucking kill us. That's dumb as hell!"

"She can hear you Pip."

"I don't care!" Pip crossed her arms, glancing behind her in case the thing was approaching. "If she can't come with us then fuck it, we'll go on our own. Come on Jay!" She reached out and grabbed Jayden's upper arm. Her fingers clamped down exactly where the cable had smacked into his flesh, and sent a stab of pain across his shoulder and up into his skull.

"I… We can't just…" Jayden wavered, blinking and stuttering. There was a scraping noise from further around the curved concrete garden wall. Jayden turned to face in that direction. "That thing is…"

Estelle stirred in her mother's arms. She wriggled in her blanket, revealed her small dark eyes to the night sky, opened her mouth, and screamed. The cry was long and as harsh as broken glass on a blackboard, cutting into the base of Jayden's skull. From the way Pip screwed up her face, he knew that she felt the same. Mia didn't even react.

"Fuck this, I'm out." Pip let go of his arm, spun around, and sprinted further down the path. Jayden could see that she was heading for the distant school gates and the main road of Kanuka Creek that lay just beyond. For a moment Jayden wondered if he should follow her. But the thought was fleeting and he knew he couldn't. He licked his lips, amazed that there was still enough moisture in his mouth to do so. He turned to face down the path.

"If it comes around the corner and sees you, we're all fucked," he muttered, more to himself than to Mia. "So I need to make sure it doesn't see you."

He rubbed his fingers across the tape that wrapped the handle of the bat. He wished that he had managed to grab the hatchet. Although a softball bat was a reassuringly heavy weight to have in one's hands, the idea of carrying something that actually had a sharp edge was even better.

"We have to deal with the world the way it is," he said, and he ran.

The bat was awkward to carry, tilting him off balance if he held it to either side, and leaving him feeling claustrophobic if he held it across his chest. He tried to dodge around as he moved out from the shelter of the gardens toward the field. There would be nowhere to hide out there. He wondered what would happen to Mia if he couldn't lead the creature away.

Estelle's cries were still echoing through the school grounds, but Jayden was relieved to notice that the echoes were bouncing from many directions. Hopefully that meant that the thing would find it harder to locate Mia and Estelle for a while. Maybe it was still far away. He risked a glance over his shoulder.

The monster was limping out from the gardens alongside the shed. In the brief glimpse Jayden felt a knot pull tight in his stomach. It had been danger-ously close to Mia. *Thank goodness I started moving when I did,* thought Jayden. Then he caught the thought and wondered at it. When was the last time he had been relieved to have brought danger and ruin upon himself? He planted the bat into the turf and used it as a pivot as he ran, turning so that he was now racing towards the tall thin rugby posts that reared up against the wisps of clouds and stars that filled the sky.

There was a roll of thunder, crashing and tum-bling from Jayden's left. *What the hell is that!? There's barely a cloud in the sky?* He turned his head in time to see a car bouncing across the entrance to the school, glass bursting in clouds of twinkling spray and metal twisting like tissue as it smashed against the road. A scream tried to rise above the tearing metal, but was cut off. The car boomed against a thick metal vertical pole that blocked the gates to traffic and rocked to a stop. Jayden kept running, but was sure he could see an arm sticking out from beneath the car. Perhaps it was a leg.

Fucking hell Pip! Why couldn't you just have stuck with us? Why did you have to go racing off for yourself? You stupid selfish- Jayden's eyes blurred as tears grew in their corners, making it hard for him to see. He was grateful for the broad flatness of the sports field as he ran, keeping him from tripping on sudden steps or having to turn around corners. He lifted the back of his arm to brush the tears aside. *She wasn't my only chance,* he told himself. *I'm going to be better. She wasn't my only chance.*

He reached the rugby posts and turned to see what he had left behind. Far across the field, the monster was still stumbling towards him. Jayden was happy to note that it was definitely limping though. Maybe flinging the hatchet had slowed it down a little.

The thing flung its tentacle towards Jayden, but he was able to dodge sideways past the metal pole of the rugby post, and the appendage missed. The pole clanged from the impact of the unnatural thing. The entire post, tall though it was, tilted in the ground like an incredibly thin Tower of Pisa.

"Yeah, you just keep coming!" he yelled. He swung the bat and managed to hit the end of the limb with a soft wet thump. It coiled away back towards the creature like a rat's tail retreating into its hole.

He ran over to the other rugby post, and then back again, trying to reduce the chance that the thing would try to spear him again. *Keep moving, keep moving,* he thought to himself. *If you stop, you'll be an easy target.* If he could avoid being hit, there was a chance he might be able to get away. If it hit him though... Those things were as brutal as a mulching machine and he knew that he would be dead very quickly.

Twice more as the thing approached, its tentacle came whipping out towards him again. It twisted through the air, the jagged bony ridge at its tip seeming to twist and seek, jutting towards Jayden's shaking and exhausted body. Each time he was able to move around the rugby posts to avoid it, though each time the harpoon got dangerously close. It rang on the metal posts, battering at them, pushing them further and further off balance until they slowly toppled to the field with a long lasting clang, like a gong, leaving Jayden standing exposed on the grass.

Jayden was wobbling on his feet. His head sagged and his eyelids felt heavier than sacks of stone. The softball bat was beginning to slip from his drooping grip. Maybe this was it. Maybe this was all he had to give. It had been a long long night, and he had come much further than he would have expected of himself at the beginning. He had probably made it further than a lot of the others would have expected actually. Further than Pip had thought he could do. And she had thought he was worth being around. She was probably his biggest supporter. He had survived longer than Mike, or Jack, even though both of them had been braver than he was. He had made it longer than Hayden, and the thought stabbed into his gut like a blade. That was unfair. He shouldn't have made it longer than Hayden. He shouldn't have outlived his own friends, Sophie and James.

But he had, and now he had to deal with it. He might be an arsehole, but that didn't matter right now. Mia was stuck nearby with a child that stood no chance if he didn't do something.

But how could he do anything? The thing was limping closer and closer, but there was no way that Jayden would be able to hurt it with the softball bat from here. He would have to run closer before he could even try throwing the bat. And if he tried to do that, the thing would impale him on that foul unnatural extension of flesh and cartilage. So what options did that leave?

Left with no better options, Jayden lifted his feet and began jogging towards the thing. He moved in fits and starts, pulling his energy together and forcing himself forward one moment at a time before sagging over his throbbing calves and summoning what he could from his dying reserves.

Jayden was shocked that the first time the creature reacted to him that it wasn't with a thick wet cable flying towards him. The thing swung an arm from side to side, and thin tendons like black barbed wires slid out from its fingers. They mostly missed Jayden, flying widely through the meters between them, but one sliced into his shoulder and pulled away. Jayden grunted as he felt a chunk of flesh rip from his arm, but he managed to push himself onward.

The second time it attacked, it did use the massive tentacle he had seen so often. Jayden twisted to avoid the worst of the blow, but screamed as its sharp edges tore into the flesh of his thigh. His lungs emptied themselves, leaving him gasping, reaching down to claw at the damp surface of the appendage. He tried to take a step, but pain roared up his nerves and blinded him momentarily. The cord jerked, tugging him off balance and he fell to the grass. *Where's that fucking bat!*

Jayden drew on every scrap of will he could find deep inside himself, stretching out in the darkness to find the bat. Pain throbbed down every limb, and he could barely focus enough to see around him. A glimpse of pale white nearby gave him a direction, and he was relieved to feel the worn tape around the bat's handle beneath his fingers when he reached out to grab at it. Then, the cable pulled.

Jayden was dragged across the field, lifted into the air and bodily carried by the horrific thing that pierced his leg. He could feel blackness pressing from the back of his skull and he knew that he might pass out at any moment. He blinked and stared forward, trying to make out the thing that was pulling him closer.

The creature's face swam into focus ahead of him, closing rapidly. The eyes bulged, milky white and pale, swelling up like the bellies of frogs. As he approached, the face split open, the lower jaw separating and swinging apart, to reveal a multiplicity of tiny segmented legs that clutched and curled around one another. *None of the others did that,* wondered Jayden briefly for a moment, before he was held up in front of the monstrous face as the tiny limbs in its jaws opened into a black and chitinous embrace.

And then, he swung.

The bat bowled into the side of the thing's head like someone stomping on a soft boiled egg. The surface of its face crunched beneath the impact of the metal bat and curled around it as it moved entirely through the head, dragging more of the face with it like wet paper. The tiny spiky legs burst aside and fell twitching around Jayden like pine needles, some tickling and pricking through his clothes.

The thing's limbs began to flail about and Jayden was heaved into the air by the limb, sending fresh waves of blood and pain down his leg. He swung down on the long tentacle and was rewarded by its sudden retreat, though the gaping wound in his leg brought him closer again to passing out. He hit the ground with a thud, and groaned. Jayden pushed the bat into the ground and used it to help lift himself to his feet.

The thing was twisting and bucking on the grass, its head a mess of curved porcelain shards and thick black sludge, oozing out onto the grass. In the starlight, all was silver and darkness. Barbed vines slid out of the fingers of the thing as it clutched at the air, whipping sideways then slipping back into whatever strange place within the monster that it hid them. The thick cord of flesh that had gashed Jayden's thigh didn't return.

Fuck you, thought Jayden as he hobbled closer, leaning on the bat like a walking stick. He could feel his strength washing out of his muscles through the wound in his leg, but he felt calm and light headed. As darkness pressed in on the edges of his vision, he stood over the thing, ignoring the scratches and slices that it managed to inflict in its death throes. *Fuck you and every other thing like you. Why would you come here and do this to us? What did they do to deserve it?*

Jayden stumbled and felt bile rise in his throat. When was the last time he had even had a mouthful of water to try and keep his system functioning? The pain in his leg was receding, though the limb didn't seem to want to keep supporting his weight any more.

Well. At least we managed to deal with this one. Jayden shifted his weight to the other leg, groaning and gasping as the muscles bunched and moved. Pins and needles ran along his side, nearly toppling him sideways. Then he lifted the bat and placed it onto the thing's head, a column of brushed metal resting upon an avant garde base of used tissue paper. The creature froze. *Yeah, you know what this means, don't you, you prick?* Jayden leaned forward, allowing his weight to slowly but inevitably squeeze down on the crumpled remains of its head. Tiny legs burst through the thin mask over the sludge, waving wildly as they attempted to find purchase, but Jayden just adjusted the column's direction to ensure he squashed there too. A pale mucus popped through the remains of the creature's face and bulged over its seams. The thing slumped onto the field and lay still.

Long seconds passed under the cold sky while Jayden stared down the shaft of the bat that he was leaning on, staring towards where its metal penetrated the body of the thing, but seeing nothing. He blinked, and became aware that he could see yellow-green snotty mucus glugging around its base. Breathing slowly, he managed to turn his head. Behind him, over the school buildings, the sky was beginning to lighten a little. The sun was coming, sun rise wasn't far. *That'll help,* thought Jayden. *Sunrise means...*

But as he continued to work on breathing properly he realised that dawn meant nothing. These things had killed people under broad daylight. They could do it again. Only, it would be easier to see people in broad daylight, so maybe those things would be worse. *Ah, fuck.* Jayden growled at nothing. A baby's cry wailed from somewhere nearby.

CHAPTER TWENTY

Jayden woke up to find himself staring at a slightly lighter sky. He felt as though his head was surrounded by cotton wool. Lying on the grass next to him was the softball bat. Jayden lifted his head and focused on the bat. His ears seemed to be ringing non-stop. He shook his head and banged on the side of it with one hand. The bat was lying on the grass, right there. Shouldn't he be holding it? He reached out to pick it up, but it was too far away. Jayden began to roll towards the bat, managing to get a grip around the handle on his second lunge. Why wasn't he using his legs? He could have just stood up and walked over to the bat. Surely that would have been easier. He tried to lift himself to his feet, but couldn't. He looked at the grass in front of himself for a moment, then blinked and took a deep breath. Was something wrong with his legs? Jayden turned to look down.

There was a large wound in his leg, still bleeding quite heavily. Jayden frowned. *That was no good.* Now that he was aware of the damage, he tried to stand using his other leg, and support himself with the bat. As he managed to get himself upright, the ringing in his ears increased in pitch until he squeezed his eyes shut and shook his head. The sound changed. What was that sound? Jayden stuck his finger into his ear and wriggled it about, trying to clear the pressure out of his head. The sound continued. *What was that?*

The buzzing noise resolved into a baby's cry with a snap and Jayden gasped. *Estelle! Shit, where is she? How long have I been lying around for?* He looked around and began hobbling across the field. He had to grit his teeth as pain bloomed from the wound in his thigh. *No wonder I hit the ground,* he thought to himself.

The sky seemed to be noticeably lightening as he stumbled across the grass. *Come on man, don't stop now.*

The crying had stopped by the time Jayden managed to return to the garden walls. He kept moving, aching, hoping that the baby was still okay. He worried that another of those monsters would have been attracted to the sound, but he hadn't seen anything as he moved closer. The pain was dulling now.

Around the corner he found a figure slumped in the shadows.

"Mia?"

The figure shifted. Her head turned towards him, eyes red and puffy. Tucked in close to her chest was the baby, suckling at her breast.

"Oh my god," she said, her voice rough. "You're back?"

"I'm back," said Jayden, leaning against the concrete wall behind her back. He felt a tremendous gravity pulling him to sit on the ground but he knew that if he succumbed to that feeling then he would never be able to pull himself up again.

"I thought you were dead. There was so much banging and then no noise at all."

Jayden focused on breathing. Deep breath in. Slow exhale out. "I'm not dead," was all he managed to say.

They sat in silence.

"My leg is pretty fucked though."

"Oh god, here," said Mia and she began unbuckling the harness that she had been using to hold Estelle. The bright blue straps and buckles dangled from her hand as she held it up to Jayden. He took it and looked at it, then looked back at Mia.

"Strap it above the wound, try and reduce the bleeding. I can't imagine how much you've already lost."

Jayden nodded, then looked back at the harness. With some fumbling and dropping and retrieving, he managed to bind the top of his thigh. Tightening the straps brought a new wave of pain, but the bleeding that had soaked through his jeans seemed to stop. He nodded again.

"I don't think we can stay out here," he said.

Mia laughed and then caught her breath before the rapid sounds could turn into sobs.

"No shit. But with a massive fucking hole in your leg, and my foot on backwards, I'm not sure that there's many options left for us." She leaned back against the wall again, cradling Estelle tightly to her chest. She sighed and stared up into the sky. Jayden looked up too.

The sky was definitely getting lighter now. There were less stars, and the blackness was turning to a deep blue. Out of the corner of his eye, off to the horizon, there was a hint of a much lighter blue beginning to spread into the darkness.

A cat yowled in the streets beyond the school.

"Hey listen to that," said Jayden, nudging Mia with his elbow. "We're not the only ones who made it through the night."

The yowl was cut off suddenly. Silence spread like spilled oil.

"Now we are," said Mia.

Jayden pursed his lips and pulled the bat closer.

"Come on," he said, as he used the bat to lever himself off the ground. "We can find somewhere else to go."

"There's no poi–"

"Come on Mia!" Jayden was shocked by the anger that flared up in his head, and he tried not to direct it at her. "We are the last ones left, but we didn't get here by ourselves. It's not like we are just special and lucky enough to be here." *Especially me,* he thought to himself. *If there was a list of people deserving of a break in this life, it wouldn't include me.* "We are only here because other people tried to get us there. They gave up their own chances of surviving, they let go of their chances, just so that we might get by for a little longer."

Mia hung her head low across Estelle. Jayden risked reaching out to place his hand on her shoulder, wincing as his body weight shifted. She shrugged off the gesture.

"He was so good to me," she whispered.

Jayden leaned closer to hear what she was murmuring.

"He supported me, he cared about me, he did so much to make sure we were ready for Estelle. He always put me first and made sure I got what I wanted." A tear dripped from the tip of her nose, splatting on the concrete beneath her. She looked up with red rimmed eyes. Jayden couldn't meet her gaze.

"And now he's gone. What do I care about any of the others? What do I care about you? He was the only thing that mattered." She looked down again.

"Well, he wasn't the only thing that mattered though, was he?" Jayden flinched at the sudden glare that she directed on him. It burned like a furnace. "I only mean, you have Estelle, right? She's, like, a continuation of Hayden."

Mia didn't move.

"So, let's try to take care of her in the same way he took care of you?"

They remained motionless for a moment more. Jayden staring down at his ex-fiancé and her child. The mother huddling over her tiny baby. Then, Mia's hair shifted, and she nodded very slightly. Jayden released a breath he hadn't realised he'd been holding.

"Come on," he said, holding out a hand. "We'll have to share this bat as a crutch."

As the sky continued to lighten, Jayden helped Mia hobble across the courtyard towards the nearest small classroom. The hatchet still sat on the concrete in the middle of the courtyard, its edge glinting with flashes of red and orange as dawn began to make itself known. Jayden tried to lean down to retrieve it, but with the weight of helping support Mia and Estelle, and the dull throb in his thigh, he couldn't manage. Just as he was going to ask Mia to wait while he picked it up, there was a long dragging noise from further inside the school, like a wet hessian sack being scraped across gravel. He decided to get the others to a safe hiding spot first, and then think about coming back for the small axe.

They arrived at the door to the small cloakroom at the back of the classroom. Through the textured glass, Jayden thought he was just able to make out the small dark space where children would be instructed to leave their bags. He leaned closer, pressing the side of his hand onto the glass and shielding his eyes. *There might even be a small children's toilet behind that door, which would hide them even better.*

He gingerly pressed on the handle. With a faint squeak of metal, it began to turn, then held firm. Locked.

"Do you think we break in?" he asked.

Mia licked her lips. She looked absolutely exhausted. Her hair was handing in threads across her face, and her cheeks seemed to have sunken into her face. Her eyes were dark, and she was clearly having trouble holding her eyelids open.

"I mean, probably not? Won't the noise let those things know that we are inside?"

Jayden narrowed his eyes as he thought about the problem.

"What if they do think we are inside, but inside somewhere else? At least we'd get some warning if they tried to come in then."

"What do you mean?"

"Wait here."

He passed the bat to Mia, who wasn't really able to hold both it and her daughter. Jayden felt awful leaving her alone, especially in such a condition, but it seemed safer and faster than trying to stumble away with her, only to return as soon as he had followed through on his idea.

He leaned close, pressing his forehead to Mia's. They stared into each other's eyes.

"I am coming back."

Jayden was surprised at how difficult it was to make his way back to the courtyard. His head began to swim and he felt as though the ground was swaying and buckling beneath his feet. He bent over and placed his hands on his knees as he breathed deeply to recover himself.

This night is never going to end, he thought as he lowered himself to the ground and picked up the hatchet. *I don't know how much longer I'm going to be able to keep going.*

He could feel the weary ache of worn out muscles in his arms. The feeling slunk down his shoulders and back. He wondered if he looked as exhausted as Mia did. *Just a little bit longer,* he said to himself, pushing himself on.

The front of the classroom faced out to the broad

emptiness of the sports field. The houses that lined the far side were gaining definition in the early light, which worried Jayden. If he was able to start making out windows and clotheslines around those distant buildings, then it stood to reason that one of the monsters roaming Kanuka Creek might spot him across the field too. He limped faster to the door of the classroom.

With a short jab, Jayden used the hatchet to break the tall narrow window next to the door. The tinkling of glass falling to the floor inside went on far longer than he was happy with. Beyond the glass he could see long shadows in the classroom, hidden and shrouded by the curtains that hung over the tall windows. Metal wires criss-crossed the room, hung with posters and artworks by small children. Directly beyond the hole that he had just made in the window was a large green piece of paper. A family was drawn on the poster in crayon and felt tip pens, using bright circles for the figure's faces. Their thin stick arms were jammed together like twigs caught in a hedgerow, but a bright red heart above the figures showed that the strange design was representing the people holding hands or hugging each other. A single roman sandal sat on the floor next to the door. It was tiny, barely the size of Jayden's hand.

He reached through the hole carefully, trying not to catch his clothing on the jagged edges of glass that remained in the frame and sucking air through his teeth every time a shard was nudged out of position and clinked to the ground. He just needed to get inside as soon as possible. He reached around to the left and twisted the lock of the door slowly, groaning when the lock thudded as it released. *Why is nothing bloody quiet?* The door creaked as it opened.

Something cracked from across the field. Jayden jumped inside and pulled the door shut behind him, as quickly as he dared. He peeked out the windows, but couldn't tell where the sound had come from. *Maybe it was just a cat or a dog or something,* he tried to convince himself. Then he turned and began pulling tables over to block the door and to clog the space around the now broken window.

The tops of the tables were lower than his knees, and coloured in bright greens and reds. Looking at the children's artwork around the room, the small toys piled in boxes and tubs near the walls, Jayden felt a wave of pain wash across the surface of his skin. *What has happened to all these children tonight,* he wondered. He noticed a laminated photo near the teacher's desk and looked sharply away, not wanting the vision of tiny faces to visit his dreams later.

Once the doorway and window were well sheltered, Jayden moved back through the classroom to the cloakroom, ducking under the paper artworks that hung from the wires criss-crossing the room just above his head. He tried not to bump into the dangling sheets, in case he set them waving and wobbling. If something came past and noticed them moving, even after he had hidden himself, all of the night could be wasted.

The cloakroom felt cold and the air was damp as Jayden moved through it. He saw the door's window of frosted squares in a grill and rushed towards it as quickly as his numb leg could carry him. His fingers fumbled on the lock, but soon he had twisted the small silver knob around and pulled open the door. Outside, he found Mia curled up on the ground.

Sighing with relief, he reached out and began pulling her inside. She jerked awake, swinging her hand out, though the bat lay useless by her side.

"It's okay, it's only me! It's just me."

Mia calmed down, but her eyes lacked direction and focus. Jayden was worried.

"Are you okay?"

Mia muttered and murmured, but Jayden couldn't understand the words she was using.

"Come on," he grunted as he reached beneath her arms and heaved her towards the cloakroom. Her shoes grated on the concrete, and the door behind him banged into the wall as he bumped into it. The wooden thump was loud in the morning air. Jayden rolled his head.

"Could the world just fucking not for a while?" he groaned.

He kept pulling Mia into the cloakroom, grateful for the smooth linoleum floor that allowed her to slide more easily towards the door to the toilets. Something crunched on a stick outside. Jayden froze.

The noise had not come from far away. He glanced over Mia to make sure that she had a good grip on Estelle. The baby was swaddled firmly in her mother's arms, but Jayden could see that Mia was losing focus and beginning to fall back asleep.

"Come on!" he urged himself, pulling on her slumped figure again. He reached back to open the toilet door, offering a silent prayer of thanks to the tiny children of this school, and their need for door handles positioned barely a foot above the floor.

He pulled Mia into the small toilet and tried to position her as comfortably as possible near the tiny porcelain sink inside. That left just enough room for the door to close. As he was about to close it, Jayden glanced back through the dim cloakroom. That was how he saw that the door to the outside was hanging wide open. A leaf blew through the empty frame and swirled across the smooth floor.

"For fuck's sake," whined Jayden. He sniffed and pulled his jeans higher on his hips, then limped out to close the door. It took three long strides, each sending a jolt through his wounded and strangely unfeeling leg. The door moved quickly and smoothly, with Jayden pushing it slowly in the last few centimetres, easing the lock back into position. Smiling, and with tension melting off his shoulders like butter, he blinked and prepared to return to Mia.

Something was shaking the bushes in the garden across the courtyard from the cloakroom.

Jayden dropped to the floor and pressed himself into the corner where the low wall met the linoleum. *Fuck these tiny children and their fucking low windows!* He heard a muffled thump from outside. Exactly the sort of sound that something heavy would make as it crawled out of the gardens and bushes before dropping to the concrete courtyard on its way to smash into a tiny primary school cloakroom so that it could rip apart the exhausted, terrified and emotionally drained people that were desperately hiding inside. *Yeah,* he thought. *It sounds just like that.*

Jayden squeezed himself further into the tiny space, trying to make sure that nothing would be able to see him if it looked down from the window into the cloakroom. He felt beads of sweat slowly form and pool and drip down from his forehead. He swallowed and shifted his head so that he could look up, watching the slim view he had of the glass pane above him.

He could just make out a thin line of blue through the gap, a glimpse of the sky far above them all. Then there was a bang as a dark shape slumped against the glass. The glass squeaked as the shape slid along the glass. Jayden held his breath.

He couldn't see it clearly, but it seemed to be the arm or shoulder of something roughly human shaped. Thick smears of grease were leaving a trail as it slid over the window, distorting the glass behind the shape. It seemed rotten and mouldy. Jayden stared directly at the shape. *If it is one of them and it leans in closer, if it looks down, will it see me?* Jayden wriggled his shoulders with deliberate slowness, trying to wedge himself further into the corner. He flicked his eyes over to the toilet door. It had closed behind him. *Maybe that thing can't see anything,* he hoped.

The high pitched sound of skin pressing along glass ceased and Jayden felt his whole head relax without the pressure of those soundwaves on it. The dark shape moved away from the thin gap and all that he could see anymore was that wisp of blue above. He exhaled, pursing his lips and blowing the air out in a single long slow breath before placing a hand on his diaphragm to try and slow down the following breath in. Even then, the rattle of air in the back of his throat sounded desperately loud in his mind.

When can I move? Jayden stared upwards, controlling his breathing. *If I even begin to roll out of this spot, and that thing is still here...* Jayden's mind was flooded with the visions and sounds of the night he had just fought through, and then those nightmares spilled over into predictions and imaginations of what could become the future of this tiny cloakroom, of what might happen to Mia and Estelle if he didn't manage to restrain himself. His back was stiff and he felt an urge to twist and stretch the muscles there. He nibbled on his lip instead, grimacing at the discomfort. After a length of time that he had no way to measure, Jayden felt that maybe he was safe. To be sure, he started counting in his head. I'll count to one hundred, he told himself. *By then there's no way the thing would still be here.* One hundred arrived before he knew it and he rolled his shoulders slightly. *Two hundred is probably a better idea.* He continued counting. *Five hundred then.* And then one thousand.

CHAPTER TWENTY-ONE

Jayden blinked. The cloakroom seemed brighter than it had moments ago. *Was I asleep? Shit, did I fall asleep?* He smacked his lips together and pressed his tongue against the roof of his mouth. *Oh god, how long was I asleep for?* He began to sit up.

Fear kept him careful, and he tried to peek sideways over the low window frame out into the courtyard. It seemed empty. He waited, trying to look into any space that might hide or shelter the things that brought so much horror. The sky was still pinkish, the shadows very long, and he was glad to think that it was still dawn. Slowly he lowered himself down again then began crawling across the cloakroom to the toilets where he had left the others.

Every inch felt as though he was a crab crawling across a beach, with seagulls circling overhead. However, he reached the door without incident and crept through, then pushed the door shut behind him. On the cool floor under the sink, Mia lay on her side, cradling Estelle in her arms. Her side rose and fell slowly, and she was snoring softly.

"Fair enough," murmured Jayden as he moved in next to them both. He wriggled into a comfortable position and pulled the hatchet across his chest. "You try and catch up on your sleep. It's been a big night."

Although his body screamed at him for doing so, Jayden forced himself to stay awake, watching the door, ears as alert as he could for any sound.

A sharp crackling sound disturbed the silence, almost like controlled thunder. Jayden narrowed his eyes, feeling the heat and exhaustion filling his head like fluff in a soft toy. He could feel Mia moving behind him.

"What was that?" she asked.

"No idea," he grumbled. His mouth tasted like damp socks.

"Shouldn't you go and find out then?"

"What?" Jayden rolled over awkwardly. "No! Why would I go out that bloody door again!?"

The tearing sound ripped through the air again. Jayden widened his eyes at Mia as if to say "See?" She just sighed.

"Go check it out Jay. I'm going to feed Estelle." She began to undo the front of her clothes. As she looked down at Estelle, she spoke quietly. "And Jay..."

He paused halfway to standing, his back sending small threads of pain sliding up and down his muscles.

"Thank you for coming back for Estelle and me. And for letting us sleep."

She didn't raise her head, so he couldn't see her eyes. Warmth grew in his chest though.

"You're welcome."

Peeking outside the toilet door, the cloakroom was well lit by now. Jayden wasn't sure how long had passed since he had closed it earlier. The room was beginning to heat up. Beyond the windows, the small school looked bright under a morning sun.

Something moved.

Jayden fell to the ground inside the toilet, grunting as the air was driven from his lungs. *Why?*

He questioned in his head. *Why can't we just get through a few hours without something shitty happening? Why?*

He tried to move from where he lay, just inside the toilet door, so that he could take a look out into the cloakroom and beyond. He lifted himself up a little on his elbows and peeked out through the gap between the toilet door and its frame once more.

Out beyond the curved concrete wall of the garden, coming around from the low green tree branches, was a figure in dark green speckled clothes. It was carrying a long black gun. *Wait? A gun?*

"What is it?" asked Mia. Jayden could hear the tension in her voice. *She must have noticed that I'm acting carefully,* he told himself as he lifted himself up from where he had thrown himself to the floor, so he could crouch beside a door and squint through a tiny gap. He considered his actions over the last few seconds. *Okay. Maybe not acting carefully so much as acting like a weirdo. If she wasn't worried, she'd be the odd one.*

"There's someone with a gun out there."

"Are they on our side?"

And that was the question, wasn't it? How would they know? If this was some over-eager vigilante, out trying to save the town, how could Jayden and Mia be sure that they would be allowed to walk out without getting shot? How could they prove to the stranger that they were safe? And even if they could emerge safely, slowly, and cautiously; how could they be sure that this wasn't one of the things that had somehow got itself a gun and decided to use it? Jayden was fairly sure that they wouldn't use a gun, but he didn't think he was sure enough to bet his life on it.

The armed figure stepped forward slowly, legs spread wide and slightly crouched. The figure turned, aiming the gun ahead of itself. It froze, looking straight at the cloakroom. Jayden held his breath. The figure raised a hand, making a series of gestures, then a second and third figure stepped out from behind the trees and bushes as well, guns leading the way.

"I think they've seen us," began Jayden, but then a red and black line fountained into his vision, erupting from somewhere to the side of the cloakroom. The harpoon smashed into the first figure, who was flung backwards, but the other two immediately opened fire. The roar and shriek of their gunfire filled the small toilet, and Mia huddled over Estelle. Then the gunfire stopped, almost as abruptly as it had begun.

The two figures dashed forward, guns still leading the way, until they disappeared from Jayden's field of view. There were two sharp cracks as they fired again. Then they reappeared, one looking for their stricken companion, and the other watching back the way they had just advanced. The first soldier knelt down next to the fallen soldier and began pulling items from pouches on his sides.

"Are you okay?" asked Jayden. He held his hand out with a thumb up and a questioning expression. He could barely hear himself over the ringing in his ears.

Mia moved her mouth, but Jayden couldn't make out what she was saying. She must have recognised the confusion on his face, so she just started nodding instead.

"I think they're on our side. We should try to join up with them." He gestured for her to move out of the toilet with him.

Mia nodded again, and stood up, carefully lifting Estelle with her. Jayden could see that the baby's eyes were wide open and she was crying. Mia tried to soothe her, running the backs of her fingers over the baby's cheeks. Jayden peered back out past the door and saw that the two soldiers were looking back at the cloakroom again. He stepped forward, pushing the door open and making sure that he kept his hands high.

By the time Mia followed, the soldiers were jogging over to the cloakroom. Jayden unlocked the door and the two burst in, passing him immediately and began to interrogate Mia.

"Are you alright miss?"

"How long have you been in here?"

"Do you know if anyone else is nearby?"

"Do you need anything for the baby?"

"No offence, but are you able to stop it crying?"

Mia answered them and was bundled out of the building. Jayden followed. As the group moved out of the shelter of the classroom buildings and back towards the gardens, the two soldiers hauled their fallen companion up and dragged him along also. His chest looked as though it was covered in red paint, shockingly bright, but the man was responding to the movement and voices of the others. Without pausing, they all continued moving alongside the garden. Jayden began to realise that they were following the path around to the school gates. The same gates that Pip had tried to run through. Jayden felt a pressure squeeze around his throat, making it tough to breathe.

The wreckage of the car was still leaning precariously against the metal pillar that blocked the driveway from being used outside of school hours. Tiny cubes of slightly blue glass covered the ground like sand. Oil and thick liquid oozed from the car, and then Jayden caught a glimpse of a limb sticking out from beneath the twisted metal. He spun away and looked up into the sky.

"What happen-" began Mia, but then she went silent. Jayden reached out blindly, unable to see where he was going. A hand met his and held him tight.

"I see, I see it. It's okay Jay." Mia's voice was

soothing and low. Jayden felt his eyes grow hot and tears begin to pool in the corners. He opened his mouth to explain, but no sound came out.

"Come on, we're nearly out." Mia stroked the back of his hand with her thumb and Jayden was able to breathe a little more easily. He lowered his gaze and took a deep breath, meeting Mia's eyes.

"It's okay," she said. "You're going to be okay."

They looked around the main street as they walked off the school grounds. Jayden coughed to clear his throat. He wanted to think about something other than what he had just seen, anything other than the sight they had passed. So he stepped closer to one of the soldiers to ask who they were and what was going on.

"How are you able to deal with these things? I thought you weren't able to cope with them breaking out in Wellington?"

"We didn't understand what we were dealing with at first, and they spread faster than we expected. We've figured them out now. Gotta use headshots or explosions."

"Because of the weird black things in the heads?"

"Yeah, gotta squash those things."

"Will your friend be okay?"

"I hope so. The medics are working fucking hard."

And they were. On the main street, just outside the gates to the school, Jayden was amazed to see ambulances, army transports, and a large group of soldiers. A handful of survivors were being escorted within a circle of watchful guards, and medics in bright gear were rushing over to them, settling them onto the asphalt in the middle of the road. A gunshot rang out and Jayden spun, heart racing. On the far side of the circle of guards, a rifle was smoking and a group of soldiers moved towards one of the houses at the side of the road. A second gunshot came and then the soldiers moved backwards into position.

"You guys really do seem to have this covered." Jayden had a hand pressed on his chest as he spoke.

"Yup. Now we know what to do, it's just a routine. Dangerous, but so's being a lumberjack, y'know?"

The soldiers who had escorted him and Mia to this gathering now moved off to speak to some of their officers, leaving Jayden and the girls with the medics. Mia and Estelle were moved into an ambulance quickly, while Jayden was sat down next to it. A medic leaned over him.

"Okay, I see this leg. Looks pretty bad, I'm impressed that you managed to walk in."

Jayden thought of Estelle, lying in the ambulance with her mother. "What else could I do?"

"I hear ya buddy. Anything else that I should know about before we start patching you up?"

Jayden shook his head. "Nothing physical."

The medic leaned closer and placed a hand on Jayden's shoulder. "I know man. But you did what you could, and you got out of there. You got a mother and her baby out of there." She gave Jayden a brief hug, one armed around his shoulders from the side. "I bet it was a world of shit. But you will be okay."

Jayden felt tears in the corners of his eyes again. He brushed them away and sniffed roughly.

"Okay, I'm going to give you something for the pain, because that leg looks bad."

Within seconds, Jayden felt the world melting and he flew away into an endless dreamless sleep.

"Hey Jay, good to see you man!" Justin was short and his ginger hair and freckles always reminded Jayden of the wise-cracking younger brother from some generic family movie. But he was enthusiastic, and pretty good at coding, and he ran the small team that Jayden had ended working with for the last year. This was the fourth week in a row that Justin had specifically walked over to Jayden's desk and asked him to come along to the StoneMasons for their Wednesday night staff drinks. The small gathering of office workers all enjoyed having a few beers and wines, and participating in the quiz that the bar put on to encourage midweek drinking. Jayden had even found that he knew the answers to a few questions, and had received huge smiles and hugs when he contributed to the group. It was quite different to the socialising he had been used to.

"Good to be here," he said, slipping onto one of the tall stools around the heavy wooden table. A young woman with a green mohawk smiled at him and then continued her conversation with her neighbour. Across the table from him sat an older woman with glasses, who leaned forward to make sure he could hear her over the buzz of conversation.

"I thought you might not make it this time, I heard that you got caught trying to fix a problem for a client?"

Jayden searched his memory for her name and was relieved when it rose to the surface. He'd worked with her a few times, but they didn't see each other much at work.

"Yeah Zoe, I thought I might be still in the office now, but luckily Robin stepped in and found me a solution I'd never heard of before!"

Zoe's shoulders bobbed as she laughed. "Love Robin! Always comes up with the best solutions."

"Right?"

Just then Jayden's pocket began vibrating and buzzing. He blinked and stuck his hand in to grab his phone. *Do I answer,* he thought. *Would that be rude to the people I'm here with?*

Zoe saw his arm move and nodded. "Go ahead, we'll be here."

"Thank you," mouthed Jayden as he pulled out the phone to see who was calling. It was Mia.

Jayden squeezed out past the others, bumping Justin as he went. The other man glanced over and saw Jayden lifting a phone to his ear and just gave a thumbs up and a smile.

Jayden put a hand over his other ear so he could hear Mia easier as he made his way outside.

"Hi Jay!" said Mia.

"Hello? Hello! Hi Mia!" said Jayden, trying not to shout at her over the crowd. He stepped through the doors and sighed in relief as quiet spread around him.

"Hello! Are you alright?"

"Yes, sorry! I'm just out at a pub so it's pretty loud."

"Oh, I'm so sorry! I was calling to catch up, it's been almost two weeks since my last call. Should I phone back another time?"

"No, it's totally fine." Jayden smiled under the orange lights outside the StoneMasons. "I love hearing from you. How have you both been?"

Mia laughed. "We're all fine. Estelle went to daycare today, and the teachers said she had fun making a huge mess of paint on a piece of paper. Maybe she's going to be an artist!"

Jayden chuckled. "Sounds great. I'd love to see what she made. And how are you today?"

"I'm good. I'm still getting used to my shifts at the cafe, but the locals are really friendly, so it's been nice and relaxed so far."

"Good to hear."

"How about you, you're at a pub? Is this the staff drinks again? Didn't you say you had been a couple of times already?"

"Yeah, and they're a fun bunch. We come out for the midweek quiz and stuff."

"Sounds perfect for you."

"It's been more fun than I might have thought." Jayden leaned back against one of the outside tables. "You have a date coming up this week, right?"

"Yeah, his name's Liam. He works at the mechanics in town, and he seems pretty sweet."

"Very cool. Well, send me some photos of Estelle, and I hope the date goes well. I better get inside before the questions start though."

"Thanks. Good luck at your quiz!"

"Cheers. See you later."

"See ya."

Jayden pressed the button to end the call and began to walk back inside the StoneMasons. He opened the doors to the heat and light and noise of the crowd, and for once, it made him smile. Inside that room were people who had asked him to join them, who had laughed with him at work, who smiled when they saw him. Whatever darkness lay behind, he could see the future that lay ahead for him was bright.

THE END

You can read two short stories for free and keep informed of any new writing by Aaron by signing up for his mailing list at: bit.ly/3kLKaaG

ACKNOWLEDGMENTS

Getting this book across the finish line was only made possible with the help of many friends.

Fleur, Kat and Emma were wonderful readers, catching far too many typos and giving me good indications of when I had sent the story down the wrong alley.

Simon is an amazing artist, and has always been incredibly generous to me, even encouraging my much earlier writing efforts.

Steff provided me with far more support than I deserved, as always.

Annalise inspired a nightmare almost 15 years before I finally got this book out. Those images have mostly made it into the novel, though the plot itself has twisted in other directions. It ended up much more positive than that nightmare did.

Any errors or missteps that remain in this book are mine.

ABOUT THE AUTHOR

Aaron Dick is a teacher living north of Auckland in New Zealand with his wife, their two daughters, and a small menagerie of household animals. They all love when his eldest daughter visits too.

He grew up as a voracious reader of science-fiction and fantasy, often to the annoyance of his unheeded family. Becoming an author was a childhood dream, alongside being a palaeontologist, or a rock star.

His stories have featured in a collection of New Zealand short stories inspired by Grimm's' Fairy Tales and in the gothic art and lifestyle magazine Nocturne.

You can read both of these stories for free, and keep informed of any new writing by Aaron, by signing up for his mailing list at: bit.ly/3kLKaaG

You can also find him on Facebook at: fb.me/AaronDickNZ